UNDER THE KISSING BOUGH

"Look at that," Stephen said, nodding upward. Directly over their heads hung a double festoon of greenery, from which was suspended an ivy-covered ball ornamented with ribbons and lady apples. "Do you realize you're standing under the kissing bough?"

Anne gave the ivy-covered ball a cursory glance. "Yes, I saw that earlier. Another of your English customs?"

"Yes," said Stephen. "Traditionally, anyone caught standing beneath it is required to pay the forfeit of a kiss." He was smiling as he spoke, but there was a question in his eyes as he looked down at her.

"I see," Anne said. Her color had risen slightly, but she made no move to step from beneath the ball. Stephen hesitated, then bent down and kissed her.

It was a longer and more intimate kiss than the one he had given her earlier in the drawing room. It was a kiss such as Anne had never experienced before . . .

ZEBRA'S REGENCY ROMANCES
DAZZLE AND DELIGHT

A BEGUILING INTRIGUE   (4441, $3.99)
by Olivia Sumner

Pretty as a picture Justine Riggs cared nothing for propriety. She dressed as a boy, sat on her horse like a jockey, and pondered the stars like a scientist. But when she tried to best the handsome Quenton Fletcher, Marquess of Devon, by proving that she was the better equestrian, he would try to prove Justine's antics were pure folly. The game he had in mind was seduction—never imagining that he might lose his heart in the process!

AN INCONVENIENT ENGAGEMENT   (4442, $3.99)
by Joy Reed

Rebecca Wentworth was furious when she saw her betrothed waltzing with another. So she decides to make him jealous by flirting with the handsomest man at the ball, John Collinwood, Earl of Stanford. The "wicked" nobleman knew exactly what the enticing miss was up. to—and he was only too happy to play along. But as Rebecca gazed into his magnificent eyes, her errant fiancé was soon utterly forgotten!

SCANDAL'S LADY   (4472, $3.99)
by Mary Kingsley

Cassandra was shocked to learn that the new Earl of Lynton was her childhood friend, Nicholas St. John. After years at sea and mixed feelings Nicholas had come home to take the family title. And although Cassandra knew her place as a governess, she could not help the thrill that went through her each time he was near. Nicholas was pleased to find that his old friend Cassandra was his new next door neighbor, but after being near her, he wondered if mere friendship would be enough . . .

HIS LORDSHIP'S REWARD   (4473, $3.99)
by Carola Dunn

As the daughter of a seasoned soldier, Fanny Ingram was accustomed to the vagaries of military life and cared not a whit about matters of rank and social standing. So she certainly never foresaw her *tendre* for handsome Viscount Roworth of Kent with whom she was forced to share lodgings, while he carried out his clandestine activities on behalf of the British Army. And though good sense told Roworth to keep his distance, he couldn't stop from taking Fanny in his arms for a kiss that made all hearts equal!

Available wherever paperbacks are sold, or order direct from the Publisher. Send cover price plus 50¢ per copy for mailing and handling to Penguin USA, P.O. Box 999, c/o Dept. 17109, Bergenfield, NJ 07621. Residents of New York and Tennessee must include sales tax. DO NOT SEND CASH.

Joy Reed

Twelfth Night

ZEBRA BOOKS
KENSINGTON PUBLISHING CORP.

ZEBRA BOOKS are published by

Kensington Publishing Corp.
850 Third Avenue
New York, NY 10022

Zebra and the Z logo Reg. U.S. Pat. & TM Off.

First Printing: November, 1995

Printed in the United States of America

One

A gust of wind sent eddies of snow swirling across the road. They looked very pretty in the light of the coachlamps, like waves on a storm-tossed sea of white, but neither the coachman crouched on the box nor the guard huddled on his seat behind found much to appreciate in the sight. Snow had been falling steadily for several hours now, and the ground was already covered with a dense blanket of white; where the road lay low the wind had driven it into great swelling drifts, so that the coach-horses had to struggle through snow as high as their harnesses. The coachman drove them remorselessly on, cracking his whip over their backs and shouting encouragement to the leaders when they foundered. His voice had grown hoarse from trying to shout above the wind, and he sat hunched on the box, his head bent low in an effort to avoid the wind's stinging blast. The guard behind was better off, being somewhat sheltered from the wind; he had wrapped himself in a couple of greatcoats and a waterproof cape and was surreptitiously warming himself with draughts of brandy and water from a pocket hip-flask.

The passengers inside the coach were spared the worst of the wind's blast, though of cold they had a plenty. There were only two passengers today, a rare thing on the Edinburgh Down Mail, but few people cared to travel in such weather, even so close to Christmastime. On this occasion it was perhaps a fortunate circumstance, for the gentleman occupying the forward seat was by himself large enough to fill most of the narrow bench which His Majesty's Mail Service had decreed sufficient accommodation for two passengers. Tall and broad-shouldered and appearing even broader in the folds of a many-caped greatcoat, he sat impassively in his seat, reaching up now and then with a gloved hand to wipe the windowpane clear of its coating of frost. He looked to be in his early thirties with dark hair and strong, clear-cut features; it would not have been too much to call him handsome, though he might with equal justice have been described as stern or even forbidding-looking. For the most part he kept his face turned toward the window and the wintry landscape outside, but every now and then his eyes strayed to the woman seated on the bench opposite.

She was very well worth looking at. A close-fitting black bombazine dress set off her slim figure and made a striking contrast to the red-gold ringlets that crowned her head and fell loose about her neck and shoulders. She had hazel eyes, pretty, delicate features, and a heart-shaped face; at the moment both face and features were drawn into an expression of deepest anxiety. Under the circumstances this could not be counted extraordinary, for the weather was certainly providing ample excuse for anxiety, but the gentleman had observed the same expression on her face when she had first entered the mailcoach several stages back, and as their journey had progressed he had noted several other anomalies about her appearance.

Chief among them was the shawl draped over her red-gold curls. It appeared to be her only head-covering, a circumstance that had struck the gentleman as extremely odd. To be sure, they were still only a few miles from the border, and even nowadays it was not uncommon for young Scottish women to dispense with hats and bonnets in favor of their native plaids. But it was not a plaid that this young woman wore; it was a fine black cashmere shawl, somber in hue but rich in texture and possessing an indefinable air of being both new and expensive. Scrutinizing her closely, the gentleman had observed that the whole of her dress had about it this same air of elegance and expense, yet she seemed to be traveling alone, unencumbered by maid or duenna, a most remarkable thing for a young woman who appeared to be of gentle birth.

Neither was she encumbered by an excess of luggage. A small jet-beaded reticule appeared to comprise the entirety of this article, and though the gentleman could suppose she had her reasons for embarking on a winter journey without bonnet, *bonne,* or baggage, he could not imagine what those reasons might be. In the end his curiosity had grown so great that he had ventured to ask a few questions of the coachman when they had stopped at a posting house to change horses.

"Aye, it's a queer thing, sir. All alone, and not a shred of bag or baggage about her." The coachman's eyes rested speculatively on the woman's figure, just visible through the window of the coach. "No, sir, I don't know her name. She wasn't on the waybill as it happens, but when she asked to be taken up last stage I hadn't the heart to refuse her. Well, sir, it's Christmastime, you know—and then, it goes against my principles to disoblige a lady, especially one that's willing to pay." With a wink and a smile, the coachman patted the pocket of his waistcoat. "What I say is, that what the lads at the post office don't know isn't likely to hurt them, and I don't see any way they're likely to know unless you or I tell them, sir. That's one good thing to be said about this infernal weather: there's not likely to be any damned informers about."

The guard, coming up in time to hear the last of this speech, had shaken his head at the coachman's words. "Something havey-cavey about the business, if you ask me," he said, looking darkly toward the woman in the mailcoach. "To look at her you'd say she's Quality, but you know as well as I do that Quality wouldn't be running around the countryside with no maid and no luggage. Her being so ready with the blunt just shows you there's something rum about her. Like as not, you and I'll both find ourselves in the suds before we've seen the end of this business."

The coachman said cheerfully that if they were to end up in the suds anyway, he might as well collect a little more blunt from the lady first. But as he turned toward the coach, the gentleman stretched out a long arm and caught him by the shoulder. "No, you don't," he said, in a voice that held an unmistakable ring of authority. "You've already got your money from her— more money than you had any right to ask, I daresay, and money that you've made free and clear above your regular pay. If you ask her for one penny more, I'll inform on you myself."

For a moment it had seemed as though the coachman might take umbrage at this speech. He bristled and gave the gentleman an ugly look, but the gentleman returned it with great steadiness, and in the end he only pulled his arm away, saying sulkily that he was sure he would never have spoken so free if he had known the gentleman was going to take the lady's part. The gentleman let it pass with a nod, and nothing more was said by either of them during the short time the coach remained in the innyard. When the gentleman went to take his place inside the coach, however, the coachman remarked to the guard *sotto voce* that there was no fathoming the ways of Quality, to which statement the guard returned a heartfelt assent.

The woman had been looking out the window, but looked around quickly as the gentleman entered the coach and resumed his seat on the forward bench. Once again he was struck by the anxiety of her expression. He gave her a civil nod, which she returned after a brief hesitation; she then drew herself further into her corner and turned her face toward the window once again. With one hand she reached up to pull the shawl a little further over her bright curls. The gentleman observed that she was without gloves, and that apart from the shawl on her head she had no wrap or mantle. Even in his greatcoat, supplemented by boots, topcoat, buckskin breeches, waistcoat, shirt, and flannel underwaistcoat, he was none too warm; he could not imagine how cold she must be in her thin robes of black bombazine.

The coach's progress had been slowing steadily throughout the afternoon. It was some two hours after this last stop that it ground to a halt altogether. Both passengers looked instinctively toward the window, but the view had long since been obscured by frost and the fall of darkness. Outside the coach, the wind soughed and sighed, and snow struck the windows with a soft hiss like handfuls of fine sand being tossed against the glass. As the two within the coach sat listening and looking about them, they heard the coachman shout, and the crack of a whip rang out sharply above the wind. The coach shuddered, lurched forward perhaps half a foot, and then settled back in its tracks with an air of finality.

Looking more alarmed than ever, the woman half rose from her seat, hesitated, and then sank down again with a quick glance at her companion. His face likewise betrayed uneasiness; reaching up to the window, he let down the glass to look outside, but such a blast of wind and snow came swirling into the coach that he quickly put it up again. Outside, the coachman and guard appeared to be holding a consultation, their voices raised up in shouts to make themselves heard above the wind. The gentleman rose to his feet.

"I'll step out and see what the problem is," he told the woman. She nodded absently, not looking at him; her eyes were still fixed anxiously on the window, endeavoring to see beyond its coating of frost. Drawing his greatcoat close around him, the gentleman went to the door of the coach and opened it.

He found himself confronted by a snowbank that stretched out in front of him level with the body of the coach. Up ahead the spent team stood dispiritedly in its harness, panting and blowing and clearly incapable of pulling the coach any farther. With a rueful look at his top boots, the gentleman stepped into the drift and waded his way to the front where the grim-faced guard and coachman were working to unbuckle the harness from the wheelers. "Lodged fast, is she?" he said.

The guard nodded, and the coachman made a noise of disgust. "Aye, there's no moving her," he said. "It's a wonder we were able to get as far as we did, the way the road's drifted in. This wind is the very devil. Goes through you like a knife, and blows the snow around so you can't see which way you're going. In all the years I've been on the road, I can't remember driving in worse weather."

The guard, who had been blowing on his half-frozen fingers in an effort to warm them, spoke up at this. "Aye, it's bad, but nothing like as bad as the winter of '99," he told his companion. "That was something to see, that was. There was drifts twice as high as your head along here and no getting a coach through for nigh on a fortnight. If you'd been through that, you wouldn't think this little dust-up was of much account."

"Even so, it appears to have involved us in difficulties," said the gentleman, glancing back at the half-buried coach. "What are you proposing to do about it?"

The coachman shrugged. "Oh, that's clear enough, as far as it goes," he said. "We've got to get the mail through, snow or no snow, at least as far as we're able. But I'm thinking that without the coach, the horses ought to make it on to Branwick all right, and as soon as we get there we'll send back a fresh team and a few stout fellows to dig you folks out. Of course you're welcome to come along with us, sir, if you'd rather. No need for you to sit here cooling your heels and waiting for help to come. Cooling your heels," he repeated with a grin. "Your heels and everything else, eh, sir? It's cold out today and no mistake."

The gentleman did not return his smile. "You were proposing to leave the lady here alone?" he said, looking from guard to coachman.

The two exchanged rather embarrassed glances. "Not much else we *can* do with her," pointed out the coachman. "I'm sure she's very welcome to ride along, too, if she likes, but you can see yourself, sir, that she's not dressed for the trip. It ain't likely to be a pleasure trip any gate," he added with a shiver, as a gust of wind caught at the skirts of his greatcoat. "To my mind, she's better off staying here with the coach. So long as the weather doesn't get any worse, it oughtn't to take us more than a couple of hours to get to Branwick, and once we're there we can send back fresh horses and a few men to fetch her and the coach along."

"And what if the weather does get worse?" inquired the gentleman. The guard and coachman merely looked blank. The gentleman looked from one to the other of them, and his brows drew together. "I see," he said. "That seems to be that, then. I'll go tell her what you've just told me, and she can decide for herself what she wants to do." Turning away, he began to wade back through the snow toward the coach.

The woman looked up quickly as he re-entered the coach. "Has there been an accident?" she said anxiously.

With a wry smile, the gentleman indicated his snow-covered boots and breeches. "No, it's the snow," he said. "We've hit a deep drift, and the men seem to think there'll be no getting the coach out of it with this team. They're unhitching them now and getting ready to ride through to the next stage."

The woman stared at him. "Ride through," she repeated. "Are we to stay with the coach, then?"

"That, or ride along with them. The decision is up to us—or rather, I should say, up to you. Do you think you could ride?"

The woman looked down at her bombazine dress. "I am not dressed for riding," she said uncertainly. "And I don't think I could ride without a saddle anyway. I am not an expert rider by any means. Will they be long sending help?"

The gentleman hesitated before answering. "They think not, but it rather depends on the weather, you know," he said carefully. "If the wind should pick up, or the snow grow heavier . . ."

He left the sentence unfinished. The woman looked at him for a moment and then looked away, biting her lip indecisively. All the while her hands were busy in her lap, nervously twisting and toying with the jet fringe of her reticule; he observed that her fingers were reddened by the cold. "I suppose I must stay with the coach," she said at last. "Will you be so good as to tell them that I will stay, sir?"

"Yes, I'll tell them. But I expect they'll be coming back to the coach in a minute anyway, once they're done with the horses. I may as well stay in here out of the wind until they do."

For several minutes the two of them sat in a silence broken only by the noise of the wind and the steady soft hiss of snow striking the windows. At last there was a rap on the door. The coachman stuck his head inside the coach; in his hand was one of the coachlamps, whose light he trained upon the passengers inside. "Well, what will it be, folks?" he said genially. "Are you staying or going?"

"I shall stay with the coach," said the woman resolutely.

"And so shall I," said the gentleman, in a voice no less resolute.

The woman caught her breath and looked at him with consternation—almost, he thought, with fear. "Oh, but it's not necessary for you to stay with me, sir," she said. "I'm sure *you* could ride with the others. And indeed, I don't mind staying here by myself."

"I'm sure you don't, but I myself would rather remain here than embark on an eight-mile ride through the snow," said the gentleman calmly. "I hope you don't object to my keeping you company?"

The woman looked as though she did object, but civility obliged her to return a negative answer. "Of course not," she said, and turned her face toward the window again with an air of vexation.

"That's settled, then," said the coachman, looking relieved. "You two sit tight, and as soon as we get to Branwick we'll send a party along to dig you out." So saying, he withdrew his head from the coach and shut the door with a slam.

Through the frost-encrusted window, the two inside the coach watched the glow of his lantern recede and vanish into the darkness. A few minutes later another lantern passed the window, this one apparently carried by the guard, for the coach shifted on its springs, and there was a creaking overhead that seemed to indicate he was retrieving his mailbags from the box. The woman sat listening to these sounds, her face rigidly averted from her companion and her hands still toying restlessly with the fringe of her reticule. The coach creaked and shifted once more as the guard dismounted from the box. Once more his lantern passed the window, and a few minutes later they heard a horse whinny somewhere in the distance. After that there was nothing to be heard but the faint hiss of snow striking the windows of the coach.

Two

For a long time there was silence within the mailcoach. The woman sat as far back in her corner as possible with her shawl pulled well over her head and her face rigidly averted from her companion. From the opposite bench he surveyed her thoughtfully. At last he leaned forward to address her in an apologetic voice.

"I don't wish to be encroaching, madam, but we are likely to be here for some time, you know. Under the circumstances, I don't think it would be out of line for us to at least introduce ourselves, do you?"

The woman turned her head and gave him a long, penetrating look. What she saw seemed to reassure her, for some of the rigidity left her figure and she nodded. "I suppose that's only sensible," she said. "As you say, we are likely to be here for some time. My name is Compton—Miss Anne Compton."

"I am very pleased to make your acquaintance, Miss Compton," said the gentleman, removing his hat and inclining his upper body in a polite bow. "My name is Etheridge. Stephen Etheridge," he added, after a brief, scarcely perceptible hesitation.

Anne nodded and turned her face toward the window once more. She remained thus for several minutes, and Stephen was just beginning to fear their acquaintance would never go beyond introductions when she spoke again, in a rather tremulous voice. "How long do you think it will be, Mr. Etheridge, before we may expect to be rescued?"

Stephen found himself disproportionately encouraged by this sign of relenting. "That's difficult to say, Miss Compton," he said with a smile. "As nearly as I can judge, we're about halfway between stages. Allowing time for our guard and coachman to ride through the snow, reach the nearest village, gather together a fresh team and a crew to dig us out, I doubt we can expect to see help arrive much before midnight."

"So long as that?" Anne looked at him worriedly. "But that's a good many hours to wait. I don't suppose it's much later than six o'clock now, in spite of its being so dark. You haven't a watch by any chance, Mr. Etheridge?"

"I have one, Miss Compton, but reading it is likely to prove difficult in this light. I could wish our companions had left us one of the lanterns, but I suppose I ought not to complain. At the moment they undoubtedly need them far more than we do." Drawing his watch from his pocket, he scrutinized it closely, turning it from side to side in an attempt to catch a gleam of light on its face. "I would guess it to be not long after six, but I'm afraid that's only a guess. It was about four o'clock the last time we changed horses, that I do know."

Anne nodded again. Stephen observed that she seemed to be deliberating further speech; even in the darkness he could see her regarding him narrowly. At last she spoke. "Why did you decide to stay with the coach, Mr. Etheridge?"

"It is as I told you before, Miss Compton. I have no desire to make a long ride in such inclement weather—and no desire to abandon my luggage, either, if it comes to that. I could hardly have carried it with me, you know." He studied her in turn, noting the pallor of her heart-shaped face against her black dress and shawl. "Why did you suppose I stayed, Miss Compton?"

She shook her head. "I don't know," she said in a constrained voice. "I wasn't thinking very clearly, I suppose. Naturally you would want to stay with your luggage. I hope you will forgive me if I seemed rather brusque earlier, Mr. Etheridge. You had as much right to wait here in the coach as I did, and I had no right to take offense at your staying."

"Oh, that's all right," said Stephen easily. "I can understand your being unhappy at the prospect of waiting here alone with a perfect stranger." It was on the tip of his tongue to ask how she came to be traveling alone in the first place, but he bit back the question, not wishing to appear overly inquisitive. Although her manner had thawed perceptibly in the last few minutes, he feared any unwary utterance on his part might make her freeze up again. A question about her final destination seemed safe enough, however. "We seem to have picked a poor day for our journey," he said, smiling at her tentatively once again. "Are you traveling far, Miss Compton?"

"No, not very far. To Harrogate in Yorkshire."

There was an edge of reserve in her voice that warned him she would not welcome further questioning on this subject. Yet he continued, drawn on by a desire to penetrate some of the mystery surrounding her. "You live in Harrogate?"

"As much as I can be said to live anywhere. I have lodgings in Harrogate, but I had not planned to stay there much longer."

The reserve in her voice was unmistakable now. Stephen did not dare go on, and for some time neither of them spoke. Anne drew herself back into her corner and turned her face toward the window again. Stephen observed that she was surreptitiously chafing her hands in her lap, however, and at last he gathered the courage to speak again.

"Look here, Miss Compton, I wonder if you might like to borrow my greatcoat. I could spare it very well, you know, for I am dressed a great deal more warmly than you are."

"Certainly not," she said, and gave him such a look of suspicion that he knew it would be futile to urge her further. He kept silence, therefore, but as the minutes passed he observed that she continued to chafe her hands in her lap; he observed also that she several times shifted her position in her seat, as though she were finding it increasingly uncomfortable. At last she stood up abruptly and reached for the door strap of the coach.

"I am going outside," she said.

Dismayed by these words and supposing that his own behavior had somehow prompted them, Stephen also rose to his feet. "Indeed, you ought not, Miss Compton," he said earnestly. "The wind's pretty sharp, and there's a drift four feet deep outside the door."

"It doesn't matter," she said, pulling open the door.

"But it does matter, Miss Compton. Since we're the only ones here, we're in the way of being responsible for each other, and I don't like to see you expose yourself unnecessarily to the cold. If you really must go outside, at least let me come with you—"

She gave him a look of exasperation mingled with embarrassment. "I thank you, Mr. Etheridge," she said. "But it is *necessary* that I go outside. *Alone.*"

"Oh," said Stephen, as her meaning finally dawned upon him. "Oh, I see." He felt singularly foolish as he sat back down on the bench. Amid a gust of wind and flurry of snow, Anne stepped out into the snowbank and pulled the door shut behind her.

She was gone only a few minutes, but when she returned, her dress and shawl were powdered with snowflakes, and there was a heavy crust of snow caking her half-boots and the lower part of her skirt. She brushed it away as well as she could, then wrapped herself in her shawl and retreated into her corner as before. But it was obvious that she was cold; once more Stephen observed that she was chafing her hands in her lap, and from time to time she was shaken by a fit of shivering she could not conceal. For several minutes he regarded her with concern, and at last he spoke.

"Miss Compton, I know you refused my coat when I offered it before, but I really must insist that you take it now. If you go on sitting there with wet feet and nothing on your hands, you'll be lucky if you don't take frostbite. You wouldn't want to lose a hand or a foot, would you?"

Anne shivered again. "I am cold," she admitted in a small voice. "But I cannot allow you to give me your coat, Mr. Etheridge. I am sure you need it yourself, whether you admit it or not."

Stephen took a deep breath. "Then share it with me," he said. "You may as well, Miss Compton, for it's going to come to that sooner or later, I'm afraid. You must have noticed that the wind's been picking up all the time we've been sitting here. It's a regular blizzard out there now, and not likely to get better before morning. At this rate our rescue party may be a long time coming, if it comes at all. I'm afraid we're going to be obliged to take drastic measures if we don't wish to freeze to death."

As though to emphasize his words, a gust of wind shook the coach with a force that set its windows rattling. Anne looked at him, trying to make up her mind. She had already looked at him once or twice that evening, but at the time she had been so distraught that she had noted little save that he was inordinately large and had the appearance of a gentleman. Now she looked closer, noting the strong jaw and clear-cut mouth, and the dark eyes that met hers steadily and without evasion. It struck her that he had a face of unusual integrity. Since she seemed to have no choice but to trust him, it was a comfort at least to find him appearing so eminently worthy of trust. "Very well, Mr. Etheridge, I will share your coat," she said, and arose from her seat to join him on the forward bench.

Stephen stood up to pull off his coat, then sat down again, spreading it carefully over them both. Anne stiffened slightly as his shoulder touched hers and made as though to draw away. He looked at her gravely. "Miss Compton, I know it's a difficult situation, but you may trust me not to presume on it. My concern is only for your welfare. If you would sit closer, you would stay very much warmer—and so should I, if that's any consideration."

She hesitated a moment, then edged closer to him on the bench. "I am being foolish, I suppose," she said with a strained smile. "But it is such a strange situation."

"Indeed it is," said Stephen with feeling. "Trapped in a mail-coach, with a roaring blizzard outside—it's almost as bad as being stranded on a desert island like Robinson Crusoe. In fact, I'm not sure it's not worse. At least *he* didn't have to worry about staying warm!"

Anne smiled again, more easily. "Yes, I would much rather be on a nice warm tropical island, given the choice," she said. "When I think how eager I was to get back to England! I would give a good deal to be somewhere warmer right now—Italy, perhaps, or Greece. Even in France it didn't get as cold as this."

"You are French, then? I noticed earlier you have a bit of an accent."

For the first time since entering the coach the anxiety left her face, and she laughed, a pretty, silvery sound of genuine amusement. "How funny that you should say that," she said. "At school they were always making fun of my *English* accent! I seem to be like Aesop's bat: neither bird nor beast, but something in between."

He smiled, thinking how pretty she looked with laughter lighting up her face. "You were educated in France?"

"No, Belgium, but of course French was the principal language there, and since Napoleon was put down I've spent some time in France, too. Mother and I were in Paris for nearly a year after the Peace was signed, so I suppose it's no wonder if I do have a trace of an accent."

"You seem to have traveled widely, Miss Compton. What brought you to England?"

"Well, I *am* English, as it happens. I was born in Southampton, though I don't remember much about it. My father died when I was very young, and my mother always had a taste for traveling. We've spent most of the past fifteen years abroad, going from place to place as the spirit moved us. But my mother became ill a couple of years ago, and when none of the foreign doctors seemed able to help her, we came back home to see what English doctors could do. I think I've visited every watering place in England during the past ten months or so."

"With Harrogate being the last?"

"Yes, the very last." She looked sorrowfully down at her black dress.

"I'm sorry," said Stephen gently. She nodded and tried to smile, but he saw a glitter of tears in her eyes as she turned her face away. Another silence ensued, which neither of them seemed eager to break. The wind outside had been steadily rising; it shrieked and howled as it swept past the coach and chilled the atmosphere within so that their breath was visible as jets of vapor in the air. Anne shivered and drew the edge of Stephen's greatcoat further over her legs. "How terrible the wind sounds," she said. "Like one of those Irish spirits that are supposed to presage disaster—banshees, I think they're called."

"Yes, and I'm afraid it does mean disaster, or at least a long and uncomfortable wait for us. With all this wind and blowing snow I doubt our rescue party will be able to set out before morning."

Anne shivered again. "Oh, I do hope you are wrong, Mr. Etheridge," she said, in a voice that was barely a whisper. "I am so very cold."

Stephen regarded her for a moment and then, with sudden decision, caught her round the waist and pulled her into his lap. She stiffened and drew in her breath in a startled gasp. "Forgive the liberty, Miss Compton," he said briskly. "But there are situations where the ordinary rules of propriety must go by the boards, and I'm afraid this is one of them. I will not sit by and let you freeze to death."

To say that Anne was surprised by his action would have been an understatement. She was astonished, and affronted, and withal, more than a little frightened. Her first impulse was to protest, her second to jump to her feet and return to her corner without delay, but a moment's reflection showed her the futility of either course. He was larger and stronger than she was and obviously very determined, and if he had designs on her purse, or her virtue, there was nothing to stop him from pursuing her to the opposite bench or anywhere else she might go. It seemed wisest to remain where she was and trust that he was as honorable as he seemed. Should it prove otherwise, she would be no worse off than if she had resisted him initially, and in the meantime there was no denying that she was warmer where she was.

Anne drew a deep breath and forced a smile. "I will take your word that desperate measures are called for, Mr. Etheridge," she said. "In truth, this whole situation seems slightly unreal to me."

For all the bravado of her manner, it was clear that she was very uncomfortable. Stephen could guess something of her fears, and rather than pretend there was nothing extraordinary about their situation he decided to address it directly by making a joke of it. "I don't wonder it seems unreal," he said. "If someone had told you earlier today that fate was about to throw you into the arms of a perfect stranger, I'll wager you'd never have believed them."

His words had not quite the effect he had hoped for. Anne began to laugh wildly, in a manner that verged on the hysterical. "Indeed, no," she said. "Out of the frying pan and into the fire, as it were!" She laughed again, rather wildly, and then turned to look at him. "You think me mad, I daresay, but if only you knew, Mr. Etheridge! Indeed, it is very ironic."

He looked at her uncertainly, curious to know the meaning of her words but not wishing to offend her a second time by asking a question she might consider overly personal. She wiped her eyes with a corner of her shawl and spoke resolutely. "You have been very tactful, Mr. Etheridge, but it cannot have escaped your notice that I am somewhat inadequately dressed to be journeying through northern England at this time of year?"

"Well, yes, I did rather wonder about that," he said apologetically.

"Prepare yourself for a shock, Mr. Etheridge. You see before you that fabled creature of romance, the abducted heiress. Yes, you may well stare, Mr. Etheridge: it still seems quite fantastic even to me, but I can assure you that it really did happen. I was abducted this very morning by a gentleman of my acquaintance—I use the word gentleman in the very loosest sense, you understand. By the meanest stratagem, this so-called gentleman succeeded in getting me into his carriage, whereupon he locked the door and immediately set off for Gretna Green. His intention, which he freely admitted, was that I should be joined to him there in unholy matrimony by a minister of the gospel who also doubled as a wheelwright. Quite an amusing situation, don't you think?"

Her listener did not look as though he found much in it to amuse him. "That is a very extraordinary story, Miss Compton," he said gravely. "How did such a thing come about?"

"It is rather a long story, Mr. Etheridge. I would not want to bore you with all the details. Oh, very well, if you insist—to be sure, we do have plenty of time on our hands, don't we? But you must stop me if you find yourself growing bored. Let me see, where to begin?

"I first made the acquaintance of my soon-to-be abductor about eight months ago, when my mother and I were staying in Bath. At the time he seemed quite an unexceptionable acquaintance—indeed, both Mother and I became very fond of him, and no wonder, for he was at pains to make himself agreeable to us. When we left Bath he followed us to Scarborough, and then to Harrogate, and when at last Mother died a few months ago he stayed on there to help me with the—the arrangements. I must do him the justice to say that he really was a great help to me at that time. There were a great many small matters that had to be arranged after Mother's death, and he took charge of them all himself, in order to make things easier for me.

"It was about two weeks ago that he asked me to marry him. He made his proposal in a perfectly honorable, aboveboard manner—and the irony of it is that I was really quite disposed to accept him, only I could not feel it right to marry or even enter into a positive engagement so soon after my mother's death. I explained all this to him, supposing that he would wait and ask me again once my first mourning was past. But it seems that the gentleman's affairs did not admit of any delay."

There was bitterness in her voice as she continued. "This morning—how long ago it seems now!—we had an engagement to drive out to Ripley very early, to see the church there and perhaps visit the castle on our way back. The gentleman took me out in his phaeton, as planned, but instead of driving me to Ripley he took me to a byway where a closed carriage was waiting. Once there, he informed me that I was to become his wife that very day, with or without my own consent. I protested, of course, but it was no use—he had his serving man there to help him, and I was shut up in his carriage and whisked off to Scotland without so much as a by-your-leave."

"What a scoundrel," said Stephen, and looked so indignant that Anne felt compelled to reassure him.

"You must not be thinking that Fran—that the gentleman who abducted me was cruel or abusive in any way," she said, in a voice of would-be gaiety. "I may have been forced into the carriage, but once I was there I was made very comfortable, with fur robes and wine and sandwiches—how I wish I had them all with me now! He really treated me very well, but of course that could not make up for the indignity of being abducted and carried off to Scotland against my will."

"You managed to escape him before you were actually married, I collect?"

"Oh, yes—indeed, I am rather proud of the way I managed it. There was nothing I could do while I was shut up in the carriage, but I was watching all the while for a chance to escape, and when we got to Scotland I found one. He took me to an odious little inn where a clergyman was waiting for us—as I said, he was really a wheelwright, but apparently in Scotland that doesn't matter, or so I was given to understand. At any rate, the clergyman was all ready for us, but apparently there was some difficulty about witnesses. It seems that there had to be witnesses to testify that I was willing, and of course since I wasn't at all willing, they had to be witnesses who didn't mind perjuring themselves. Well, the clergyman said he knew of some who would do it for a price, and after a little grumbling my bridegroom agreed to pay the extra cost. He then took me into the inn parlor to wait while our clergyman went off to find his friends.

"It was horribly cold in the inn parlor, almost as cold as it is here in this coach, and my bridegroom swore a little, shouted for the servants to bring more coal, and set about trying to poke up the fire. But he made the mistake of turning his back on me while he was doing it. There was a nice heavy set of fire-irons right there, all ready to hand—really, I thought it seemed almost like providence."

"And so you hit him with the poker?" said Stephen, regarding her with a sort of fearful admiration.

"No, *he* was using the poker; I had to hit him with the tongs. And I wish I could think I had really hurt him, but he was already starting to revive by the time I left. He had made me take off my pelisse and bonnet and gloves when we first came in, so I had to leave them behind, but I did have my shawl and reticule with me, which was a great piece of good fortune. And I thought it even more fortunate that I got to the coaching house in time to get a seat on the south-going mailcoach—but now it seems as though perhaps that wasn't such a good thing after all."

"Indeed," said Stephen, regarding her with fascination. "If you could escape from a situation like that, Miss Compton, I shouldn't think a mere blizzard would be much of an obstacle to you! You seem to be an uncommonly resourceful young woman. My mother would enjoy hearing your story—she is always railing against the heroines in storybooks who make no effort to defend themselves against their abductors. She called Pamela a spineless idiot, I recall, and said no woman with an ounce of spirit would behave like such a ninnyhammer."

"Your mother is still living, then?" said Anne. Stephen nodded, and she drew a sigh. "How I wish mine was. In a way her death was a merciful release, for she suffered a great deal toward the end, but still I cannot help missing her very much."

"I'm sorry," said Stephen again, with a look of contrition.

"I do keep putting my foot in it, don't I? It was thoughtless of me to bring up such a subject."

"Oh, but I really don't mind talking about it, Mr. Etheridge— at least, not with you. It's actually a relief to talk about it with someone who doesn't rush in with platitudes every time the subject arises. The woman Mother and I were lodging with in Harrogate, for instance—she is an excellent woman in her way and has been very kind to me, but whenever I try to talk about Mother's death she just tells me I mustn't dwell on it and changes the subject as soon as possible. Well, I don't mean to dwell on it, but she *was* my mother, after all. I knew and loved her for twenty-one years, and I would not want to forget her overnight, even if I could."

Stephen could only nod in sympathy. Anne's eyes had once again filled with tears, but she blinked them back and smiled at him. "You are a very good listener, Mr. Etheridge," she said. "I've told you practically the whole story of my life; now I'll turn the tables and let you tell me about yours. What impelled you to do something as mad as traveling down from Scotland in the middle of December?"

Stephen hesitated a little before speaking. "My story is also a rather long one, but not so interesting as yours, I'm afraid. I was staying with a friend in Scotland and received a letter from my mother urging me to come home for Christmas. On an impulse I decided to do it—and the result is what you see now."

He seemed so reluctant to talk that Anne's interest was aroused. "Your friend was sorry to see you go, I suppose?" she said, observing him closely.

He smiled and shook his head. "Rob thought I was mad to set out in such threatening weather and told me so in no uncertain terms! I'm sure he would say I was well-served by my present dilemma."

Anne noted that he seemed not at all reticent on this subject, at least. "Where in Scotland does your friend live?" she asked.

"It's a few miles south of Inverness, up in the highlands. Robert McGuire is his name, Sir Robert McGuire, to give him his proper title—he inherited the baronetcy a few years ago, along with the family home, which happens to be a castle. Not a very large castle, mind you, and not at all watertight, but very ancient and picturesque. During my stay at Castle McGuire, Rob did his best to induct me into the mysteries of deer-hunting and salmon fishing and all the other sports with which Scottish gentlemen while away their leisure hours."

"And how does Lady McGuire while away *her* leisure hours?" inquired Anne.

Stephen laughed and shook his head once again. "There is no such creature, Miss Compton! I'm afraid Sir Robert is something of a misogynist. The only female inhabitant of Castle McGuire is Rob's housekeeper, who's about a hundred years old—at least, she's always boasting of how Bonnie Prince Charlie kissed her once when she was a canty lass of sixteen, so she can't be too many years short of that."

Since he seemed perfectly willing to talk on this subject, Anne encouraged him to tell her more about Castle McGuire and its occupants. He responded with a highly colored, highly entertaining account of Sir Robert's *ménage*. Anne laughed at his descriptions, but even as she laughed she found herself wondering why he had shown such reticence earlier when he had spoken of returning home. When he came to the end of his account, she could not resist touching on the subject a second time. "It sounds as though you made quite a long stay in Scotland," she said. "I expect you are looking forward to seeing your own home again?"

His face immediately clouded over. "Yes and no," he said slowly. "To be perfectly honest, there are circumstances that would have made me glad to stay away from it even longer. I'm not at all certain that I'm doing the right thing by returning even now, but my mother's letter was very persuasive—and I suppose, too, that I had some sort of nostalgic longing to see the place again after being away so long. You might almost say I'm a prodigal son, returning home after an extended absence and not at all sure what kind of welcome is awaiting me."

He looked and sounded so grim as he spoke that Anne was

rather alarmed. She immediately set about smoothing over her gaffe. "Oh, I should think your welcome is secure, if your mother is encouraging you to return," she said lightly. "The fatted calf is probably already on the spit!"

He smiled at little at that. "If so, I wish I had it here," he said. "Roast veal would taste very good about now."

"Yes, I am getting hungry, too. I keep thinking about all those lovely sandwiches that I refused to eat this afternoon."

"And *I* keep thinking of the chops I paid for and didn't have time to eat, when we changed horses a couple of stages back."

"It's terrible to be hungry, isn't it? I don't think I've ever been in a situation before where there was absolutely nothing to eat. What I wouldn't give right now for those sandwiches—or better yet, a loaf of fresh-baked bread with butter and honey. Have you ever noticed that when you're really, really hungry, it's the simplest foods that seem most appealing?"

"I'm afraid that with me, it's the simplest foods that always seem most appealing, Miss Compton!"

"Therein speaks the Englishman," said Anne with a smile. "I suppose you share the national predilection for roast beef and boiled vegetables, Mr. Etheridge?"

"Not for boiled vegetables, but I should think myself a poor Englishman if I had not a partiality for roast beef. I take it from your tone that you do not, Miss Compton? Oh, but that is bad, very bad—you must try to cultivate a taste for it now that you're back in England. To find fault with roast beef here is akin to heresy, you know."

"To tell the truth, I have never cared much for roast beef," confessed Anne. "It always seems so terribly dry and uninteresting."

"Ah, but that's only because you've never had *proper* roast beef. Living abroad all this time, it stands to reason that you wouldn't—no, nor living in English lodging houses, either. I've spent enough time in lodgings myself to know what a travesty passes for roast beef on your average lodging house table. Proper roast beef is something else altogether. You may insult

English manners, or English morals, but don't let me hear you speak lightly of English roast beef, Miss Compton—at least not until you've had a chance to try it for yourself!"

Anne laughed, rather wistfully. "I would try it with the greatest pleasure if I had it now," she said with a sigh. "How long it seems since breakfast." Again she sighed, but a moment later her face grew thoughtful; she sat quietly for a minute or two, gazing pensively into space as though meditating a problem of great complexity. Stephen watched her curiously. At last she spoke, with an air of decision.

"Consommé to start with, I think," she said. "Yes, a nice light consommé, just enough to pique the appetite without dulling it—"

"I beg your pardon?" he said, with some surprise.

She turned toward him a face alight with laughter. "I'm ordering dinner, Mr. Etheridge," she said. "Since it appears I have no hope of actually getting any, I've decided to amuse myself by ordering what I would choose, if I might have anything at all. Yes, consommé to start with, and for fish I would have whiting, or perhaps a nice slice of turbot—no, on second thought I believe I would have shrimps. I may not have a proper appreciation for English roast beef, Mr. Etheridge, but it will gratify you to know that I have conceived a veritable passion for English shrimps! Shrimps, then, and after that I would have a roasted chicken—or perhaps ham—or perhaps both, together with—let's see—French beans and mushroom fritters. And for dessert I would have sponge cake, strawberries, and cream. There now, I've ordered *my* dinner, Mr. Etheridge; what will you have for yours? Anything you like, and price no object: you observe that I did not scruple to order strawberries in December!"

Stephen gave the question a long and serious consideration. "I think that for my part, I would dispense with soup and fish altogether and proceed directly to a large beefsteak," was his eventual pronouncement. "Rare beefsteak, with perhaps a few fried potatoes—that would comprise *my* ideal dinner."

"Your tastes *are* simple, Mr. Etheridge! Simple, and some might even say barbaric, though I personally have no objection to rare meat. And what dessert would you choose to finish off this barbaric repast of yours?"

"If I had my beefsteak and potatoes, I would be more than happy to dispense with dessert along with the soup and fish, Miss Compton! But since you insist, I suppose I would choose—say, apple tart. Not a very original menu, is it?" He smiled at her, then suddenly slapped his thigh. "We are fools," he exclaimed. "Here we are, going on and on about being hungry, when ten to one there's something edible stowed outside in the boot."

"Do you think so?" said Anne hopefully.

"It's practically a certainty. These mailcoaches do a deal of that sort of business, you know; they're the usual means of sending game and garden stuff back and forth across the country. Let's hope some good Scotswoman has been kind enough to send a relative a Christmas pie or one of her home-cured hams as a Christmas gift."

He had already thrown the greatcoat aside as he spoke, and Anne got quickly to her feet so that he might do likewise. She watched as he turned up the collar of his topcoat and pulled his hat low over his eyes. "Aren't you going to take your greatcoat?" she said with surprise, as he moved toward the door.

"I'll only be gone a minute," he said. "You may as well keep it for me. Don't let anyone take my place while I'm gone," he added with a flash of a smile, before stepping out into the storm.

Three

After the door had shut behind him, Anne wrapped herself snugly in the abandoned greatcoat and sat listening to the wind howl while she waited for him to reappear. He returned a few minutes later, cold, crestfallen, and empty-handed. "Not even an undressed goose," he said, stamping his feet to rid them of snow before sinking down beside her on the bench. "I checked both the front and hind boots and the cradle on the axle, but there's nothing in the way of foodstuffs in any of them. I'm afraid we're doomed to fast until help arrives."

"Then our beefsteak and roast chicken will taste all the better when we finally get them," said Anne in a determinedly cheerful voice. She stood up to let him resume his place on the bench, then sat down on his lap, drawing the greatcoat over them both. "Oh, but you are cold, Mr. Etheridge," she exclaimed, as the chill of his garments began to make itself felt through her own. "You ought to have taken your coat to go outside, even if it was for only a few minutes." For a moment she hesitated, then resolutely put her arms around him and lay her head against his chest. "If you can be noble, then so can I," she said. "It is foolish to stand upon ceremony when we are freezing to death."

He did not reply, but his arms encircled her and drew her tightly against him. For several minutes they clung together without speaking. "How strange this is," said Anne presently, in a small voice. "To sit here, waiting to die perhaps, and there's not a thing we can do to save ourselves. It's such a helpless feeling."

"Yes, but you mustn't lose hope, Miss Compton," said Stephen, looking down at her. "If we stay as close as possible and don't open the door any more than necessary, I think it entirely possible that we can survive until help comes. Are you comfortable as you are?"

"Yes," said Anne. It was not quite true, for even in his arms the cold was inescapable, but for all that, there was comfort in the near presence of another human being. In the extremity of their situation she had forgotten her initial distrust and was now disposed to regard him, if not quite as a friend, at least as a fellow sufferer and a most welcome bulwark against the cold.

With an inward smile she reflected that she had never known a gentleman better fitted to serve in this latter capacity. The chest against which she laid her head was broad and nearly as solid as a wall, and the arms that encircled her felt reassuringly strong and protective. It was strange to be in a position of such intimacy with a near stranger, but Anne no longer had any qualms on that account; the situation was so clearly out of the ordinary that ordinary considerations did not seem to apply.

Following this line of thought, she said aloud, "It's very easy to lose sight of the things that are really important, isn't it? Things like being alive and warm and having enough to eat. If I live through this I don't think I shall ever look at life quite the same way."

Stephen was quiet for a moment. At last he said, with a kind of sigh, "Yes, I know what you mean. An experience like this tends to make one regret all the time and opportunities one's wasted in the past. Or perhaps I should say rather that it makes me regret mine. I doubt you've as much cause for regret as I have, Miss Compton."

Anne tilted up her face to look at him. He was looking straight ahead of him with an expression both sad and stern. She felt instinctively that his thoughts had hearkened back to the subject they had been discussing earlier, and that his regrets were in some way connected with his long absence from home. "Have you then a great many things to regret, Mr. Etheridge?" she said softly.

Her voice seemed to recall him from his thoughts. He looked down at her for a moment, and when he spoke it was in an altered tone, gentler than she had heard him use before. "I wish you would call me Stephen," he said. "I know it's rather early in our acquaintance to be Christian-naming each other, but since fate seems to have thrown us together I see no reason why we may not dispense with some of the formalities if we choose. As you say, it is foolish to stand upon ceremony in a situation like this—and then, too, I am rather out of the habit of being called Mr. Etheridge, as it happens. Will you call me Stephen?"

"Yes . . . yes, I will. I will call you Stephen, and you may call me Anne, if you wish. Have you many things to regret, Stephen?"

"Not a great many things, but a few—yes, definitely a few. For one thing I regret that I waited until now to return home. If something should happen to me—if we should not be rescued in time, you know, it would be such a blow to my family. It strikes me that I have been behaving rather irresponsibly these past few years, though I never quite saw it in that light until now. Have you anything to regret, Miss Compton—or Anne, as I should say?"

Anne considered the question, her eyes fixed reflectively on the frost-covered window. "A few things, I suppose," she said. "I shouldn't think there was anyone, anywhere, who couldn't look back on his life and find something to regret, should you? It's easy to sit here now and say, 'Oh, I should never have done that; I should have done thus and thus instead,' but at the time things are never so clear. I know I've wished many times that I had insisted on coming back to England when Mother first fell ill, but at the time we both thought it was only a minor illness and that a month or two at Baden would set her to rights. It's the same way with most other things, I suspect. If we could know the consequences of our actions at the outset, then of course we would order our lives differently, but since we can't, it seems to me worse than futile to torture ourselves over what can't be changed. In that respect I think my landlady is quite right: it's unhealthy to spend too much time dwelling upon the past. To use one of her favorite cliches, 'what's done is done'—one can only go on and resolve not to make the same mistake twice. Unfortunately, that's advice easier given than taken, as I know from my own experience."

Stephen was silent so long that Anne began to wonder if he intended to respond at all. Stealing another look at him, she saw that he was looking straight ahead of him as before, but that his expression had grown thoughtful.

"Indeed," he said at last, with another sigh. "Much easier given than taken, but at least I've the comfort of knowing that my particular mistakes are pretty much beyond repeating. The opportunity to bungle on such a grand scale isn't likely to be granted to me twice in one lifetime."

There was such a weight of regret in his voice that Anne hardly knew how to respond. She made a sympathetic noise and waited to see if he would go on, but he did not, and the minutes dragged by in silence until she felt she must say something, even if it were something inane. Trying to inject a jocular note into her voice, she said, "At the moment, I must confess that my chief regret is not having eaten those sandwiches when I had the chance! I do wish I had at least put one in my reticule, instead of spurning them all in an excess of injured virtue. And why could there not have been a ham in the boot, as we had every right to expect? I am rather put out with that Scotswoman of ours, Stephen. If she could not spare one of her hams, she might at least have sent a pie or pudding, even if it were only one of those horrible puddings the Scotch make out of sheep's stomachs. What is it they're called?"

"Haggis?" suggested Stephen. His voice had regained its normal tone, Anne was relieved to note; he even sounded as if he might be smiling.

"Yes, a haggis. It's a desperate statement, but I think I am almost hungry enough to welcome a dinner of sheep's entrails!"

Stephen laughed, but Anne could detect in his voice a trace of his earlier emotion. "Are you?" he said. "For myself, I passed that stage of desperation some time ago. I would be very happy to dine upon haggis—or husks."

A gust of wind shook the coach, drowning out any reply Anne might have made. She shivered, and Stephen drew the greatcoat closer around her. For a time they sat without speaking, listening to the howling of the wind outside. They sat so long at last that Anne began to lose track of time and to succumb by degrees to an urgent and irresistible drowsiness. Her eyelids grew heavier and heavier, until she could no longer keep them open, and the rise and fall of the wind blurred into a steady, monotonous murmur that further lulled her wearied senses. She slept, only to awake with a start some time later. There were tears on her cheeks, icy cold, and for a moment she was gripped by panic, unable to remember where she was or what had happened to her.

"Anne?" Stephen's voice, pitched cautiously low, came out of the darkness beside her. "Were you asleep?"

"I suppose I was," she said, shifting her position a little so that she could look up at him. "It must have been the wind that woke me. No, it couldn't have been that, for the wind's died down, hasn't it? I dreamed I heard my mother calling me. I tried and tried to find her, but I couldn't—and then I woke up."

Though he was not a superstitious man, Stephen felt the hair rise on the back of his neck. "It was only a dream," he said, with more conviction than he felt. "Nothing but a dream. Go ahead and go back to sleep, if you can."

Anne nodded, and Stephen could see the tears sparkling on her cheeks. On an impulse he reached down and wiped them gently away with his hand. The next instant he was sorry, fearing he had been guilty of presumption, but she only gave him a tremulous smile and laid her head on his chest once again. It was a gesture so childlike and trusting that he was emboldened to go a step further and pat her on the back, as though she really were a child in need of comfort. He then put his arms around her as before and sat listening to the soft sighing of the wind as she settled down to sleep.

Four

It was a long and thoroughly miserable night, which passed for Anne in a haze of suffering. She drifted in and out of sleep, dozing fitfully, waking, then dozing again, conscious even while she slept of the cold and the discomfort of her cramped position. If her companion slept, she was unaware of it. Whenever she opened her eyes she found him awake and looking toward the window, where the snow continued to hiss and the wind to sigh with ever-diminishing voice.

Both wind and snow had stopped, and a pale gray light had begun to glow in the east when Anne finally awoke for good. She was stiff with cold and cramped from sleeping in a sitting position, but these discomforts were more than outweighed by the exquisite relief of finding herself alive to face another day. Stephen was already awake, if indeed he had ever been asleep; he looked down at her with a smile as she sat up and looked around her. She smiled back rather wanly.

"Good morning," she said. "Gracious, but I'm stiff and sore. I feel as though I've aged about thirty years since yesterday, which isn't surprising when I think about it. Last night seemed to go on forever. Did you manage to sleep at all?"

"A little, I think. The wind kept me awake at first, but toward morning I think I slept for an hour or two." Surreptitiously he shrugged his shoulders in an effort to relieve his cramped muscles. Anne saw the movement and got quickly to her feet, wincing a little as her own muscles gave protest.

"You must be very tired of holding me on your lap all this

time, Mr. Etheridge. It was very chivalrous of you to let me sleep, but I'm afraid I robbed you of the chance to get any sleep yourself."

He disclaimed the idea with a smile, but his expression was quizzical as he surveyed her. "Our acquaintance appears to have taken a step backward overnight," he said. "You just called me Mr. Etheridge. Does that mean we are back to terms of formality once more?"

"No, of course not, Stephen," said Anne quickly. Yet she found herself a little uncomfortable using his first name now, as though she were presuming on an intimacy that no longer existed. What had seemed perfectly natural last night in a situation of darkness and danger seemed less natural now that day had dawned and the worst of the danger seemed to have passed.

"No, of course not, Stephen," she repeated, and hurried on in an effort to hide her discomfort. "It looks as though the storm is over, doesn't it? I wonder if it would be premature to hope we might be rescued before too much longer."

"Not premature at all, I should think," said Stephen. He was greatly disappointed by the reserve that had crept back into her manner, and in hopes of breaking it down, he had recourse to humor once more. "Yes, our rescue can be only a matter of hours away. You'd better be reviewing your dinner menu so you'll have it all ready when we finally get back to civilization!"

She smiled at that, but shook her head. "It's odd, but I'm not nearly so hungry now as I was last night. I really believe I'm more thirsty than hungry. At the moment I'd trade my whole menu for a nice long drink of water—even Harrogate water!"

Stephen laughed, then stopped suddenly with an arrested expression. "You may be about to get your wish," he said. "Did you hear that?"

"What?" said Anne, listening.

"I'm sure I heard something—it sounded like someone shouting. Yes, there it is again," he said, as a halloo rang out in the distance. The two of them exchanged startled, hopeful glances and hurried to the window. Anne, who was already on her feet, got there first; she let down the glass and leaned out to look. The sun had just begun to peep over the horizon, bathing the eastern sky in a rosy light and turning the snow-covered countryside into a vista of dazzling whiteness as far as the eye could see. Anne spared no glance for its beauty, however; her eyes were turned toward the south, where a party of men on horseback was making its way slowly along the road.

"Oh, Stephen, we are saved," she said joyously. "There's a whole troop of men on horseback heading toward us right now."

Stephen joined her at the window, observing with inward pleasure that in her excitement she had used his Christian name quite naturally. "Eight horses," he said, leaning out to look at the distant cavalcade. "They're not taking half measures, are they? But I suppose a double team might come in useful if there are other bigger drifts further on. I remember the guard talking yesterday about the winter of '99 and how the roads along here were closed for weeks because the snow was so deep. It's a relief to see that our storm didn't measure up to that one. I kept thinking about it all last night, wondering if we weren't going to make history, too."

Anne laughed and shivered at the same time. "So that's why you couldn't sleep," she said. "It was considerate of you not to share your fears with me. I was worried enough at the thought of surviving just *one* night!"

Stephen turned his head to smile at her. It struck Anne that he was looking much more relaxed and cheerful this morning, even in spite of his sleepless night; she would hardly have recognized him for the stern-faced gentleman who had sat opposite her during the journey of the previous day. She gave him a quick smile in return before turning her eyes toward the team of men and horses who were now approaching within a few hundred yards of the mailcoach.

"They'll have some heavy digging to do before we'll be able to move the coach," said Stephen, also watching their approach. "I'd better go and give them a hand. You can stay here in the

coach with my greatcoat. Yes, indeed, Anne; once again I must
insist. I won't be needing it if I'm shoveling snow, I assure you!"

Anne protested at this further instance of chivalry, but let
herself be persuaded into keeping the greatcoat for the time
being, on the condition that he resume it for the journey back.
This he promised to do, and he left her wrapped snugly in its
folds while he went out to join the rescue party.

They had by now reached the snowbound mailcoach, and the
air was filled with the sound of rough north country accents as
the men dismounted their horses, shouldered shovels and
spades, and set to work digging the coach out of its snowbank.
They were half-a-dozen red-faced countrymen garbed in home-
spun garments and heavy boots, but to Anne they appeared like
angels from heaven as she watched them from the coach window. An occasional grunt or oath accompanied their labors, but
their voices rang out cheerily in the frosty morning air, and the
scraping of their shovels made a music very pleasant to her
ears. Stephen reappeared at intervals to report on their progress,
and once to offer her a drink from a leather-bound flask.

"It's not water, I'm afraid, but at least it's wet, and it definitely
ought to keep you warm! That fellow over there asked me to
give it to you, with his compliments." Stephen nodded toward
one of the countrymen, who gave her a shy smile and then
ducked his head in an abashed manner. "It's likely to be afternoon before we can get anything else, so I thought you'd better
have it. Drink as much as you can, and I'll pick up the bottle
next time I come around."

Anne thanked him with a smile and smiled also at her home-
spun benefactor, who ducked his head again and grew quite red
with pleasure. After Stephen had left, she uncorked the flask
and tilted it cautiously to her lips. The potency of the spirit
made her gasp and choke, but she swallowed the draught cou-
rageously and was rewarded a moment later by a pleasant sense
of warmth and well-being which rapidly pervaded her being.
But the flavor was so distasteful that she could not drink enough
to allay her thirst; and when she found, in addition, that it had

a tendency to make her head swim, she had no hesitation about returning the flask to Stephen on his next visit.

Soon after this the sound of shovels ceased; and Anne, peering from the window, saw that the men were harnessing the fresh horses to the mailcoach. A few minutes later the coach gave a jerk and moved forward a few feet, then rolled back in its tracks. Several minutes elapsed, during which there was much shouting and more scraping of shovels; then at last the mailcoach was pulled free of the snowbank where it had resided so long. Having achieved their object, the men loaded their shovels and themselves on the outside of the mailcoach; and with one of their party appointed coachman, they set off down the road toward the south.

Anne had no opportunity to return the greatcoat, after all, for Stephen very cagily chose to ride outside with the other men and left her in unrivaled possession of it during the journey south. This journey proceeded very slowly, and was accomplished with no small degree of peril. Although the storm had ceased, the road was icy in places and heavily drifted in others; twice more the coach had to be dug out of drifts, and once it only narrowly escaped sliding into a ravine. But early in the afternoon they arrived at last in Branwick, a small village some twenty miles south of the border.

The village boasted only one inn, a low rambling structure of wattle-and-daub that gave the appearance of having seen better days. Anne had no fault to find with its appearance, however, any more than she had been in a mood to find fault with the homely character of her rescuers. Her thirst had by this time grown to nearly unbearable proportions, as had her hunger; and though the brandy and greatcoat had kept her from feeling the cold too painfully, she was almost as eager for fire as for food and drink. As soon as the coach turned into the innyard she was on her feet, pulling off the greatcoat with the intention of restoring it to its owner whenever he should appear.

He appeared very shortly in the doorway of the coach, but once again Anne's intentions were frustrated. When she presented him with the greatcoat, he simply draped it around her own shoulders, swept her up in his arms, and proceeded to carry her across the snowy innyard. Anne alternately laughed and scolded at this high-handed treatment, but Stephen remained smilingly deaf to her objections. He did not set her on her feet again until they had attained the inn's public room, a small dingy room with a sanded floor which was at present deserted of company.

"Upon my word, Stephen, this is carrying chivalry too far," said Anne, shaking out her skirts and then laying her hands against her cheeks in an effort to warm the former and cool the latter. "I was perfectly able to walk across that innyard by myself."

"I know you were, my dear, but I didn't see any point in your wetting your boots when mine were already wet through." As Stephen spoke these words, he became aware that a third person had entered the public room, a dour-looking dame of middle years clad in a mobcap and a none-too-clean apron. She was standing in the doorway with elbows akimbo, regarding them both with an expression of marked disapprobation.

"Good afternoon, madam," said Stephen, who had taken in the cap and apron along with the woman's proprietary stance and had correctly identified her as his hostess. "I trust we do not discommode you by our entrance. My name is Etheridge, and my companion and I are half-frozen and in an advanced state of starvation. We require food, fire, drink, and a private parlor, not necessarily in that order."

The landlady's expression of disfavor became even more marked. She looked him up and down, not bothering to conceal the suspicion in her eyes. "Oh, you do, do you? And who might you be, sir?" she said belligerently.

"I just told you, madam: my name is Etheridge, Stephen Etheridge. The lady and I have just passed a most cold and miserable night, and if you would be so good as to show us to a private parlor—"

"Oh, you'll be the ones as was snowed up in the mailcoach,"

said the landlady with sudden enlightenment. "This way, sir; there's a fire burning in the taproom. We haven't such a thing as a private parlor here, but you're welcome to use my own sitting room if you like. I'll call Betsy and have her build you a bit of a fire. She ought to be somewhere about, if she's not off flirting with the stable lads again, the lazy slut. Betsy!" Shouting repeatedly for her handmaiden, the landlady led Anne and Stephen to the taproom and flung open the door.

The fire in the taproom was so small as to warm virtually nothing of the room beyond the immediate area of the grate. Anne lost no time in dropping to her knees before it, however, and holding out her hands to its meager blaze. Stephen paused only to remove his hat and gloves before doing the same.

"Doesn't that feel wonderful?" said Anne, flexing her stiff and reddened fingers over the fire. The landlady had lingered in the doorway to watch them both with undisguised curiosity, and Anne gave her a friendly smile. "You can't conceive, ma'am, what a relief it is to be here after being cold and hungry for so long," she told the woman. "If it wouldn't be too much trouble, do you think I might have a glass of water?"

"Water, miss?" said the landlady, looking at her incredulously. "I'd say tea or a spot of rum and water'd be more to the purpose."

"Yes, we will want something more later on, no doubt, but for now the lady would like a glass of water," said Stephen, producing a couple of coins from his pocket and clinking them together suggestively. The landlady gave them both another incredulous look, but trotted off obediently in search of water.

"What a miserable little fire," said Anne, as soon as the door had shut behind her. "I hope Betsy is building us a better one in the sitting room. Our landlady is clearly a stingy soul. There aren't even any fire-irons here to build it up."

"You're right," said Stephen, looking about the hearth. "But miserliness might not be the motive for that, you know—or at least not the only motive. Possibly they've heard reports of young women using them as weaponry on their male guests."

A look distinctly mischievous accompanied these words,

which surprised a gurgle of laughter from Anne. She was still
a trifle flown from the effects of brandy and water on an empty
stomach, and her mood had been made even giddier by the relief
of finding herself safe after the trials of the last twenty-four
hours. She suspected her companion must be feeling some of
the same effects, to judge from his behavior since reaching the
inn: the way he had carried her into the taproom, for instance,
and the levity—almost the hilarity—of his manner of addressing the landlady. Anne laughed, therefore, and shook her head.

"I cannot believe now that all that really happened," she said.
"The past day and a half seems like some kind of mad dream—
more like a nightmare really, I suppose. If it weren't that I'm
so hungry and thirsty, I'd be tempted to think I did dream it."

Stephen was prevented from responding by the landlady, who
had just come back into the taproom with a glass of water in
her hand. This she presented to Anne, who took it with a word
of thanks and drank it off at a draught. The landlady watched
her incredulously and received back the empty glass with the
air of one who had witnessed a singular act of folly.

"Now food," said Stephen. Rising to his feet, he turned to
the landlady and addressed her with a courtly bow. "Dear
madam, we require—let us see—I believe it was a clear soup
to start with, wasn't it?" His manner was perfectly solemn, but
there was laughter in the dark eyes turned inquiringly toward
Anne. "Follow that with some ham and a hot roast chicken, if
you please. Oh, I'm forgetting the shrimps, aren't I? Shrimps,
and *then* the ham and roast chicken—"

"And the gentleman will have a large beefsteak," said Anne,
entering into the game with zest and endeavoring to imitate her
companion's solemn manner. "Rare beefsteak and fried potatoes. And for dessert an apple tart—"

"No, sponge cake with strawberries and cream!"

During this exchange, the landlady's head had been swiveling
back and forth like a spectator at a game of battledore and
shuttlecock. When they were done, she spoke in a flat voice:
"There's not a thing in the house but a cold pork pie."

"Good enough," they said in unison, and burst out laughing like a pair of lunatics. The landlady regarded them for a long moment, then left the room shaking her head and muttering under her breath.

"Do you know, I get the distinct feeling that woman doesn't approve of us," said Anne, her voice unsteady with laughter.

"I get the same feeling," said Stephen. "Possibly she has never been in the presence of two people who have narrowly escaped a frosty death."

"It does give one a different outlook, doesn't it? I don't think I shall ever look at life the same way again. In the past I must confess that I used to grow vexed at quite small things—when my landlady used to call me deary, for instance, or when my dinner was late or ill-dressed. But no more: from now on I shall accept all the vicissitudes of boarding house life with perfect good humor and thank heaven that I am alive to endure them."

Stephen laughed. "A fine philosophical statement, Miss Compton! I agree with it in theory, but though dinner may be an unimportant issue in the overall scheme of things, just at present I am finding it an issue of some moment."

"Yes, now that I've had something to drink, I feel twice as hungry as before. I suppose I should wash my hands and see about smoothing my hair and dress before we sit down to eat. I wonder if there's an empty bedchamber somewhere that I might use for a few minutes?"

Anne repeated this question to a slatternly maidservant, presumably Betsy, who came into the taproom a few minutes later to minister to the dying fire. The girl nodded and showed her to a bleak, sparsely furnished chamber on the upper floor of the inn. At Anne's further behest she fetched a basin of tepid water and then clumped her way back downstairs while Anne washed her face and hands and took stock of her appearance in the small dark looking glass over the washstand. Her hair was coming undone, and her dress was rather rumpled; she smoothed the latter as best she could and took her hair down altogether, combing it out with one of her sidecombs and pinning it neatly up again.

"At least I appear respectable from the neck up," she told herself, as she set the pins into place. She had given no thought to her appearance since leaving Harrogate the day before, but now she found herself taking great pains with her toilette, possessed by a determination to look her best before she went downstairs again. It did not take her long to realize what had inspired this determination, and when she did, she laughed aloud at her own folly.

"He is certainly a very attractive gentleman, and a very agreeable one, too, but that's no reason to make a fool of yourself," she told her reflection. "You mustn't go trying to read anything romantic into the situation. Given the circumstances, it's only natural that we should have become somewhat intimate, but only a fool would refine too much on such an intimacy. If he hasn't already forgotten, he's probably regretting that he lowered himself to discuss his personal affairs with a perfect stranger. I know I'm embarrassed to think how I discussed mine with him—and then the way I cried all over his shoulder last night, simply because I had a bad dream! If he thinks anything at all of me, I expect he thinks me a perfect wet-goose."

As Anne's thoughts continued in this vein, she wondered again what he had done in the past that seemed to cause him so much regret. His offense must have been serious indeed if it had caused him to be cast off by his family, as she had gathered to be the case. His remarks about the prodigal son would seem to indicate that there had been profligacy, at the very least; and for the first time it occurred to her that she might be doing an unwise thing in continuing her acquaintance with such a man. Of course she could not avoid his company altogether while they remained at the same inn, but there was certainly no necessity to take her meals with him. She might easily send down a message to the landlady and have her dinner brought to her room. Then she recalled how he had shared his greatcoat with her the night before and had stayed awake so that she might sleep, and she grew ashamed. No matter what he had done in the past, he must have atoned for it by the way he had treated her during those long hours of cold and uncertainty.

"No one could have been more of a gentleman," she told herself. "But gentleman or not, from now on I must be on my guard. It's obvious that I'm not indifferent to him, or I wouldn't have spent the last fifteen minutes primping myself here in front of the glass. And it really won't do, Anne; only a fool would let herself become involved with a man she knows nothing about. Especially one who seems to have so many dark secrets in his past . . ."

While Anne was making these resolutions in the inn's best bedchamber, Stephen was in the room next door making a few alterations to his own appearance. He could not do as much as he would have liked, for he had left his friend's house in such a hurry that he had brought only a few essentials with him in a valise; his other things were to have been packed and sent on later under care of his valet. In consequence he could not change his jacket, which like Anne's dress was rather creased from being slept in, but he was able to change his shirt and neckcloth, a change that made him feel very much better.

He washed, and combed his hair, and ran a hand appraisingly over the day's growth of beard on his face, but decided to postpone shaving lest he make himself late for dinner. He was looking forward to that dinner with great eagerness, and as he went down the stairs it occurred to him that his eagerness had, upon the whole, very little to do with hunger. Certainly there was an excitement in his breast which could not be explained solely by the prospect of cold pork pie. He paused at the foot of the stairs to analyze this sensation. Being a man of good sense and reasonable intelligence, an explanation was not long in occurring to him.

"Good lord," he said aloud, and then a moment later, "Well, but why not? It's damnably ill-timed, of course, and I wouldn't have chosen this particular method of introduction, but on the other hand it's quite likely that I never would have met her at all if I had waited for any other. I must go slowly, that's all, particularly here at first. She will need time to get over that other business, no doubt, and as for me—I must get my affairs in order before I can legitimately go paying court to anyone. After that—we shall see. I intend to try, anyway."

And having delivered himself of these sentiments, he continued on his way into the sitting room quite as though nothing had happened.

Five

Anne arrived in the sitting room a few minutes after Stephen did and found the table already laid for two.

"Our board awaits, you see," he said with a smile. He was doing his best to keep his manner exactly as it had been before, but feared he must be betraying himself by every look and word. As he helped Anne seat herself at the table, he observed her closely, trying to judge by her behavior how far she might be aware of his feelings and, still more importantly, how far she might go toward sharing them. What he observed was disappointing. She thanked him politely for his assistance, yet it seemed to him that her manner was cooler than it had been earlier that afternoon. This might well be due to hunger, however; he reflected that she must be near to fainting after being so many hours without food. Taking his own seat, he quickly set about helping her to the several dishes that were awaiting them on the table.

Besides the promised pork pie, there were a couple of bowls containing spinach and boiled potatoes and a third that held an apple dumpling still steaming from the oven. "It would appear that our landlady understated her resources," said Stephen, as he passed Anne her plate. "It looks better than I dared expect, but I'm afraid it's much closer to my ideal menu rather than yours."

"Perhaps, but I'm sure it will taste wonderful," said Anne. She spoke more warmly than she intended, for the smell and sight of the food had affected her so strongly that she forgot all about her resolution to treat him with greater reserve. Indeed, it took considerable effort to force herself to use knife and fork like a civilized person instead of tearing into the food like a voracious animal. "Oh, this is so good," she said fervently. "I don't think I've ever properly appreciated pork pie before. Or boiled potatoes!"

"It's a case of hunger making the best sauce, I suppose," said Stephen. "Although I will say that our landlady's cooking is much better than her appearance would lead one to suppose."

"It is, isn't it?" said Anne, shutting her eyes to enjoy a particularly savory bite. Having emptied her plate, she passed it to him to fill again and unashamedly embarked on second helpings all around. He himself had already finished his own second plateful and was working his way through a large serving of apple dumpling; they ate in companionable silence broken only by the clink of cutlery on china. At last Anne pushed her plate away with a sigh.

"Can I help you to anything else?" inquired Stephen.

"No, not a thing. At the moment I am perfectly satisfied. Indeed, more than satisfied—it feels absolutely heavenly to be alive and warm and full of good food after being cold and hungry for so long. And I owe it all to you, Stephen." Anne looked at him soberly from across the table. "You saved my life, you know. If you had chosen to ride on with the others I know quite well I would not be sitting at this table now. I could never have survived last night without you and your greatcoat."

Stephen shook his head. "You don't owe me a thing," he said. "Our survival was a joint effort, and you did quite as much for me as I did for you."

"I find that rather difficult to believe, Stephen," said Anne, regarding him skeptically. "Tell me truly now, would you have stayed with the coach if I hadn't been there? I have a strong suspicion that you wouldn't have, luggage or no luggage!"

Stephen hesitated. He had no wish to prevaricate, but it seemed a little early in their acquaintance to reveal his real motives for staying. "Perhaps not," he said cautiously. "Still, I can say now that I am glad I did stay, for several reasons. If nothing else, it has been a valuable lesson to me not to take life for granted. One is so apt to assume that one is immortal, you know, until mortality actually stares one in the face. I've wasted a lot of my life brooding over mistakes I've made in the past—mistakes that are past mending. When I finally made the decision yesterday to go home and face my responsibilities, I'd gone one step in the right direction, and now it seems almost as though this experience was sent to hurry me along a little. In any case, it's made me resolve to put the past behind me once and for all and not let it poison any more of the future."

Once again Anne felt a burning curiosity to know what deed had prompted so much regret. "Indeed?" she said encouragingly. He only smiled, however, and shook his head.

"I'm sorry, I don't mean to make a mystery of my past. Someday, perhaps, I'll tell you all about it, but it's a long and rather sordid tale, and this is supposed to be a celebration. And that being the case, I think we ought to have a toast, don't you? A toast to celebrate our victory over storm and snow."

"Yes, certainly," said Anne, a trifle disappointed by his reticence, but rallying gamely. "Only I doubt whether our landlady has any champagne in her cellars!"

"Yes, it really ought to be champagne, of course, but I'm afraid we'll have to make do with our landlady's homebrew—which isn't half bad, I am happy to say."

"I think I would prefer to make do with water," said Anne, regarding the amber liquid in Stephen's tankard with a dubious eye.

Stephen laughed. "No, my dear, you cannot drink a solemn toast with water," he told her. "I'll give you half a glass, and you can work on acquiring a taste for English beer along with English beef. Are you ready? Well, then, to life! May neither of us ever take it for granted again."

Anne raised the glass to her lips, took a cautious sip, and set it down hastily. "I don't think I like English beer any more than I like English beef," she said. "Much less, in fact."

Again Stephen laughed. "First you insult roast beef, and now honest homebrew—what kind of an Englishwoman are you, Miss Compton? Well, never mind; I'll drink the beer, and we can ring for the landlady and order you a pot of tea."

He had no sooner spoken these words than the landlady herself appeared in the doorway of the sitting room. She was wearing a slightly more friendly expression than she had earlier, and in her hands she carried a tray containing a steaming bowl and a couple of glasses. "I just wondered, sir, if you and the lady mightn't care for a drop of punch to warm you up," she said, holding the tray invitingly before him and Anne. "We make as good a bowl of punch here as you'll taste anywhere in England, if I do say so myself."

"Thank you, Mrs.—Mrs.—I don't think I know your name, ma'am—"

"Mrs. Campbell, sir."

"Thank you, Mrs. Campbell. I wouldn't mind a glass or two of punch, and perhaps the lady will join me for a glass, too, if I can persuade her to give over drinking your fine beer." He smiled at Anne, who laughed and made a face at him. The landlady set the bowl and glasses upon the table, but when this was done she did not leave the room, as Stephen had expected. Instead, she continued to stand beside the table, wiping her hands on her apron and surveying both him and Anne with an expression at once indecisive and calculating.

"Well, Mrs. Campbell?" he said, rather impatiently.

"I was just thinking, sir . . ." The air of calculation in the landlady's manner was very pronounced as she looked from him to Anne. "I was thinking that if you and the lady was looking to be married, sir, I've a cousin just across the border who could do the business for you. A proper parson he is, too—none of your rubbishing smiths, or anything of that sort. The roads'll be clear by tomorrow, they say, and if you and the lady wanted to nip over to Gretna I know Andrew'd be happy to tie the knot for you."

These words struck Stephen like a direct blow to the solar

plexus. It was clear from Anne's face that she had sustained a similar shock; she was staring at the landlady with dismay written large on every feature.

"What makes you think that the lady and I stand in need of your cousin's services?" said Stephen, as soon as he had recovered enough to speak.

"Why, what should I think, sir? A gentleman and a lady so friendly-like, laughing and joking and traveling together so close to the border—well, it's as plain as the nose on your face, if you'll pardon me for saying so, sir. And if you wasn't planning to marry, all I can say is that it's more shame to the both of you, considering how the two of you spent last night!"

"I see," said Stephen, and with an effort managed to keep his voice level. "Well, I thank you very much for your recommendation, Mrs. Campbell. The lady and I will keep your cousin in mind, should we find ourselves in need of his services." With a hand only slightly unsteady, he reached out to ladle a glass of punch from the bowl.

Mrs. Campbell looked dissatisfied, but the dismissal in his voice was unmistakable. Slowly she shuffled out of the room, casting a backwards glance at them both before shutting the door behind her.

"Oh, Stephen, what shall we do?" said Anne. Her voice sounded near tears as she continued, "It never entered my head that anyone would expect us to—no, it can't be possible. It was all an accident, a wretched accident, and surely people would not think it necessary for us to marry only because we happened to be caught in a snowstorm for a few hours?"

Stephen drank off half a glass of punch before replying. He felt rather dazed by the recent turn of events. "But you see, people *do* think it necessary, people like Mrs. Campbell at any rate," he said. "And I'm afraid a large part of the world would be similarly censorious."

"But it's so stupid," said Anne passionately. "To marry, only because an accident put us in the same mailcoach on the day of a blizzard! And it's not as though anyone need know about it, Stephen. If we were to leave here immediately and go our separate ways—"

"No, I'm afraid that wouldn't serve. The thing is, you know, that quite a few people already *do* know about it," said Stephen. He was surprised by how cool and logical his voice sounded, quite the opposite from what he was feeling. He continued, "Our landlady, and the guard and coachman—even the men who dug us out of the drift this morning. They all know about it, and it won't take long for the word to spread. A snowed-in mailcoach is always news. I wouldn't be surprised if it didn't rate a paragraph in the London newspapers."

Anne shook her head distractedly. "I cannot believe this is happening. And here we thought our difficulties would be over, once we got out of that snowbank! Oh, Stephen, what shall we do?"

Stephen took another drink of punch and thought rapidly. For his part, he would not have been averse to taking the landlady's advice and nipping over the border to take advantage of her cousin's services, but he could appreciate Anne's reservations; even for a man well on his way to being in love, he felt things were happening a little fast. A marriage begun with an unwilling bride was not likely to be a felicitous one.

"I have an idea," he said finally. "A compromise, if you will. Instead of getting married immediately, perhaps we could pass ourselves off as a betrothed couple for a few weeks."

"What good would that do?" said Anne despairingly. "Everyone would still expect us to marry in the end."

"As a first step, it would help quiet Mrs. Campbell's tongue. And it would buy us a little time— time to see how serious the situation is likely to prove and to decide what we want to do about it."

"Yes, I suppose it would do that much," agreed Anne.

"We could stay here long enough for you to send for your luggage in Harrogate," Stephen went on, with a quick look at her downcast face. "And then I could take you to my home for a few weeks while we waited to see which way the cat was going to jump. The betrothal wouldn't be formally announced, you understand; we would merely let it be understood among my family that we are engaged. Your mourning would be reason enough to postpone any formal announcement."

"And then?"

"And then, if at the end of a few weeks it looks as though the thing's going to die down by itself, we can declare our engagement null and void and go our separate ways." Stephen felt a chill within him as he pronounced these words. He took another sip of punch to fortify himself before continuing in a matter-of-fact voice. "And if the thing *doesn't* look as though it will die down—well, then, we get married."

Anne was quiet for several minutes as she thought this over. "It's not a bad plan," she said at last, rather grudgingly. "But won't your family think it very odd for you to arrive home for Christmas with a perfectly strange young woman in tow and calmly announce her as your fiancée?"

"My family will not mind that. In fact—well, I don't wish to influence your decision one way or another, but the fact is that I would be very glad to have you there with me, Anne. You've probably gathered from what I told you that my homecoming was likely to prove somewhat awkward. The presence of another person would do a great deal to mitigate the awkwardness—it would remove the focus of the occasion from me, so to speak."

Anne hesitated a moment longer, then nodded. "If you are quite certain your family will not mind my being there, then I suppose there would be no harm in my accompanying you," she said. "But I still cannot believe it's really necessary. What a lot of bother I am causing you, Stephen. First you have to save my life, and now it looks as though you're going to have to save my reputation, too."

"I don't mind doing either one," said Stephen stoutly.

Anne smiled with a trace of her old spirit. "You really are too good to be true, you know," she said. "A regular Galahad, rushing to the defense of a damsel in distress! I suppose all the damsels you rescue tell you that?"

"No, but I've been told once or twice that I have an overdeveloped sense of responsibility, and that probably amounts to much the same thing. In the present case my responsibility is clear, however—and I truly am glad to be of service to you, Anne." Fearing he was about to betray himself, he hurried on to a less perilous subject. "I hope spending Christmas at my house won't upset any plans you've already made?"

"No, indeed. The only plans I had made involved a gentleman whose acquaintance I intend to cut hereafter. Your invitation is actually in the nature of a Godsend, or would be, if it weren't prompted by such an unfortunate necessity. But even so, I must confess that I am rather looking forward to experiencing a real English Christmas for the first time since I was a child. Do you and your family do all the old-fashioned things like Yule logs and boars' heads?"

"Oh, yes," Stephen assured her with a smile. "My mother is a fiend for tradition and an inveterate party-giver. I can promise you that you'll have your fill of old-fashioned Yuletide merriment at Etheridge Hall."

"Etheridge Hall," repeated Anne. "It sounds . . . impressive."

"I think you will like it. Of course, it's been some time since I've seen it myself, but I have no reason to think it's gone downhill in my absence." In another abrupt change of subject, he gestured toward the table with its burden of half-empty dishes and soiled plates. "If we're done eating, we may as well ring for Mrs. Campbell and tell her we're done with dinner. At the same time we can drop her a hint or two about our betrothal. Perhaps we can be discussing wedding dates when she comes into the room, and that will lead into the subject quite naturally."

Anne assented to this idea without much enthusiasism. "I suppose I must get used to the idea of play-acting for the next few weeks," she said with a sigh. "But it does seem hard that we must go to all this trouble only because that old busybody and two or three others want to make a scandal out of something perfectly innocent."

"Yes, it is very unfortunate. I could kick myself for making such a point of introducing myself when we first came in. If it hadn't been for that, we might have escaped without anyone knowing our names at all. No, I'm forgetting, my name would have been on the waybill of the mailcoach. Yours wasn't, of course—"

"No, but the guard knew it. He asked me for my name and direction at one of the stops, and though I didn't like to tell him, I was afraid he'd put me off if I didn't. I think he had the impression I was a fugitive from Bow Street!"

"That settles it, then. There'll be no escape for either of us if the story gets abroad. It's enough to make me wish I'd traveled under an assumed name—but it could have been worse, I suppose. At least I had sense enough not to use my title."

Anne, who had been sitting slumped dejectedly in her chair, suddenly sprang to attention at these words. "Title?" she said sharply. "What title do you mean?"

Stephen gave her a rather embarrassed smile. "I'm afraid I wasn't being perfectly frank when I introduced myself to you last night," he said. "My name really is Etheridge, but it's Lord Etheridge, not Mr. Etheridge—"

"Oh, no!" Anne was sitting straight up in her chair now, staring at him as if he had suddenly grown horns. *"Lord* Etheridge—oh, why did you not tell me sooner? I never would have agreed to any of this if I had known. To accompany you to your home—and to pretend to be betrothed to you—no, I never would have agreed to it. Indeed, I cannot agree to it now, my lord."

The violence of her reaction rather astonished Stephen, who had not supposed her the woman to be intimidated by a title "No, you mustn't be 'my-lording' me now, Anne, not after all we've been through together," he said, hoping to laugh her out of her mood. "The title's not one I particularly care for, and you needn't care for it, either. It's not even a very impressive title as such things go. I'm not a member of the upper nobility—not a duke, or a marquess, or even an earl. Only a lowly viscount, and not a very experienced viscount at that. I've only held the title for a couple of years."

His assurances fell on deaf ears. Anne, in a trembling voice, repeated that he should have told her sooner that he was a nobleman, and that she never would have consented to be betrothed to him even in pretense if she had known the truth.

It soon dawned upon Stephen that her distress was much greater than could be accounted for by a mistaken sense of unworthiness, or even by resentment at having been initially deceived. But he had no opportunity to discover from whence sprang her reservations. She was already on her feet and moving toward the door, and he had all he could do, first, to persuade her to stay in the room; second, to induce her to resume her seat; and third, to convince her to listen to what he had to say.

"I know you don't like it, Anne. I don't like it either, as it happens, but if we can stave off a scandal by pretending to be engaged for a few weeks, it seems to me a small price to pay. You must see that we haven't much alternative at this point."

"Yes, I see," she said, in a voice charged with hostility. Stephen eyed her apprehensively for a moment before going on.

"So you agree to the idea of a temporary engagement? And you will accompany me to my home for the holidays, as we agreed before?"

"I suppose I must," said Anne. She spoke grudgingly, however—so grudgingly that Stephen felt her consent had better be ratified through some immediate and positive action. Accordingly, he rang for the landlady and requested her to bring paper, pen, and wafers.

"And you might also give me the direction of your cousin in Gretna," he added casually. "I don't say we'll need it immediately, but there's definitely a trip to the altar somewhere in our future. Isn't there, my dear?" he said, with a tender look at Anne.

She forced her features into a semblance of a smile and nodded. Mrs. Campbell grunted her approbation and went off to fetch the writing materials. When she had laid them on the table in front of them and departed again, Stephen turned to Anne.

"You must write and send for your things in Harrogate as soon as possible," he said. "We may as well stay on here until they arrive. This place isn't exactly luxurious, but at least it's quiet, and at this stage the fewer people privy to our situation the better. I suppose I ought to send off a letter, too, while I'm at it."

"To your mother?" said Anne, reluctantly pulling a sheet of paper toward her and uncorking the ink-bottle.

"No, to the Archbishop of Canterbury. It's just occurred to me that if news of our adventure does get about—if we find we must go through with the betrothal, you know—it would be of great advantage to have a special license on hand. If nothing else, it would save us the trouble of making a mad dash for the border and Cousin Andrew," Stephen finished, in a rather forlorn attempt at humor.

Anne did not laugh, or even smile. Her head was bent low over the letter she was writing, and as the pen moved over the paper, a noise like a sob broke from her lips.

Six

From her seat inside the post-chaise, Anne looked out at the passing countryside. Ahead of her she could see the postilions' backs bobbing up and down as they rode astride the post-horses; beside them rode Stephen on a bay hack hired from the last posting house. He rode well and made an impressive figure on horseback, but the sight of him filled Anne with an acute discomfort. Although several days had passed since she had agreed to play the role of his fiancée, time had not yet brought her to an acceptance of her new situation.

On the seat beside her rode Parker, her dressing woman, sitting stiffly erect with her eyes fixed straight ahead of her and her hands resting protectively on Anne's jewel case. She had arrived at the inn the day before in company with Anne's luggage and had immediately set to work putting her mistress's tangled affairs in order. Certainly her arrival had done a great deal to restore Anne's credit with her landlady. Mrs. Campbell's belligerence was no match for Parker at her most top-lofty, and a few hours had been enough to reduce the landlady to a state of cringing subservience. This had been amply demonstrated by a snatch of conversation Anne had overheard while passing the inn kitchen that morning.

"Of course it may seem strange to *you,* Mrs. Campbell, not being used to the ways of Quality," Parker was telling the landlady in a patronizing voice. "But I can assure you that to those of us accustomed to moving in the best circles—"

The kitchen door had swung shut just then, depriving Anne

of the last of this speech, but she got the benefit of it in the form of improved service from Mrs. Campbell and the other inn servants. Parker's arrival had also relieved Anne of other, more pressing difficulties having to do with her wardrobe. It was a relief to be able to change her dress at last, even if it were only for another black one, and to finally assume her own sable-lined cloak in place of Stephen's greatcoat.

She wore the cloak now along with a wide-brimmed black silk bonnet, a pair of black chamois gloves, and a large sable muff. Parker was also dressed in black out of deference to her mistress's mourning; she looked very severe and unbending as she sat gazing impassively ahead of her at the shabby interior of the post-chaise. Anne wondered what she was thinking. She could hardly have helped feeling curious about her mistress's sudden, mysterious disappearance from Harrogate and her equally mysterious reappearance at the Scottish border a few days later as the betrothed wife of an English viscount.

Yet Parker had shown no curiosity, asked no questions, and accepted the whole situation with an imperturbability that seemed to Anne well-nigh inhuman. On the whole she was grateful for her serving woman's reticence, but now and then she found herself wishing that Parker were not quite so conscientious about preserving the proper respectful distance between herself and her employer. There had been many times in the past few days when Anne had felt sorely in need of a confidante.

As the chaise rattled over the snow-covered road, she wondered what lay ahead of her at Etheridge Hall. During the past few days, Stephen had told her a little more about his home, its history, and its inhabitants, and from his words she had gathered that Etheridge Hall was not an ancient, ghost-ridden family manor but rather a comfortable, relatively modern country residence.

"Our name is a fairly old one, but the title only goes back sixty years or so," Stephen had explained a couple of days earlier, when she had expressed a desire to learn more about the place she was going to. "It was the first Viscount Etheridge who built Etheridge Hall, probably feeling that a simple farm-house wasn't in keeping with the dignity of his new position. But he didn't let it go to his head too badly. The Hall isn't a moated castle, or a great unwieldy place like some noblemen's seats. The house itself is really quite livable, though it's larger than we need for just the few of us who live there now."

This had led naturally into a discussion of the inhabitants of Etheridge Hall. "Well, firstly there's my mother," said Stephen. "You will recall my mentioning her earlier, in connection with parties and family traditions! She does have rather a bee in her bonnet about those, but I think you will like her, Anne."

"Yes, but will she like me?" Anne had said frankly.

Stephen had given her a long, meditative look. "Yes, I believe she will," he said. "I have reason to think she would welcome any woman I brought home as a prospective bride, but you I think she will like for yourself. And for your red hair," he had added with a smile. "You must know that she has red hair herself and holds it to be a most superior coloring! She often regrets that neither Diana nor I inherited it."

"Diana is your sister?"

"Yes, my younger sister. She is considerably younger than I am—her sixteenth birthday would have been just a few weeks ago."

"So she's still in the schoolroom?"

"Ye—es. Yes, in a manner of speaking." Stephen's voice had held a trace of doubt. "I suppose you might call Diana a school-girl for want of a better word, but she's like no other schoolgirl I've ever encountered. Diana is—different. Different, and some-times difficult—at least, she was last time I saw her. She may have outgrown some of her more trying characteristics since then."

"You don't think she'll like me," said Anne, once again voic-ing the concern that was uppermost in her mind. But Stephen had shaken his head.

"No, I think Diana will like you very well, Anne. She will probably be glad to have another young woman in the house.

Etheridge Hall is rather isolated in its locale, and so is Ash Grove, the estate where she and I both spent most of our childhood years. There aren't many families in the neighborhood with girls her age. Sometimes I think that may be part of the reason why Diana is so different from the general run of schoolgirls."

This had sounded rather formidable to Anne, who had mentally resolved to tread warily around the different and difficult Diana Etheridge. "Is that all your family that lives at Etheridge Hall?" was her next question. "Just your mother and your sister?"

"No, I have also a cousin who lives there—a cousin by marriage, I should say. Lady Etheridge, my cousin Marcus's widow, still lives at the Hall along with her young daughter. It was from Marcus that I inherited the house and title on the occasion of his death a couple of years ago."

Anne had sensed a change in Stephen's voice when he spoke of his cousin, a quality of restraint that hinted at some strong underlying emotion. It was the same quality she had noticed that night in the mailcoach, when he had spoken of returning home as the prodigal son. "You and your cousin did not get on?" she had asked, observing him curiously.

"We got on very well until a few years ago. Both of us were the same age, or nearly so, and we were brought up practically as brothers. Marcus was orphaned very young, and my parents took him and raised him as one of their own. We went to Eton together, and to Oxford, and even after Marcus came into his inheritance he spent almost as much time at my father's estate in northern Yorkshire as he did at Etheridge Hall. Marcus and I were very close for most of our lives, but after he married we—grew apart."

Once again Stephen's voice had held that odd note of restraint. Anne had deduced that the late Lord Etheridge's marriage had been rather a sore point with Stephen; she wondered if perhaps he had disapproved of his cousin's choice of brides. Not wishing to trespass on what appeared to be sensitive ground, she had remained discreetly silent, and after a brief pause he had gone on to speak of his cousin's death.

"I still find it hard to believe he's really gone. His death was very sudden, very unexpected—I think it came as a shock to everyone who knew him. From what I have been able to learn, it seems that he was out in the fields one afternoon helping with the harvest, and he happened to cut his hand on one of the worker's scythes. That was all—but the cut became infected, and within a few days he was dead, just like that. A simple thing to cause a man to lose his life, isn't it? I was in Scotland at the time, and I didn't learn of it until he was already dead and buried. It is a source of never-ending regret to me that I wasn't able to see him before he died."

Although the statement was quietly made, it was evident from Stephen's voice how much he meant it. In light of her own recent bereavement, Anne could not help but feel for him, and though she well knew the inadequacy of language to ease such a loss, she had lain her hand on his arm and spoken a few words of earnest sympathy. He had appreciated the gesture, she thought; at any rate, his expression had softened, and he had taken her hand in his and held it for a moment with a pressure that was almost painful.

By mutual accord, they had gone on to speak of other things. Stephen had never again alluded to the subject of the late Lord Etheridge, but it was a subject very much in Anne's thoughts in the days that followed. She felt certain that there was some mystery connected with that gentleman and his sudden demise, and just as certainly she felt that the mystery must somehow involve Stephen. Exactly what the mystery was, she could not guess, but it would seem to have been rather a serious matter if it could separate two men who had been raised as brothers. The thing had rather a sinister appearance, in fact, though common sense kept Anne from jumping to any very lurid conclusions. The manner of the late Lord Etheridge's death made it obvious that Stephen could have played no part in it, even inadvertently, and there was in any case ample evidence to show that he had been in Scotland during the period when it had taken place. It was clear that no mystery lay there, but that a mystery did exist somewhere Anne could not doubt; and as the post-chaise rolled on its way toward Etheridge Hall she wondered if she were soon to be enlightened.

It was late afternoon when the chaise drew up before a pair of ornate wrought-iron gates set in a high stone wall. Through the chaise window Anne watched Stephen dismount from his horse to speak to a wizened little old man, evidently the gate-keeper, who had come out of the gatehouse to open the gates for them. As soon as they had passed through, Stephen re-mounted his horse and rode alongside the chaise as it rattled up the drive. Anne let down the chaise window to talk to him.

"I had no idea there were woods like these in northern England," she said. "Does all this belong to you, Stephen?"

"Yes," he said, looking about him at the grove of oaks and beeches through which they were passing. The sight seemed to cause him as much agitation as pleasure. Anne thought both emotions natural, considering his long absence from the place and the circumstances of his return. She put up the window again and leaned back against the seat as the chaise rolled down the drive. A few minutes later the drive emerged into the open, at a point where a stone bridge crossed a stream whose waters continued to flow sluggishly beneath a thick layer of ice. On the opposite bank, surrounded by an expanse of snow-covered lawn, stood Etheridge Hall.

The Hall was built of pinkish-gray stone with white stone facings. It made a striking picture against its wintry backdrop of snowy hills and barren trees, interspersed here and there with a cluster of dark green evergreens. The house consisted of a large central block with a pillared portico in front; two smaller wings stood on either side, and a long, low stable building was connected to it by a covered walkway. On the hill behind the house Anne observed a narrow cylindrical tower, also built of pinkish stone, of which the upper level appeared to be an open gallery. She supposed it to be some kind of garden folly; there

also appeared to be formal gardens laid out to the east and south
of the house, though at this season they naturally presented a
rather bleak appearance.

As the chaise drew up in front of the portico, a handsome
middle-aged woman wearing a cap and a green silk dress came
hurrying down the front steps. Stephen had just swung himself
down from his mount, and she ran toward him, threw her arms
around him, and embraced him exuberantly.

"Oh, Stephen! Oh, my dear, how good it is to see you again,"
she cried. "I am so very glad you decided to come after all,
Stephen. You can't imagine how much we all have missed you.
Oh, but you are grown thinner, Stephen! You're nothing but skin
and bones, upon my word. Did they not *feed* you in Scotland?"

Stephen laughed and enveloped the woman in his arms. "Yes,
Mother, they fed me very well," he said. "You're the one who
looks as though she's nothing but skin and bones. Don't say
you've been fretting yourself over my absence?"

The woman smiled, but her voice was serious as she answered, "It would be no wonder if I had. I cannot say how glad
I am that you have returned, Stephen. This is where you belong,
and if it had been up to me, you would never have left."

Anne, meanwhile, had descended from the chaise and stood
hesitating near the foot of the steps, feeling herself very much
an intruder on the scene. But Stephen, after good-humoredly
answering his mother's anxious inquiries about his health, soon
directed her attention toward his companion.

"Before you go making an invalid of me, Mother, there's
someone I want you to meet. Mother, this is my fiancée, Miss
Anne Compton; Anne, this is Mrs. Walter Etheridge, my honored and over-anxious mother."

Anne was unprepared for the expression of pure joy that
spread across Mrs. Etheridge's face. "My dear! Your fiancée!
Oh, Stephen, and you never breathed a word of this in your
letters! How like you to simply show up and astonish us all
with the news. Yes, and I am very pleased to meet *you,* my
dear—truly, you can't imagine how pleased I am." She accom-

panied her words with an warm hug, then stood back to examine
Anne with happy interest. "Oh, and she has red hair, Stephen!
Excellent taste on your part! You must know that my own used
to be red, too, Miss Compton—yes, even redder than yours is,
though you wouldn't know it to look at it now." Mrs. Etheridge
touched her graying locks with a disparaging smile. "I approve
of her already, Stephen, and my only complaint is that you didn't
bring her to meet us sooner."

While she was speaking, a tall slim girl in Lincoln green had
come out of the house and descended the steps to where they
stood. She was a strikingly beautiful girl with very dark hair,
very fair skin, and features of a perfection more often seen in
classical statuary than in life. Her large dark eyes appraised Anne
curiously before turning to Stephen. "Hullo, Stephen," she said.

Stephen laughed and embraced her. " 'Hullo, Stephen'—and
is that the utmost enthusiasm you can summon up for the appearance of your long-lost brother? You have grown taller since
I saw you last, Di. I take it from your dress that you're still at
the archery?"

"Yes, and you will find me much improved since you went
away," said the young lady with pride. But her eyes had turned
again toward Anne as she spoke; and Stephen, noting the direction of her gaze, hastened to perform introductions.

"Anne, this is my sister, Miss Diana Etheridge. Diana, this
is Miss Anne Compton, my fiancée."

Diana looked surprised but not ill-pleased by her brother's
announcement. "I am very pleased to make your acquaintance,
Miss Compton," she said, dropping a graceful curtsy. Anne observed that though young, there was nothing immature or awkward about her. She had the face and figure of a mature woman,
and a self-possessed manner that many a mature woman might
have envied. "So you are to marry, Stephen," she said, looking
Anne up and down with grave interest. "I suppose you two met
while he was staying in Scotland. Are you Scotch yourself?"

"No, I was merely visiting friends there, Miss Etheridge,"

said Anne, keeping to the story she and Stephen had agreed upon. "I met your brother at one of the Edinburgh assemblies."

Diana nodded. "I see," she said. "Well, I'm sure I wish you and Stephen happy, Miss Compton. Lydia *will* be surprised."

There was satisfaction in her voice and also, Anne thought, a shade of malice. Her words were followed by an embarrassed silence, which was broken at last by Stephen. "I suppose I must go and pay my respects to Lydia," he said. "Is she in the house?"

"Yes, in the drawing room," said Diana. As she turned to go back into the house, she added over her shoulder, "You will find her grown rather broad in the beam since you last saw her, Stephen."

Stephen took Anne's arm, and together they followed Diana up the steps of the house. Anne could feel the tension in his figure; she wondered if it was the circumstance of his entering Etheridge Hall again after being so long away that accounted for it, or the prospect of meeting the unknown Lydia. On the whole, she felt it was probably the latter. A little calculation had shown her that Lydia must be the late Lord Etheridge's wife, and—in all probability—the cause of the discord that had developed between him and Stephen in their later years. If Stephen had disapproved of his cousin's bride, then it was only natural that that lady would hold him in little esteem, and equally natural that he would be rather diffident about approaching her now.

With a feeling that she was drawing very near to the heart of the mystery, Anne took a tighter hold on Stephen's arm and walked through the handsome double portal that formed the front entrance to Etheridge Hall.

She found herself in a vestibule fronting a large rectangular entrance hall that ran the full width of the house from front to back. The hall was lit from above by a leaded glass skylight, and its floor was paved in squares of black and white marble. A graceful double staircase stood in the center of the room, leading to a gallery that ran around three sides of the hall and gave access to the rooms on the upper floor.

Diana, who had preceded Anne and Stephen into the hall,

continued on through it until she reached another set of double doors at the far end. These appeared to open onto a terrace at the rear of the house, but Stephen did not follow his sister outside. Instead, he led Anne to a door on the left side of the hall, one of several that lined its delicately entablatured walls. It seemed to Anne that he hesitated an instant before laying his hand on the knob. If so, it was a very brief hesitation, and he gave no other sign that he felt nervous about confronting his cousin's widow. It was rather Anne who was conscious of a flutter of nerves as he pushed open the door. This he did seem to feel, for he gave her a reassuring smile as he stood aside to let her pass through the doorway.

The room was a formal withdrawing room, elegantly decorated with heavy gold-fringed hangings, a gold and white striped wallpaper, and dainty gilded furniture. There were only two people in the room, a small dark-haired girl of about three years of age, and a plump, chestnut-haired woman in a white dress who was seated on the sofa in front of the fireplace. As Anne and Stephen came into the room, the woman was pushing the little girl impatiently from her lap.

"No, I don't want you in my lap; your fingers are sticky," she told the girl. "You ruined my best blue silk last week by getting jam on it, and I don't intend that you shall ruin another. And don't cry about it—you're getting too big a girl to be crying at every little thing, as if you were still a baby. If you can't behave any better than this, I'll ring for Molly to take you back to the nursery."

The little girl was just turning away with a disconsolate face when she caught sight of Anne and Stephen in the doorway. For a moment she stared at them with round eyes, then turned and plucked at the woman's sleeve. "Mama," she said. "Mama!"

The woman turned on her in a fury. "I just told you not to—oh, my God." The last words were spoken in a whisper. For a moment the woman sat staring with wide eyes and parted lips, and then a slow smile illuminated her face. Rising from the sofa, she ran toward Stephen with outstretched arms. "Oh,

Stephen, I knew you would come back," she said exultantly. "I knew it—I knew it."

"Hello, Lydia," said Stephen quietly, and submitted to the woman's embrace. Anne, watching them, was shocked by the sharp surge of jealousy that went through her at the sight. Lydia was in no wise as beautiful a woman as Diana, and she was undoubtedly grown rather "broad in the beam," yet there was an attraction about her that could not be denied. Her glossy chestnut hair was drawn smoothly back from her oval face, madonna-fashion; her skin was thick and creamy, of the sort that never shows a blush; and her narrow eyes were as brilliantly green as a cat's. She looked like a cat that had just obtained access to the cream pitcher as she smiled up at Stephen.

"Dear Stephen" she said softly. "It's so very good to have you back. Amélie, this is your Uncle Stephen," she told the little girl in a sugary voice.

The little girl, who had been regarding her and Stephen all the while with her fingers in her mouth, removed them long enough to speak. "My name is Amy," she said with great distinctness, and promptly put her fingers back in her mouth.

Lydia frowned. "No darling, your name is Amélie. Am-è-lie," she repeated, laying an exaggerated stress on each syllable. "I know Grandmother and Aunt Diana call you Amy, but Mother prefers that you be called by your proper name."

"Amèlie, is it?" Stephen squatted down, so that he might address the child on her own level. "Well, Miss Amèlie—or Miss Amy, as you prefer—I am very pleased to make your acquaintance." He offered her his hand, and after a brief hesitation she took it and shook it with a grown-up air that was very entertaining to see.

"My name is Amy Etheridge, and I am three years old," she told him confidingly. "And I have a nurse named Molly, and a kitten named Orion. Aunt Diana calls him that because he is a great hunter—he caught a mouse once when he was hardly bigger than a mouse himself. And I have also a canary bird—"

"That's enough, darling," said Lydia impatiently. "Run off and find Molly now, and let Mama talk to Uncle Stephen."

"You may go to Molly in a minute, but first there's someone else you ought to meet," said Stephen. Rising to his feet, he turned toward Anne and took her by the arm. "And you, too, Lydia. I would like to introduce to you my fiancée, Miss Anne Compton. Anne, this is Lydia, Lady Etheridge, and this—" he bowed gravely toward the little girl, "this is Amy, otherwise known as Miss Amèlie Etheridge."

Amy curtsied politely, but Lydia stood stock-still, staring at Anne with green eyes grown suddenly dilated. "Fiancée," she whispered, then turned and ran out of the room. Stephen looked uncomfortable, and Amy put her fingers back in her mouth; Anne was glad when Mrs. Etheridge came bustling into the drawing room.

"I saw Lydia leave," she said in a hushed voice. "I suppose she was very upset? I thought it better to stay away while you broke the news to her—and indeed, I had to speak to Mrs. Gibbons about making up a bedroom for Miss Compton. It was really too bad of you, Stephen, just to bring her here without giving us any chance to prepare for her. For all you knew, we might have had a house full of company and nowhere to put the poor girl. Only think what a shocking thing that would have been!"

"You would have managed somehow, Mother; you always do, you know," said Stephen. He was smiling now and seemed already to have forgotten the awkward scene that had taken place only a moment before. "And by the by, I must congratulate you upon the way you've managed the place in my absence. Everything looks just as it always did, if not better."

Mrs. Etheridge did not return his smile. "It has not been easy, you know, Stephen. There have been times when we needed you quite badly. Diana and I can manage the house well enough, but when it comes to matters of business—"

"Why, Mother, has not John Laughton been doing his duty?"

"John Laughton is a treasure, as always, but it was *you* we wanted, Stephen. However, I'm more willing to excuse you now that I've seen what's been keeping you away." She gave Anne a laughing look. "If you would like to come with me now, my dear, I'll show you to your room. You will want to change your dress and rest before dinner, I'm sure. You may as well come along with us, Amy," she told the little girl kindly. "We will take you back upstairs to the nursery. I expect Molly is looking for you."

"Yes, Grandmother," said Amy. She took Mrs. Etheridge's hand and accompanied her and Anne out of the drawing room. They crossed the hall, climbed the stairs, and started down the main hallway that led off the gallery into the north wing. Midway down they met a small, round, mob-capped maidservant who curtsied to Mrs. Etheridge and then turned to Amy.

"There you are, Miss Amy," she said cheerily. "I was just coming downstairs to fetch you. Come with me, now, and we'll go up to the nursery and get you ready for supper."

"All right, Molly," said Amy. She turned first to bestow a hug on Mrs. Etheridge and another polite curtsy on Anne before taking the maidservant's hand and accompanying her toward the backstairs at the far end of the hallway. Anne and Mrs. Etheridge also continued down the hallway until they came to a door near its farthest end. This Mrs. Etheridge announced to be the room that had been prepared for Anne's reception.

"I do hope my arrival hasn't put you out, Lady Etheridge," said Anne, who had been feeling rather guilty on this score. "Stephen ought to have written you beforehand that I was coming—"

"No, no trouble at all, my dear, but you really mustn't call me Lady Etheridge, you know. That is Lydia's title. I daresay it does seem a bit confusing, but you see my husband died several years before Marcus, so that when *he* died the title passed directly to Stephen. And very glad I am of it, too. At my age I would find it very difficult to find myself, 'my lady,' " after all these years of being plain Mrs. Etheridge. And can you imagine how impossible it would be to have *three* women in the house called Lady Etheridge?—for of course when you marry Stephen that will be your title, too. We would have to work out some kind of a system to keep us all straight!"

Mrs. Etheridge laughed merrily as she opened the bedroom door. "This will be your room, my dear," she said, disclosing a pretty bedchamber hung with rose-colored chintz. "And let me say again how glad—how very glad we are to have you here. I am afraid we did not make you as welcome as we ought when you first arrived. You must have thought us very ungracious, but that was only because we were all so surprised. I can assure you that Diana and I, at least, are very happy to have you here. But I am afraid you are going to have problems with Lydia."

Mrs. Etheridge sunk her voice to a whisper as she continued. "In a way I feel almost sorry for Lydia—not that Stephen owes her the least consideration after the way she treated him, but still it must have been a shock to her to hear of you and Stephen's engagement without any warning. I think she had hopes of snaring him again, after all that's passed—and really, you know, we were none of us altogether certain that she wouldn't. That's part of the reason why I'm so very glad to see you, my dear. Not that we wouldn't love you for your own sake, but you can't know how much we were dreading to see Stephen fall into Lydia's toils again. A most unprincipled woman—and of course it's such bad *ton* to marry your cousin's widow, especially after you've just inherited his house and title. It has a very ugly look about it, if you see what I mean. People do tend to talk, and there was already enough talk when Lydia threw over Stephen and married Marcus."

"Yes, I can imagine that there was," said Anne, trying to keep the shock out of her voice. "But surely—but surely there was not an actual *engagement* between Stephen and Lydia?"

"Well, to be sure, their engagement hadn't been formally announced, but still it was quite an understood thing. I know Stephen felt it very deeply at the time. But he must be rejoicing now that things turned out as they did. It's terrible of me to say such things, I know, but Lydia truly is unprincipled. I was never so glad in my life when she decided to marry Marcus instead of Stephen. Not that I would have wished ill on *him,* poor boy, but if it had to be one of them, I would rather it be he than Stephen—one's own blood does count for something when all is said and done, I suppose.

"And then, of course, Marcus was fortunate enough to die only a year and a half after he married Lydia, before he could become completely disillusioned with her. That's another terrible thing to say, but it's the truth—much as I hate to speak ill of my own sex, I have to say that Lydia is completely impossible, and there have been times when I've wondered if she might not be actually unbalanced. I can't tell you what Diana and I have had to put up with these last few years. Living together is difficult enough, you know, even with people you love, but when there's actual antagonism—well, I always think it must be a good deal like living in hell, or at least purgatory."

"Indeed?" said Anne, rather faintly.

"Indeed, yes. I don't know what you and Stephen mean to do about Lydia, but you mustn't think Diana and I mean to be any bother to you after you're married. If the two of you would rather be on your own for a while, we would both be more than happy to remove to Ash Grove. Ash Grove was our home long before this place was, you know, though of course we had both stayed at Etheridge Hall many times before, when Marcus was alive. But there, we needn't go into all that right now."

Mrs. Etheridge laid her hand on Anne's arm and squeezed it affectionately. "You're looking fatigued, my dear, and no wonder. Such a long journey, and then to have me standing here gossiping on and on, when you only want to rest—you should have stopped me sooner. I'll leave you in peace now. I see the maids have made up the bed, so you can lie down for a little while if you like, before dinner. Please don't hesitate to ring for anything you might need."

Smiling warmly, Mrs. Etheridge hurried out of the rose-colored bedroom, leaving Anne prey to some very unpleasant reflections.

Seven

Anne went down to dinner that evening with a good deal of reluctance. The mystery was solved; the rift between Stephen and his cousin now fully explained; but though the truth was much milder than some of Anne's imaginings, she had still been shocked to learn of his one-time engagement to the present Lady Etheridge. She dreaded the thought of facing Lydia at the dinner table, and almost as much she dreaded facing Mrs. Etheridge, whose kindness had made her feel the worst kind of interloper.

Alone at the inn with Stephen it had seemed a small matter to play the part of his fiancée for a few weeks, but here at Etheridge Hall, among his friends, family, and servants, she found her role unexpectedly distasteful. Anne sighed aloud as she went down the graceful curving staircase, and she entered the drawing room with strong misgivings about the evening ahead.

It proved to be not such a great ordeal as she had feared. Dinner was served in the breakfast parlor, a snug apartment tucked behind the formal dining room, and only Anne, Stephen, Mrs. Etheridge, and Diana took their places around its circular mahogany table. Amy, it appeared, took most of her meals in the nursery, and Lydia had chosen to absent herself from dinner that evening under plea of indisposition. Anne was very glad to be spared that cross, at least. She found it difficult enough to play her role with only Mrs. Etheridge and Diana for an audience. The two of them had naturally a great curiosity to learn more about her, and they questioned her throughout the meal about her background and upbringing, and the circum-

stances of her meeting with Stephen. Stephen did his best to
help her, but a good many of their questions found her unprepared, and she had to exercise considerable ingenuity to avoid
contradicting herself.

"So it was after your mother's death that you met Stephen,"
said Mrs. Etheridge thoughtfully. "But then it all must have
happened quite recently, mustn't it, my dear?—for I see by your
dress that you are still in your first mourning. And yet you say
that you met him at an assembly?"

Anne rolled an agonized eye toward Stephen, who quickly
came to her aid. "Yes, but it was a private assembly, not a public
one, Mother," he said. "A small party at the home of one of
Rob's friends. I had come along rather unwillingly, for you
know I don't much care for that sort of thing. Having success-
fully foiled all my hostess's attempts to get me to dance, I fell
into conversation with Anne, who wasn't dancing either, owing
to her mourning—"

"And that was how it all began," finished Mrs. Etheridge
with a sentimental smile. "That will teach you to despise assemblies, Stephen! You owe your existence to one as it happens,
for it was at an assembly that I first made the acquaintance of
Mr. Etheridge. A mutual friend introduced us, and we danced
two dances together. . . . I was wearing a white dress, I recall,
and my hair in curls down my back. How long ago it all seems."

Diana broke in upon these reminiscences to address another
question to Anne. "Before your mother's illness you traveled a
great deal, I think you said?"

"Yes, a very great deal," said Anne. Feeling herself to be on
safer ground with this subject, she went on to describe in some
detail her stay at the Belgian *pensionnat* and her subsequent
travels throughout Europe. Diana listened to it all with close
attention, but it seemed to be the subject of Anne's education
that interested her most.

"You must speak French very well, after attending a Belgian
school and then spending all those years in France. Do you
speak any other languages?"

"Not very well. I can manage a conversation in Italian, but I never learned the grammar of it, and German was completely beyond me. I studied it in school, but what I learned never seemed to stay with me."

"You must know that Diana prides herself on being something of a linguist," said Stephen, smiling at his sister. "Before I left, she had already passed me in Greek and Latin, and *I* had the advantage of an Oxford education!"

Diana looked more discontented than pleased by this speech. "I wish *I* could attend Oxford," she said. "I would like beyond anything to go to lectures, and visit the library, and make a proper study of philology under a tutor. It seems terribly unfair that I cannot, only because I am a girl."

Stephen laughed. "I hate to destroy your illusions, Diana, but I'm afraid Oxford isn't quite the hotbed of learning you envision! You've probably learned more studying with Doctor Schultz this last year than I did my whole three years at university."

"Yes, but he is not very able in the modern languages, except for German, of course. Perhaps *you* could help me, Miss Compton." Diana turned eagerly to Anne. "I'm not busy with my regular studies right now, for my tutor Doctor Schultz is visiting friends at Cambridge over the holidays. If you would help me with my French for the next few weeks, I could help you with your German—or with Greek or Latin, if you preferred."

"Why, of course I would be happy to help you, Miss Etheridge," said Anne, trying to disguise her dismay at this prospect. "But even though I speak French tolerably well, I've never had any experience in teaching it to anyone. I'm afraid I wouldn't be very good at it."

"Yes, Diana, and you must remember that Anne is here as a guest," added Stephen. "You mustn't be bullying her into shutting herself up in the library with you for hours on end. Not everyone has such a boundless thirst for self-improvement as you have, you know."

"But she must do *something* with herself, Stephen. The evenings are so long and dull at this time of year. You wouldn't want her to sit on the sofa and eat bonbons like Lydia, would you?"

"That will do, Diana," said Mrs. Etheridge. Her voice was a little unsteady as she continued, "I'm sure Miss Compton will find plenty to do with herself while she's here. With the holidays so close, we will be doing quite a bit of entertaining—in fact, our biggest festivity is coming up tomorrow night on Christmas Eve. It's always been the custom at Etheridge Hall to invite everyone from the village and all the tenants and neighbors, and have a big noisy party with everyone all together and lots of dancing and eating and drinking. You remember our Christmas Eve celebrations from years past, don't you, Stephen?"

"Yes, of course, although I hadn't realized this year's was so close," said Stephen, looking rather startled. "What with one thing and another, I seem to have lost a day or two out of this past week."

He looked at Anne as he spoke, and the corners of his mouth quirked up in a conspiratorial smile. Anne smiled back weakly; then, perceiving that Diana was regarding them both curiously, she turned hurriedly to Mrs. Etheridge.

"Stephen tells me you do all the old-fashioned things for Christmas, ma'am," she said. "Yule logs and boars' heads, and all the rest of it. As a matter of fact, that was one of chief lures he used to get me here. I haven't passed a Christmas in this country since I was very young, and it's one of the things I've missed most while I've been abroad. Now that I'm back, I'm eager to experience again all the festivities of a real Old English Christmas."

"Well, I do try to keep up the old customs," said Mrs. Etheridge modestly. "Certainly we will have a Yule log. Stephen, you'll have to go with the men tomorrow and help them bring it in. And I always do serve a boar's head, though I don't think many people eat it nowadays—and we have frumenty for Christmas Eve supper, and plum pudding for Christmas dinner, and Twelfth cake on Twelfth Night. And tomorrow we will be decorating the house with greenery for the party. That's a nice old custom, I always think, and one that you could certainly participate in, if you wished, Miss Compton."

"Indeed, I do wish, Mrs. Etheridge. It sounds delightful, and if there's any other way I can help, I'd be more than happy to do it."

"That's very kind of you, my dear." Mrs. Etheridge beamed at Anne from across the table. "I don't know that there will be much for you to do apart from the decorations, for most of the preparations are already complete for this year's party. The staff have all done this so many times, you know, and so have I—I played hostess at the Etheridge Hall Christmas parties all the time Marcus was growing up, right up to the time he married, and then again after he died. So it is all quite familiar to us, but of course it is all new to you, my dear, and you are very welcome to look on and lend a hand if you like. It will be good training for you later on, after you and Stephen are married."

Anne made a weak noise of assent and looked down at her plate. She could feel Stephen's eyes upon her. Mrs. Etheridge, meanwhile, was still intent on the subject of the Christmas Eve party.

"Having lost your mother so recently, I quite understand that you may not be in the mood for noisy festivity this year," she told Anne. "You must do just as you wish, but I do hope you will at least put in an appearance tomorrow night. No one will expect you to dance, but all the neighbors will be wanting to get a look at you, and it will be a fine opportunity for you to become acquainted with some of the people hereabouts."

Anne made another feeble noise of assent. "You must remember, Mother, that we are not planning to announce the engagement formally until Anne is out of mourning," put in Stephen quickly. "There's no need for her to meet the whole of county society tomorrow night."

"Of course not—but you must realize that news of these things does get around, Stephen. I expect most of the neighbors already know that Lord Etheridge has brought a young lady home with him for the holidays. From there, they will not be slow to put two and two together, I assure you."

Anne shot Stephen a look of dismay. He returned it with a slight negative shake of his head and a reassuring smile. Mrs. Etheridge observed these signs of intelligence passing between them and smiled indulgently. "You two will want a little time to yourselves, I expect," she said, pushing back her chair from the table. "Diana, why don't you come along with me to the drawing room? Miss Compton and Stephen can join us there later for tea."

After Mrs. Etheridge and Diana had gone out of the room, Anne also rose from her chair and went over to stand in front of the fireplace. "This gets worse and worse," she said in a choked voice. "I feel such a fraud, Stephen. Deceiving your mother and sister—and now it sounds as though the whole neighborhood is going to hear about our engagement. This isn't at all how we planned it."

"Then we will have to change our plans," said Stephen. Rising from his own chair, he came over to join Anne beside the fireplace. "You mustn't be worrying about how this will affect me, you know," he said, looking down at her. "What concerns me is how it will affect you. Do you think you can endure it for the next few weeks?"

"Oh, yes. Your mother has been so kind to me—but in a way that only makes it worse. I feel as though I were accepting her hospitality under false pretenses."

"Don't let it worry you. I will make all the necessary explanations, if and when it should be necessary. For the present, you need only go on as you are doing. I hope it will not be too much of a strain on you." Stephen's face wore a look of concern as he continued to look down at her. "Dinner tonight was rather an ordeal, but I think the worst is probably over. Now that Mother and Diana have had a chance to satisfy their curiosity, they probably won't bother you with too many more questions, especially since they'll have preparations for the party tomorrow night to keep them busy."

"Yes, but all this talk of Christmas has reminded me of another thing, Stephen. Do you and your family exchange gifts at Christmastime? In France and Belgium it was only the children who got them, but I have heard that the custom is more general here."

"Yes, as a matter of fact we do exchange gifts, but that needn't be of any concern to you, Anne. I'm sure everyone will understand that you didn't have time to prepare anything—"

"Yes, but you're forgetting, Stephen. As far as they know, I've been planning all along to come here with you. That's certainly the impression we've been trying to give, and it would look very odd if I didn't have any gifts for your family. They would have expected you to tell me about your customs. I shall have to go through my things and see what I can contrive in the way of presents."

"I hope you won't go to too much trouble," said Stephen, still eyeing her worriedly. "The gifts needn't be anything expensive or elaborate, you know. And I would be happy to reimburse you for any cost you might incur—"

"Certainly not! I would be very glad for a chance to do something for your family in return for all they're doing for me. Especially your mother—I can't help seeing that my coming here has put her to a great deal of trouble."

"You mustn't think of that, Anne. I am sure she would say so herself, if she were here. And for myself, I can say that I am very glad that you chose to accompany me. Very glad indeed."

In speaking he took a step toward her, laying a hand on her shoulder. It was a comforting gesture, and Anne felt comforted, until she raised her eyes to his face. There was something in the way he was looking at her that gave his words a more than ordinary significance.

For an instant Anne felt a quick, responsive glow of pleasure, but the next instant there flashed through her mind a picture of Lydia embracing him with an exultant smile on her face. It was evident that she still cherished strong feelings for her former fiancé. And was it not likely that the reverse was true? By all accounts, Stephen had been badly upset when Lydia had jilted him for his cousin, and it appeared now as though his exile in Scotland had been for no other purpose than to nurse a heart wounded by her betrayal.

The thought brought a chill with it, which caused the glow in Anne's heart to subside as quickly as it had come. Involuntarily she drew away from him a little. Stephen let his arm drop down to his side, and for a moment neither of them spoke.

"I hope you will have a pleasant stay here at Etheridge Hall," said Stephen, in a more formal voice than he had used before. "You find your rooms comfortable, I hope?"

"Yes, very comfortable," said Anne, also rather formally. She hesitated a moment before adding, "I suppose we ought to join your mother and sister now?"

"As you wish," said Stephen. He offered her his arm, and together they went into the drawing room.

This conversation was still in Stephen's thoughts later that evening as he left the drawing room and went slowly up the stairs. Upon the whole he had found it rather an unsatisfactory conversation, but for that he was inclined to blame himself. In his eagerness to assure Anne that she was welcome at Etheridge Hall, he feared he had gone too far and betrayed an ardor that was inappropriate under the circumstances.

He reminded himself that she had entered into their engagement only with the utmost reluctance, and that if he wished to win her to a fuller acceptance he must give her time to adjust to the status quo before throwing her off balance with any new and possibly unwelcome revelations.

So much he had resolved even before he and Anne had left the dining room, but their conversation there had reminded him of another issue that remained unresolved. This was the issue of Anne's Christmas present. He had not yet provided himself with a gift for her, and it had at once struck him how strange, not to say suspicious, such an omission would appear to his family.

Stephen had thought long and hard on the subject as he had

sat on the drawing room sofa beside Anne, drinking tea and listening to his mother retail the latest neighborhood gossip. His conclusion had been that the most logical gift for a newly engaged man to give his fiancée would be an engagement ring. But would Anne accept a ring from him, even to further the pretense of an engagement between them? That was the question, and it was a question Stephen had not altogether settled in his own mind by the time he reached the door of his mother's room.

A tap on the door admitted him to Mrs. Etheridge's dressing room, where that lady was in the midst of having her hair put up in curl-papers for the night.

"Stephen," she exclaimed, with unaffected pleasure. "No, dearest, that's quite all right; you are not interrupting in the least. You can sit on the settee over there and talk to me while Esther finishes with my hair. I look a perfect guy in these curl-papers, I know, but since the party is tomorrow night I did want to look my best. Ridiculous, isn't it, at my age? You would have thought I had outgrown vanity long ago, but somehow I cannot reconcile myself to wearing a cap on such an occasion."

"I don't see what age has to do with it, Mother," said Stephen, dropping a kiss on her cheek before seating himself on the settee. "You've as much right to vanity as any woman I know. Is Colonel Lambeth still pursuing you as doggedly as ever?"

Mrs. Etheridge laughed, and for a moment looked rather arch. "Yes, I'm afraid so. Poor man, I've told him 'no' half a hundred times, but it doesn't seem to discourage him in the least. I should think that's why he made such a success in the army, shouldn't you? He must have been quite an indomitable foe on the battlefield. But you didn't come here to quiz me about Colonel Lambeth, did you, Stephen?"

"No, there was something else I wished to discuss with you, when you had a moment free," said Stephen, with a significant look at the dressing woman. Mrs. Etheridge nodded understandingly and as soon as the woman finished arranging her hair in papers, she dismissed her with a word of thanks and came over to sit beside her son on the settee.

"Now, my dear, what was it you wished to discuss?" she said, regarding him quizzically. "Are you here to ask my blessing on your engagement? If so, you have it, along with my most sincere congratulations. I like your Anne very well, Stephen. She is just the sort of girl I would have picked myself, if it had been up to me to choose one for you."

"I thought you would like her," said Stephen, much gratified by this praise of his intended. "And I appreciate having your blessing, Mother, though I must confess that that's not the reason I'm here. The thing is, you see, that I haven't yet given Anne a betrothal ring, and since Christmas is the day after tomorrow I thought it would be an appropriate occasion to give her one. If it wouldn't be putting you to too much trouble, I had hoped you might go through the family jewelry with me tonight and help me choose something appropriate. Do you keep it up here, or in the safe downstairs?"

"I keep my own jewelry up here, but I'm afraid that won't do you much good, Stephen. Unless you would like to give her my betrothal ring? It's not as showy as some of the other rings, but the diamond in it is very fine, and you are very welcome to it if you think it would suit Anne. My joints have swollen so these past few years that I've had to give up wearing rings altogether."

"That's a generous offer, Mother, but I would prefer to look through all the jewelry before making up my mind. Where do you keep the other pieces?"

Mrs. Etheridge looked embarrassed. "Well, that's just it, Stephen. I don't have any of the family jewelry; Lydia does. She was so upset after Marcus died that I didn't like to insist she give it up—and indeed, I don't know that I had any right to. Yes, I know the jewels were entailed upon you, Stephen, but I am only your mother, you know. I wasn't sure how far my rights extended in the case."

Stephen's expression was grim. "I'll speak to Lydia tomorrow about turning them over," he said. "I trust she has recovered from her upset by now."

Mrs. Etheridge hesitated. "I don't know if you ought to do

that, Stephen. Of course she should be over the shock of Marcus's death by now, but you must know that your engagement to Anne has come as another shock to her—perhaps an even greater shock than the other. It might be kinder to wait a day or two before you approach her about the jewels. In the meantime, why don't you take a look at that ring of mine and see if it might do?"

Not waiting for a reply, Mrs. Etheridge rose from the settee and went into her sitting room. She returned a few minutes later with a ring box which she put into Stephen's hand. "There it is, Stephen. As I said, it's not as large and showy as some of the Etheridge family jewels, but the stone is very fine. And this is the wedding band that goes with it, here beside it in the box."

The frown on Stephen's face lifted slightly as he surveyed the rings in their nest of blue velvet. "It is a nice stone, isn't it?" he said, picking up the engagement ring to examine it more closely. "I believe this might do very well, Mother—if you're sure you don't mind parting with it?"

"Quite sure, my dear. It would give me great pleasure to see your Anne wearing it. I only hope it suits her—but if it doesn't, you can easily exchange it for one of the other rings later on, of course."

"Yes, of course, assuming I can prize them away from Lydia," said Stephen in a hard voice. Mrs. Etheridge gave him a quick, worried look and seemed about to speak. "No, don't worry, Mother," he said, dropping another kiss on her cheek and getting to his feet. "I'll take your advice and give Lydia a day or two to reconcile herself, but I intend to have those jewels by New Year's even if it sends her into a full-blown fit of the spasms! Good night, Mother, and thank you." Tucking the ring box into his coat pocket, he started for the door.

"Good night, Stephen," said Mrs. Etheridge, looking after him pensively. Under her breath she added, "Still a little bitter, but that's not to be wondered at. Thank heaven he is over her at last."

Eight

Anne slept late the following morning, and when she came downstairs to the breakfast parlor she found no one there but Diana.

"Stephen had to go out on some business about the estate," Diana informed her. "He told me to make his apologies to you and to tell you he would be back sometime early this afternoon. Mother's in the kitchen seeing to the refreshments for the party tonight, and Lydia's off sulking somewhere, so it's just you and I this morning. Would you like me to show you around the house? After that you could come out and watch while I practice my archery."

Anne agreed to both these proposals, and as soon as she had finished her breakfast Diana took her on a tour of Etheridge Hall that began in the cellars, ended in the attics, and included nearly every room in between.

It was a rather more extensive tour than Anne had bargained for, but Diana took it for granted that the future mistress of Etheridge Hall would take an interest in even its smallest details, and so Anne was called upon to admire stillrooms and sculleries, ale cellars and servant's halls, linen cupboards and housemaids' pantries. She dutifully admired everything and found, incidentally, much that was really worthy of her admiration. As Stephen had said, the first Viscount Etheridge had shown commendable restraint in the building of his new house. Etheridge Hall was neither unnecessarily large nor excessively fine, but a spacious, elegant residence fitted up with a great deal of good taste.

After the two young women had finished their tour of the house's upper regions, they paid a brief call upon Amy in the nursery and then went to their rooms to put on their outside garments.

When Anne had donned her cloak and bonnet, she joined Diana downstairs in the hall. The two of them left the house through the double doors at the far end of the hall, which opened onto a paved terrace walk that led around the house to the south. It was a beautiful winter's day, clear and cold and still, with the sun shining brightly on the snow-covered trees and lawns. Anne breathed deeply of the frosty air as she followed Diana to an open area on the south lawn where a couple of straw-stuffed targets stood propped against wooden supports.

It was obvious that Diana took her archery practice very seriously. She was correctly attired in a habit of Lincoln green cloth with a plumed hat atop her dark head, bracers of Spanish leather on her arms, and a quiver of arrows slung over her shoulder. Anne watched as she fit an arrow to her bow and sent it flying to the heart of the nearer target. After some half-dozen arrows had followed the first, she politely offered Anne the use of the bow.

Anne took it rather gingerly and attempted to follow her companion's instructions as to stance and grip, but her arrow fell many yards short of the target. None of her subsequent efforts came much closer, and after she had painfully snapped her wrist a couple of times with the bowstring, she returned the bow to Diana and told her she would prefer merely to watch.

"You shoot very well, Miss Etheridge," she said, watching as Diana sent arrow after arrow flying into the target. "Do you ever shoot anything besides targets?"

"Yes, now and then. Sometimes I used to go out hunting grouse and pheasants with Stephen and Marcus when I was younger. It is much more difficult to hit a moving bird than a stationary target, but I generally did as well as they did with their guns, and sometimes better."

Anne shuddered. "I don't see how you could," she said. "It

disturbs me even to step on an insect. They often used to tease me about it at the *pensionnat*. I'm too soft-hearted, I suppose."

"It used to bother me, too," said Diana. "In fact, it still does, a little. And yet I am as fond of a dish of grouse or pheasant as anybody. It seems to me hypocritical to object to the killing part and still sit down to roasted pheasant at dinner-time—and I refuse to be either a hypocrite or give up eating pheasant. Therefore, I make myself go out shooting, even though I would really rather not. It is an exercise in self-discipline, if you will."

"You are an extraordinary girl," said Anne, regarding her with astonishment. "Do you always force yourself to do things you don't want to do?"

"Not always, but sometimes. That's what self-discipline is, isn't it? And it has been my experience that if you make the effort to face the things you find difficult or disturbing, they generally become easier and sometimes quite enjoyable. I will never really enjoy killing birds, but there is certainly an enjoyment in making a good shot, or simply in challenging oneself with a difficult target. Do you see what I mean?"

"I suppose I do," said Anne, revolving the matter in her mind. "But I don't think I could carry it as far as you do, Miss Etheridge. I shall continue a hypocrite to the end of my days, I'm afraid, and eat my grouse and pheasant while trying very hard not to think how they came to be on the table!"

Diana smiled tolerantly and went out to gather her arrows from the target. When she returned, she took up her stance opposite the farther target and fitted an arrow to her bow. "You can't be half such a hypocrite as Lydia," she said, as she lifted the bow to her shoulder. "She's been having hysterics ever since she learned about you and Stephen's engagement, and yet *she* was the one who threw *him* over! Do you find it difficult, staying in the same house with her?"

"A little," admitted Anne.

"He never knew her." Diana drew back the bow and sent the arrow twanging savagely to the center of the target. "She was always sweet as honey around him, but if he had lived with her a year or two like the rest of us, he'd realize what a narrow escape he'd had. I find her positively loathsome."

Scowling, Diana sent two more arrows flying in quick succession after the first. "Do you know what Lydia reminds me of?'' she continued, as she fitted another arrow to her bow. "A great big lazy over-fed cat. All purrs until she doesn't get what she wants, and then—watch out for her claws! And then she's such a shiftless thing. Most of the time she never stirs from the house, but just sits on the sofa and eats sweets all day long, as I was saying at dinner last night. That's the whole reason she's as big as she is—she used to be quite slim years ago, but as soon as she married Marcus she quit walking and riding and dancing and took up eating instead."

"Don't you think that's a little unfair, Miss Etheridge? She has had a child, you know, and childbirth does often tend to thicken the figure. And taking care of her daughter probably doesn't leave her much time for exercise—"

"That won't wash," said Diana scornfully. "She was getting fat even before she had Amy, and having one child shouldn't have made her swell up like a balloon. Why, look at Mother: *she* had Stephen and me and two more children besides who died when they were babies, but she's not nearly as big as Lydia. And as for spending time taking care of her daughter, that's a joke. Mother has done far more toward raising Amy than Lydia ever did. I think that's the most despicable thing about her, next to her marrying Marcus: she won't have anything to do with her own daughter, because Amy is 'tiresome,' and 'temperamental,' and musses her hair or rumples her dress every now and then."

"Oh," was all Anne could think to say. Diana finished shooting the last of her arrows, then went out to the target to gather them up again. When she returned, she took up the conversation where she had left off.

"I hope you don't mind my speaking so frankly, Miss Compton. But if you must live in the same house with Lydia, it's only fair that you know what you're likely to encounter. I don't suppose Stephen told you much about her—and in any case he couldn't tell you as well as I could, because he doesn't know her as I do, even if he *was* engaged to her once.

"Living in the same house with her, I have had plenty of opportunities to study her character, let me tell you! And actually it has been quite an interesting study, or would have been if there hadn't been so much personal annoyance involved in making it. I think, you know, that Lydia really did love Stephen, at least as much as she could love anyone besides herself. It was only that she couldn't resist the chance to be a viscountess, and live at the Hall, and have finer clothes and carriages than any woman in the neighborhood.

"So she married Marcus, and what happened after that was just what you'd expect. As soon as she got all the things she wanted, she stopped caring about them and started wanting the one thing she couldn't have, which was Stephen. It's strange, isn't it, how people always do seem to want worst the things they can't have?

"I think it was like that with Lydia. After she'd lost Stephen she wanted him more than ever, and the idea that she couldn't have him just kept eating away at her—and all the time she really was eating away, and hardly stirring out of the house even to flaunt the new clothes and carriages she'd worked so hard to get. It's rather pathetic, isn't it? I could feel almost sorry for Lydia if the whole situation weren't so manifestly her own fault."

"Yes, but I don't see how it could be completely her fault, Miss Etheridge," said Anne, still struggling to be fair. "Of course, I don't know all the facts, but it seems to me that your cousin must have been at fault, too, if he proposed marriage to a woman who was already engaged to someone else. Or is Lydia supposed to have tricked him into it somehow?"

"That is a rather good question, Miss Compton." There was a renewed respect in Diana's face as she regarded Anne. "A very good question, but I'm not sure that I can answer it. At the time it happened I was quite young and living at Ash Grove, and it wasn't much talked of there, as you can probably imagine. Mother will have it that it was all Lydia's artfulness, but then she raised Marcus from a boy, you know, and naturally she would seek to excuse him if she could. Based on my own knowledge of Marcus, I would say that he probably did know what he was doing, even if he refused to acknowledge it to himself."

"But Miss Etheridge, that makes his action even more reprehensible! For a man in his position to deliberately woo away the fiancée of another man—and a man who had been like a brother to him at that—"

"Yes, it does sound rather reprehensible, doesn't it? But you have to understand what Marcus was like, Miss Compton. He wasn't what you could call a deep thinker, but he was witty enough in a superficial way—always laughing and joking, and what most people would have called very charming. He made friends easily—much more easily than Stephen, who was always rather quiet—but for all that, I think Marcus was always a little jealous of Stephen.

"He was the eldest by almost a year, but Stephen was always bigger and stronger and better at games and sports than he was—yes, and very much better-looking, too, for that matter. Marcus had his title, of course, which ought to have evened things out, but still I think it galled him that Stephen was superior to him in so many ways. I don't suppose Stephen was aware of it. Marcus was accustomed to make jokes about everything, and if he did refer to it now and then in a joking way, Stephen probably just took it at face value and laughed it off. He wasn't jealous of Marcus, so it never would have occurred to him that Marcus might be jealous of him."

"So you think your cousin married Lydia as a means of settling old scores?"

"I think it very likely. Mind you, I don't say that was the only reason. Lydia probably gave him plenty of encouragement, and there's no denying that she can be very winning when she wants to be. When Marcus found he might have her for the

taking, he probably told himself that all's fair in love and war
and simply shut his eyes to the other implications."

Anne was silent for a moment, thinking the matter over. "I'm
glad you told me all this, Miss Etheridge," she said finally. "I
had often wondered about your cousin—what sort of man he
was, and how he could have behaved as he did when he and
Stephen were supposed to be so close. Now I feel as though I
understand him much better. And Lydia, too—I must say, I cannot help feeling a little sorry for her, in spite of it all. She has
undoubtedly behaved wrongly, but it appears to me that her
wrongdoing has hurt no one more than herself."

"Don't waste your pity on her, Miss Compton. I would advise
you rather to watch your back! I know Lydia, you see, and I
am perfectly sure that even in her darkest hour she never gave
up hope of getting Stephen back someday. And I don't think
she's given up now."

Diana's face was grave as she looked at Anne. "You must
know that it has become a regular obsession with her, Miss
Compton. Marcus was hardly in his grave before she was talking about marrying Stephen, just as though everything that had
happened before counted for nothing. You can imagine how
odious that was to Mother and me, having to listen to her go
on and on about it and not being in a position to contradict her.
And though your coming here has taken the wind out of her
sails for the moment, I don't believe she'll stand back and
tamely relinquish the thing she's wanted so badly all these years.

"Mark my words, Miss Compton: before another day goes
by you'll see her making up to Stephen one way or another, and
I wouldn't be surprised to see her leaving off the bonbons and
going for long walks, too. That's the one really admirable thing
about Lydia: when she sets out to do a thing, she does it thoroughly, with no half measures."

Having exhausted her supply of arrows once more, Diana
went out to retrieve them from the target. When she returned,
she announced to Anne that she had had enough practice for

that day. Anne nodded, and together the two of them returned to the house.

As the day wore on Anne found herself thinking often of Diana's words. She thought about them as she helped Mrs. Etheridge and the maidservants decorate the house with Christmas greenery, and she thought about them later when Stephen and the other men of the household came laughing in, bearing the great oaken log that was to occupy a place of honor in the hall fireplace. She was still thinking about them when she went upstairs late that afternoon to dress for the party.

The efficient Parker had already laid out the gown she was to wear, an evening dress of black crepe over silk with long sleeves, a low square neckline, and a short train. The dress had trimmings of jet about the neck and hem, and there was a necklace and earrings of the same material to go with it.

Once Anne was dressed and arrayed in these ornaments, Parker arranged her hair in its usual style, with loose curls in front and a low knot at the back of her head. Above the knot she set another jet ornament from which was suspended a black lace veil that hung over Anne's back and shoulders. All in all, it was rather a somber costume, but a very effective one in combination with Anne's fair coloring; and she did herself less than justice when, after a prolonged survey in the mirror, she shook her head and mentally denounced it as drab.

She felt drabber than ever when she got down to the drawing room. Lydia was there, robed in a dress of creamy white satin that set off her rich brunette beauty to perfection. The dress's extreme décolletage served to draw attention away from the width of her derrière, and she looked as lovely and voluptuous as one of Ruben's nymphs as she reclined upon the sofa, her chestnut head resting on one jeweled hand. She looked up quickly as Anne came rustling into the room. Having taken in the details of Anne's costume in one quick, jealous glance, she looked away again with affected disinterest. Mrs. Etheridge was also there, garbed in mauve silk with a dashing mauve and silver striped evening toque perched atop her gray curls; she smiled at Anne and beckoned her toward the couch where she was sitting.

"You look very elegant, my dear," she said, as Anne sat down beside her. "It's not everyone who looks well in black, but you contrive to make it look positively stylish. I'm sure no one who sees you tonight will wonder that Stephen lost his heart to you."

From the sofa, Lydia gave an audible sniff. Mrs. Etheridge appeared not to hear it, but she lowered her voice a little as she continued, "And that reminds me, my dear. I quite understand that you and Stephen do not want your engagement announced at present, but would you mind very much if I just mentioned it to one or two people tonight? Only a very few people, and all in the strictest confidence—it would not be a general announcement in any sense of the word." Lowering her voice still further, she added, "There has been quite a bit of talk, you know, what with one thing and another. If I were to just drop a word in the ear of one or two of the people most concerned, it might serve to set straight some of the foolish rumors that are going around. You would not mind if I did that, would you, my dear?"

Under Mrs. Etheridge's expectant gaze and Lydia's malicious one, Anne felt herself powerless to object. "No, I would not mind at all, ma'am," she said unhappily.

She had no sooner spoken these words than the drawing room door opened. "Ah, here is Stephen," said Mrs. Etheridge. Both Lydia and Anne looked around quickly, but it proved to be not Stephen but Diana, leading Amy by the hand.

Diana looked as beautiful as a Grecian statue in a simple dress of white muslin enlivened by a festive-looking crimson sash. Amy was likewise dressed in white and crimson, and her eyes were round with excitement as she looked about the drawing room with its garlands of holly and ivy. Anne observed that when Diana released her hand, it was to Mrs. Etheridge that she ran rather than her mother.

"Grandmother," she said breathlessly, "Grandmother, the house is beautiful! Is it Christmas yet?"

"Not yet, darling, but it soon will be," said Mrs. Etheridge, leaning down to give her a hug. "This is Christmas Eve, and when you wake up tomorrow, Christmas will be here. Ah, here is your uncle Stephen at last. Stephen, you wretch, what has been keeping you?"

"Business with John Laughton, Mother," he said, taking the hand she offered him and saluting it gracefully.

Anne, watching him, thought she had never seen a man whom the austerity of formal evening dress better suited. His jacket of black superfine fit without a wrinkle across his broad shoulders; the shirt and waistcoat underneath were pristine white, as were the form-fitting trousers that accentuated the lean muscularity of his lower body.

Having greeted his mother and bestowed a formal bow on Lydia, he turned next to Anne. For a moment he looked her gravely up and down, then bent down to kiss her deliberately on the lips. "You look beautiful, Anne," he said in a husky voice.

"Thank you, Stephen," said Anne. She felt very uncomfortable, partly because of the kiss (which she had not at all expected), but even more because of the attention it had drawn to her. Mrs. Etheridge was smiling approvingly, while Lydia regarded her with smouldering eyes, and even Diana was looking at her with an expression that was hard to read. Anne was grateful when Amy hopped off Mrs. Etheridge's lap and seized Stephen by the hand.

"Come see the dining room, Uncle Stephen," she said eagerly. "Molly and I and Aunt Diana have been decorating it, and it looks beautiful."

"Not now, Amèlie," said Lydia peevishly. "Your uncle just got here, and he doesn't want to go running off again just to see the dining room. We'll all be seeing it later anyway, when we eat."

Amy's face fell, but Stephen smiled and took her hand more firmly in his. "Indeed, I would like to see the dining room very much," he told her. "We'll go see it together, shall we?"

"Yes," said Amy happily, and led him off in the direction of the dining room. They made a quaint looking couple, the one so large and the other so small. Mrs. Etheridge looked after them with a fond smile.

"Dear Stephen has such a kind heart," she said. "Not many men would bother themselves to indulge a child's whim in that way. I have often thought he would make a wonderful father." Although her words were not addressed to anyone in particular, Anne felt their inference was meant for her and was hard put not to blush.

Not long after this, the first guests began arriving. Anne soon saw that when Mrs. Etheridge had described the Etheridge Hall Christmas Eve festivities as a "big, noisy party," she had been guilty of no exaggeration. The party was both large and loud and seemed to include guests of every imaginable age and social station.

There were toothless octogenarians and wailing babies; members of the local gentry, tradespeople from the village, and a number of Stephen's tenant families. Anne was introduced to countless people and soon gave up trying to remember their names; she comforted herself with the reflection that it did not really matter, since in all probability she would be leaving Etheridge Hall within a few weeks and would never have occasion to return. Yet it was a reflection that brought her very little comfort, upon the whole. As she looked around the hall, she found herself thinking that there was something very attractive about the scene in which she was taking part.

The great entrance hall appeared an entirely different place from the elegant, rather austere room it had been the day before. Decked with Christmas greenery and blazing with the light of innumerable lamps and candles, the room was made still more brilliant by the guests in holiday attire who packed it solidly from wall to wall. The buzz of conversation within the room was very nearly deafening, but not so loud as to completely drown out the sound of music from the servant's hall down the corridor, where country dances were taking place.

Through the glass doors at the rear of the hall was visible the light of a great bonfire that had been kindled on the lawn to give warmth and festivity to those revelers who preferred to remain outside. This group appeared to be exclusively male and to consist largely of members of the tenant and villager classes, although there were also a few gentlemen among them; to judge from their gestures, they were regaling one another with sporting stories while imbibing quantities of ale, lamb's wool, and rum punch. More substantial refreshment was available in the dining room, where Mrs. Etheridge had provided a standing supper of cold roasts, meat pies, fruit, bonbons, and other sweetmeats. Guests holding plates and cups streamed in and out, eating and drinking, laughing and talking; squires rubbed shoulders with shopkeepers and *grandes dames* with gardener's daughters in a scene that held as much jollity as confusion.

The members of the Etheridge family had entered with enthusiasm into the festivities. Amy and several of the village children ran about the hall, shrieking with laughter and adding greatly to the atmosphere of noise and confusion. Amy's small face was bright with smiles and smeared from ear to ear with the remains of a mince pie which she and her companions had seized earlier in a daring raid on the dining room sideboard.

At the far end of the room, oblivious to the unruly behavior of her offspring, Lydia stood talking animatedly to a well-dressed couple who appeared to be members of the local gentry. Diana glided among the guests, coolly fending off the advances of a couple of infatuated-looking youths who trailed along behind her; and in the very midst of the throng, standing a good head taller than anyone around him, was the master of Etheridge Hall himself.

Anne had been watching him throughout the evening as he moved about the hall, bestowing a smile here and a bow there, and pausing now and then to converse for a few minutes with one of the guests. At the moment he was listening with courteous attention to an elderly gentleman who appeared to be holding forth on the subject of politics. Not for the first time,

Anne found herself thinking how handsome he looked, and how completely at home in his role as host. But since such reflections tended only to increase the discomfort of her own role, she put them hastily aside and turned her attention back to the task at hand, which was the task of greeting the guests as they came into the hall.

She had been busy with this task for over an hour now. As each group of guests was announced, Mrs. Etheridge would come forward to greet them, then introduce them to Anne or she to them as their positions warranted. They had both been kept very busy earlier in the evening, but now the flow of incoming guests was finally beginning to subside. For several minutes there had been no new arrivals at all, and Mrs. Etheridge had fallen into conversation with an elderly couple who had been among the last group of guests to enter the hall. Their conversation held little interest for Anne, dealing as it did with people and events completely unknown to her. She did her best to appear interested, but as they continued to talk her thoughts began to wander. They had not wandered far, however, when her reverie was abruptly shattered by an announcement from the footman stationed at the front door.

"Sir Thomas and Lady Moorhaven," he intoned in a sonorous voice. "Miss Moorhaven—and Lord Francis Rowland."

Nine

The footman's words made Anne catch her breath and turn quickly toward the door. The party who had just been announced stood in the vestibule, divesting themselves of their outer garments. Foremost of the party was a stout middle-aged gentleman with sandy whiskers and an air of consequence; on his arm was an elegantly dressed lady who appeared to be his wife, and behind him stood a much younger lady with long blond curls who was obviously his daughter. At the moment she was being helped out of her pelisse by the fourth member of the party, a slim, fair-haired gentleman clad in a rather theatrical-looking black evening cloak. It was upon this gentleman that Anne's eyes immediately fastened.

As soon as he had finished helping his companion with her pelisse, the fair-haired gentleman removed his cloak with a dramatic swirl and handed it to one of the waiting footmen. This done, he glanced about the hall with an air of mild interest. Almost at once his eyes lit upon Anne, and a pleased smile appeared on his face. The elder lady and gentleman had already come forward to greet Mrs. Etheridge, who had broken off her conversation with the other couple to return their greetings. The slim gentleman followed behind them with the blonde young lady on his arm. She was saying something to him in a confidential voice, smiling up at him as she spoke; his head was bent low to catch her words, but all the while his eyes remained fixed unwaveringly on Anne's face.

"Sir Thomas, I am so glad you and Lady Moorhaven could

attend," said Mrs. Etheridge, giving her hand to the older lady and gentleman. "And Chloe, too—my dear, you are become quite a young lady! Where is Tom tonight?"

"He is on the injured list as usual, Mrs. Etheridge," said the young lady with a laugh. "Like an idiot, he tried to jump a five-barred gate when he was out riding this afternoon and got thrown from his horse."

"Poor boy! I hope he did not break his leg again?"

"No, the doctor tells us it is only a fractured collarbone this time. When we left he was sitting up in bed surrounded by racing lists and sporting papers and shouting for the servants to bring him something to drink. I think the thing that pained him most was the thought of missing your party tonight, Mrs. Etheridge!"

Mrs. Etheridge smiled and said she hoped Mr. Moorhaven would soon be feeling better. Turning to Anne, she said, "Anne, I must introduce you to the Moorhavens, who are near neighbors of ours. This is Sir Thomas and Lady Moorhaven, and this is their daughter Chloe. This is Miss Anne Compton, who is staying with us over the holidays," she informed the Moorhavens. "She is English by birth, but has spent most of her life traveling around the Continent with her mother, who recently passed away. Stephen made her acquaintance when she was visiting Scotland a few months ago and brought her home with him to experience a real old English Christmas."

Sir Thomas and his wife and daughter all expressed themselves pleased to make Miss Compton's acquaintance. Anne managed to make the proper polite responses, but her eyes kept returning to the gentleman holding Miss Moorhaven's arm. After Mrs. Etheridge and the Moorhavens had exchanged a few more pleasantries, Lady Moorhaven turned and beckoned him forward.

"And now I must introduce to you and Miss Compton a gentleman who is staying with us, Mrs. Etheridge," she said. "I know it is unforgivable to bring along a guest without an invitation, but since Tom could not come I hoped it might be admissible to bring a substitute in his place. Lord Francis had a great desire to attend, and as your party is so large—"

Mrs. Etheridge assured her warmly that she was welcome to bring along any number of guests. "For we do not stand upon ceremony at Christmastime, you know," she told the gentleman. "I am very pleased to have you with us, sir."

"You are very good, Mrs. Etheridge," he returned with a low bow. "Lord Francis Rowland, at your service. Good evening, Anne," he added, with another bow and a rather mocking smile. "Imagine meeting you here. It's a small world, isn't it?"

"You know each other?" said Mrs. Etheridge, looking from him to Anne in surprise.

"Yes, we are old friends—or perhaps I should say we *were* old friends, until circumstances conspired to separate us. Anne, I hope you will give me a dance later on. I am most eager to renew our acquaintance."

"I am not dancing tonight, Francis," said Anne coldly. "You must see that I am still in black gloves."

"So you are! How foolish of me. I cannot think how it came to escape my notice. But then I suffered an injury to my head a few days ago which has possibly rendered me less acute than usual. No, nothing serious, Mrs. Etheridge; I don't believe any lasting damage was done, but it is very kind of you to be concerned. Anne, if you cannot dance with me, I hope you will at least sit with me for a few minutes, sometime during the evening? As I said, I am most eager to renew our acquaintance."

With the Moorhavens and Mrs. Etheridge looking on, Anne had no choice but to murmur her assent. Lord Francis smiled. "I will be looking forward to it, Anne," he told her in a low, intimate voice. She made no reply, but turned away with a flush of displeasure.

Across the room, Stephen was doing his best to appear interested in his companion's tirade on Tory politics, but his eyes were on Anne. In truth, they had seldom strayed from her figure throughout the evening. He had thought her lovely in the plain black dress she had worn during their stay at the inn; but in the splendor of full evening dress, with her neck and shoulders bared by the fashionable low neckline of her dress and her hair shining coppery-gold in the light of the candlelit chandelier, he thought her beautiful, easily the best-looking woman in the room.

All through the evening he had stolen frequent glances in her direction, admiring the elegance of her figure and the well-bred composure with which she greeted guests at his mother's side. The sight of her standing there had more than ever filled him with a determination to make the arrangement a permanent one.

He had been standing near the dining room door, ostensibly listening to Colonel Lambeth but in reality watching Anne, when Lord Francis Rowland had come into the hall. He had observed Anne's start of surprise and subsequent flush of annoyance; and while he made appropriate responses to his companion's diatribe he had pondered to himself what might be their meaning. Lord Francis was slightly known to him as a younger son of a noble family; it appeared now that he must also be known to Anne, and known in no very favorable light if one were to judge from her reaction. As soon as he could, Stephen excused himself to Colonel Lambeth and made his way over to where she stood.

She greeted him pleasantly, but he thought he detected a shadow in her eyes and a touch of strain in her smile. "There ought not to be many more people arriving this late," he said, laying a hand on her arm. "You've been on your feet for a couple of hours now. What do you say we go to the dining room and get something to eat?"

"Yes, my dear, you go on with Stephen," said Mrs. Etheridge, smiling at her. "I daresay you're ready to sit down for a while. There's nothing so fatiguing as meeting dozens and dozens of people you don't know, is there? Go and get yourself something to eat, and if you don't feel equal to returning when you're done, I will quite understand. You need only send word to me through Stephen, and I'll make your excuses to everyone."

Stephen took Anne's arm and led her through the crowd to the dining room. The greater number of the guests had already supped, and the room was empty except for the attendant footmen. Stephen accepted a plate from one of these worthies and went to the table.

"It looks like our dearest wish of a week ago, doesn't it?" he said, casting a glance around the table with its load of beef, brawn, and meat pies.

Anne smiled a little as she looked at the table of food. "Indeed it does. But really I am not very hungry right now, Stephen. If I could just have something to drink, perhaps . . ."

"You ought to eat something," he said firmly. "Do you care for mince pie? Or here's something that ought to interest you— it's frumenty, one of those old English customs you're so interested in. If I remember aright, eating it on Christmas Eve is supposed to insure good luck throughout the coming year. Would you like to try some?"

Anne looked dubiously at the dish he indicated. "What is it, exactly?" she said.

"Boiled grain with milk and spices—a sort of sweet porridge."

Anne wrinkled her nose. "I'm sure it is delicious, Stephen, but I think I would rather have chicken if it's all the same to you," she said frankly.

Stephen laughed and helped her to the chicken. "There's roast beef, too—cold roast beef, alas, but still probably better than your average boardinghouse fare."

She shook her head, smiling. "You'll never give up trying to convert me to the cause of roast beef, will you, Stephen? I promise to give it a fair trial sometime soon, but for now I would rather have just chicken, and perhaps a little of that custard."

After he had filled her plate in accordance with her wishes, Stephen carried it for her into the adjoining breakfast parlor and helped seat her at the table. He then returned to the dining room to fetch her a glass of wine. He fetched a glass for himself at the same time and sat beside her at the table drinking it and watching her while she ate.

"Aren't you hungry?" she asked, looking up from her plate.

"No, I supped earlier in the evening with some of my tenants. It was an enlightening experience, and a rather humbling one, too—I find there's a lot I don't know about running a place this large. It's enough to make me wish I'd come home a couple of years ago instead of staying on with Rob."

Anne glanced at him briefly, then looked away. The mention of his prolonged stay in Scotland had reminded her that it was Lydia who had been the cause of it; and this in turn reminded her of the resolution she had made at the inn and renewed only the night before, to be on her guard around him.

Stephen observed the change in Anne's expression and wondered at it. He had been toying with the idea of asking her how she had come to be acquainted with Lord Francis Rowland, but the sudden chill in her manner made him decide against it. "You're looking rather tired, Anne," he said instead. "I think you should take my mother's advice and go upstairs when you're done eating."

For a moment she looked uncertain, then nodded with sudden resolution. "I *am* rather tired," she said. "I believe I will, Stephen, if you don't mind."

"Not at all. We will miss you, of course, but given the circumstances, I'm sure everyone will understand. I'll see you in the morning, Anne." Taking her hand in his, Stephen carried it to his lips. "Merry Christmas, my dear," he said gently.

"Merry Christmas, Stephen," she said, looking rather startled. Withdrawing her hand from his, she flashed him a nervous smile and hurried out of the room.

He followed at a more leisurely pace and was just in time to catch a glimpse of her as she vanished into the gallery at the top of the stairs. As he stood meditatively looking after her, he noticed Lord Francis's slim, nattily dressed figure detach itself from the crowd and mount the stairs after her. Stephen made an instinctive move in the same direction, but was prevented from following by a small gloved hand that came out of nowhere to seize him in a grip of iron.

"Stephen," said a lilting voice. "It's been ages since I've seen you. Do you remember me?—Chloe Moorhaven, from over at Moorhaven Manor. You and Marcus used to come over during the holidays to visit my brother Tom."

"Of course I remember," he lied politely, his eyes still fixed on the gallery overhead where Lord Francis's form had momentarily appeared and then disappeared. "You look very lovely tonight, Miss Moorhaven."

"You haven't even looked at me," she said, laughing. "Indeed, that is no way to treat an old acquaintance, Stephen. You must make amends by dancing the next set with me—yes, indeed you must."

Rather vexed by her insistence but not wishing to appear any ruder than he already had, Stephen accompanied Miss Moorhaven to the servants' hall and took his place on the floor with the other couples taking part in the dance. As he advanced and retreated, turned and bowed along with the other dancers, he wondered what was transpiring upstairs.

Anne had just reached the first floor landing when she heard Lord Francis's voice behind her, calling her name. "Anne," he said softly, and then in a louder voice, "Just a moment, Anne, if you please. I really do need to speak with you most urgently."

Anne whirled around to face him. "What are you doing here, Francis?" she said angrily.

"I might ask you the same question. What are *you* doing here, masquerading as Etheridge's fiancée?"

"That's none of your business, Francis. After the way you behaved, I have absolutely nothing to say to you."

"Wrong on both counts, my dear. It *is* my business, and I insist you stay and hear me out. Oh, I don't blame you for being rather irked with me about that business last week. I don't even blame you for that whack on the head you dealt me with the fire-irons, though I do think it was rather unsporting of you to attack me while my back was turned. But I can make allowance for your state of mind at the time and am willing to forgive you—"

"Kind of you, Francis, but I don't want your forgiveness!"

"But I forgive you nevertheless, my dear. That's very handsome of me, I think, considering that in addition to giving me a devil of a headache, you ended up costing me a deal of money which I could very ill afford. Why, I had to pay a hundred pounds to the parson alone, and then the scoundrel refused to give it back when you turned up missing. He said he'd kept his part of the bargain, and that it was my own fault if I didn't keep mine. Upon my word, I think I have been very badly used."

Anne merely gave him a disgusted look, then turned and began to walk away. Lord Francis followed after her, however, and caught her by the arm.

"Take your hands off me, Francis," she said through her teeth. "I've already told you I have nothing to say to you. You may think yourself lucky that I haven't hailed you into court for trying to abduct me."

"Ah, but that would reflect on you, too, wouldn't it, my dear? That sort of publicity is always so damaging to a lady's reputation. But I do not mean to be offensive," he added in a milder tone. "As I said, I can quite understand your being angry with me. What I cannot understand is how you came to turn up here of all places, the betrothed wife of our friend, the Right Honourable the Viscount Etheridge."

"I've already told you that's none of your business, Francis."

"And I've already told you that it is—and you might be surprised by how much I already know about it. When I was making my way back from the border a few days ago, I happened to stop at an inn where I heard a very interesting story about a lady and gentleman who were trapped overnight in a southbound mailcoach. The gentleman's name was Etheridge, I understand, and though I wasn't able to discover the lady's name, from the description I was given she seems to have borne a strong resemblance to you, my dear."

Anne merely looked at him without speaking. Lord Francis gave her a sympathetic smile. "Quite right, my dear; you needn't trouble to deny it. I had full particulars of the incident, and I know very well that it was you and Etheridge in that mailcoach. The question is, what are we going to do about it?"

"I don't think 'we' are going to do anything about it, Francis!"

"I fear you are mistaken, my dear. This betrothal story may serve well enough for the present, but there are plenty of people like myself who can look at the facts and piece the real story together. Etheridge may be willing to save your skin by passing himself off as your fiancée for a few weeks, but you don't seriously expect him to marry you, do you?"

Anne's temper was already running high, and the amusement in Lord Francis's voice made it flare even higher. "Why, yes, as a matter of fact I do, Francis," she said bitingly. "Unlike some people of my acquaintance, Lord Etheridge is a gentleman as well as a nobleman."

Lord Francis only smiled and shook his head. "My, you are bitter, aren't you? But it won't do, my dear—no, assuredly it won't do. I am positive that Etheridge knows the value of his title quite as well as I know the value of mine. Would that we might exchange with each other! This whole situation might have been avoided if I had only had the fortune to be born an elder rather than a younger son. I would willingly trade my name, ancient and honored though it is, for Etheridge's viscountcy and a snug estate like this one. But I suppose there is no use in repining. Unless some kind fate should suddenly sweep away my older brothers and all their offspring, I must remain what I am, which is to say, a well-born but sadly impoverished younger son. That is nothing to the purpose at present, however. What is to the purpose is that, though I *am* only a younger son, I am perfectly willing to marry you, Anne—and I assure you that Etheridge is not. Should worst come to worst and news of

your little escapade get about—through the agency of some
third party who took an interest in the affair, for instance—I
think you would find him very unwilling to come to the point.
Whereas I, on the other hand, am willing to marry you at the
drop of a hat—yes, even with the certain knowledge that you've
already spent at least one night with another man."

Anne raised her hand and slapped him hard across the face.
It was some satisfaction to see his smile disappear, but still he
managed to maintain his equanimity. "I shall not hold that
against you, either," he said calmly. "I can quite understand
your disliking to have your hand forced; I daresay I should feel
just the same, if our situations were reversed. But I must re-
spectfully point out that I *do* hold the trump card in this situation, and I think you will come around to my point of view
once you've had a chance to cool down and reflect a little—"

"Never! I shall never marry you, Francis."

Lord Francis sighed and rubbed his cheek ruefully. "You do
have a temper, don't you? First my head, and now my face—but
as I said, I shan't hold it against you. Neither shall I expect an
answer from you immediately. You may have a day or two to
think it over, and I feel quite confident that at the end of that
time you will have reached the conclusion that your best option
is to marry me. I really do find you very attractive, Anne," he
said, looking her over with ingenuous pleasure. "Even if you
weren't an heiress, I would be tempted to have you, and for a
man in my position that's saying a great deal.

"Shall we arrange to meet in, say, three days' time to discuss
your decision? Three days from today, out on the grounds somewhere. Let's see . . . on the drive over here, I recall seeing a
little pavilion down by the river that would do excellently for
a meeting place. I daresay you would have no difficulty slipping
away from Etheridge for a few minutes and meeting me there
sometime during the afternoon—"

"I shall not be there, Francis."

"Three days from today, at the pavilion down by the river.
Until then, dear Anne." Smiling, he swept her a low bow, then

turned and strolled back down the hallway in the direction of the stairs.

Downstairs in the servants' hall, Stephen was undergoing a smiling interrogation from Miss Moorhaven.

"I made the acquaintance of your Miss Compton this evening," she told him, as they went down the line of dancers. "I say *your* Miss Compton, because in spite of your mother's attempt to pass her off as a mere guest, rumor has it that she is destined to be the next Lady Etheridge. Are you planning to marry her, Stephen?"

"Yes," said Stephen, with a determination that made Miss Moorhaven open her eyes.

"Gracious, you sound quite fierce about it! I'm sure you have my sincerest congratulations, Stephen. She seems a charming girl, and certainly she is very lovely. You must bring her over to visit us at the Manor sometime. I know Tom would enjoy meeting her—he always enjoys meeting pretty girls—and I'm sure he would like to see you again, too, after all this time. How many years has it been since you were at Etheridge Hall?"

Stephen was spared answering by the steps of the dance, which forced Miss Moorhaven to leave off her interrogation at this point and retire to the opposite end of the room with the other ladies. When she and Stephen were subsequently reunited, he was ready with a few questions of his own.

"We've been so busy talking about my guest that I haven't had a chance to ask you about yours, Miss Moorhaven. I noticed you came in on the arm of Lord Francis Rowland. Is he staying at the Manor over the holidays?"

"Yes, he is—at least, I do not know how long he intends to stay, but he is certainly with us for a few days. Mama was a little annoyed about it because he came without being invited—just dropped in on us yesterday without any warning—but because he is one of Tom's particular friends she could hardly object. And she is even more annoyed with him after what happened today."

"Oh, yes?" said Stephen, trying not to show how deeply this story interested him. "What happened today, Miss Moorhaven?"

"Well, it seems that when Francis and Tom were out riding this afternoon, Francis bet Tom that he couldn't jump his horse over a five-barred gate, Of course Tom took the challenge, but when he tried to do it, he took a tumble and ended up fracturing his collarbone. That was certainly very naughty of Francis, but it was Tom's fault as much as his, and Francis apologized for his part in it very nicely. And I think even Mama forgave him in the end. It was she who suggested he accompany us here tonight—or perhaps it was he who mentioned it first—but in any case she made no objection, and she spoke to him quite civilly on the drive over here. Francis can certainly be very charming, even if he *is* a sad rattle."

Having thus summarily disposed of the subject of Lord Francis Rowland, Miss Moorhaven returned perseveringly to the subject of Stephen's engagement. "I am sure your mother must be delighted, Stephen. She will be looking forward to the fun of a wedding, and the pleasure of spoiling her grandchildren later on. But how is Lydia taking the news?"

It was the kind of sly remark that would have disturbed Stephen very much not too many months earlier. Now he felt no emotion stronger than annoyance as he replied, "I do not know what Lydia's plans are. She knows she is welcome to stay on here at Etheridge Hall as long as she likes, but it may be that she would prefer to retire to Ash Grove with my mother and sister when Anne and I marry. We really have not had time to discuss the subject as yet."

Disappointed of scandal, Miss Moorhaven congratulated Stephen once more upon his engagement and then spent the rest of the dance telling him about the wonderful success she had enjoyed during her first London Season the previous spring. When the dance finally ended, Stephen thanked her for standing up with him, led her back to her mother, and headed for the stairs.

At the first landing he met Lord Francis, who was coming down as he was going up. For an instant their eyes met, and it seemed to Stephen that the expression on the other man's face more nearly resembled a smirk than a smile. Stephen looked after him frowningly, then turned and hurried on up the stairs.

He found Anne still standing motionless in the middle of the upstairs hall. At his approach, she turned to look at him, and he saw that her face wore a look of blank despair. "Oh, Stephen, the most dreadful thing has happened," she said brokenly.

He felt a powerful impulse to gather her into his arms. With an effort, he withstood the impulse and took her by the hand instead. "It can't be as bad as that," he said firmly. "Tell me what has happened, Anne."

Too upset to dissimulate, she told him all that had passed between her and Lord Francis. "I had no idea that he would follow me here and try to see me again. I was so sure that I had seen the last of him back in Scotland. Oh, Stephen, what are we to do?"

Stephen shook his head in amazement. "And so it was Francis Rowland who abducted you? I can scarcely believe it . . . and yet, now that I think about it, I *have* heard some rather dark stories about him in the past. One tends to discount the rumors one hears because the man himself is so likable."

"Yes, he is. Even when he was threatening me just now, he was quite smiling and pleasant about it, but still it was a threat, Stephen. If I don't agree to marry him, he will tell everyone about that night we spent in the mailcoach. Oh, Stephen, what are we to do?"

"Well, there's really only one thing that we can do, isn't there? We must get married ourselves, as soon as possible."

Stephen made this statement with outward composure but inward trepidation. Anne made a small stifled noise and turned her face away. He came a step nearer, looking down at her with compassion. "I know it is hard, Anne, but I truly don't see any other way. Francis may be mercenary, but I don't believe he's malicious. If we were to marry, he wouldn't have any incentive to spread stories about us, and it's ten to one that the whole business would die away without a breath of scandal. And if he should go ahead and try to cause a scandal anyway—well, at least if we were married, I'd be in a position to do something about it." Stephen smiled rather grimly. "Thank heaven I had the foresight to send off for that special license."

"Oh, Stephen, I can't let you do this," said Anne. There was a catch in her voice, but the face she turned to him was both dry-eyed and determined. "You have done so much for me already. I couldn't live with myself if I let you do any more, especially such a thing as that. To expect you to sacrifice your whole future for a woman you hardly know—no one could expect it. I'd sooner marry Francis than ask you to do such a thing."

Stephen cleared his throat. "Well, as it happens, Anne, I would not consider it much of a sacrifice. It's true that I have not known you long, but the nature of our acquaintance has been exceptionally close—closer perhaps than most people could obtain in a year's ordinary intercourse. I can say with all sincerity that there is no woman I know whom I would rather marry than you."

Half amazed and half incredulous, Anne lifted her face to look at him. "Truly, Stephen?"

"Truly, Anne," he said, returning her look steadily.

Looking into his eyes, Anne felt a strange stirring of emotion. She had been feeling a good many emotions since her interview with Lord Francis, but this was an emotion very different from shock or grief or anger: a feeling of relief verging almost upon exultation. Without giving any real credence to Lord Francis's words, she had nevertheless wondered if he were right in saying Stephen would never marry her if worst came to worst; now the worst had come to pass, and it was clear that he *was* willing to marry her. Anne was inexpressibly glad to find him true to his word. Amidst all the conflicting emotions she was feeling at that moment, a single conviction had begun to emerge, and that conviction was, that though very sorry to be marrying under such circumstances, she was not sorry to be marrying *him*.

"Very well, Stephen," she said aloud. "Let us be married then, as soon as possible. It will have to be tomorrow or the next day if we are to thwart Francis's schemes."

"The sooner the better," said Stephen briskly. "If Reverend Healy hasn't already left, I'll speak to him tonight; otherwise, I'll have a word with him after services tomorrow."

Anne nodded. "And I suppose we ought also to tell your mother and sister tonight, to prepare them," she said.

"I'll tell them," said Stephen immediately. "You go on to your room and let me take care of the whole."

Anne shook her head with a ghost of a smile. "No, you've been shouldering more than your share of the responsibilities ever since we've met, Stephen," she said. "If we are indeed to marry, then from now on we must deal on equal terms, with me doing my own share. Shall we go downstairs?"

Stephen took her arm, then smiled suddenly. They were standing in the middle of the upstairs hall where it joined with the corridor leading to the servants' quarters. Directly over their heads hung a double festoon of greenery, from which was suspended an ivy covered ball ornamented with ribbons and lady apples.

"Look at that," said Stephen, nodding upward. "Do you realize you're standing under the kissing bush?"

Anne gave the ivy-covered ball a cursory glance. "Yes, I saw that earlier," she said. "There's one downstairs in the drawing room, too. Another of your English customs?"

"Yes," said Stephen. "Traditionally anyone caught standing beneath it is required to pay the forfeit of a kiss." He was smiling as he spoke, but there was a question in his eyes as he looked down at her.

"I see," said Anne. Her color had risen slightly, but she made no move to step from beneath the ball. Stephen hesitated, then bent down and kissed her.

It was a longer and more intimate kiss than the one he had given her earlier in the drawing room. It was a kiss such as Anne had never experienced before. She found it strange but not unpleasant.

With her eyes shut, her other senses seemed heightened; she was intensely aware of the way he smelled and felt and tasted, of the scent of soap and fresh-laundered linen that clung to him, the solid warmth of his body next to hers, and the faint tang of wine on his breath. Most of all she was aware of the gentle yet persuasive pressure of his mouth on hers, drawing from her a response almost against her will.

When he released her at last, Anne felt curiously shaken. She had the sensation of having passed some invisible boundary which, having once passed, she might not now retreat from. The thought made her shiver a little.

"You are cold," he said, drawing her arm protectively within his own. "Do you need to go to your room to fetch a shawl before we go downstairs?"

"No, I am not cold, Stephen. Let us go find your mother and sister." Laying her hand on his arm, she accompanied him down the hallway, toward the blaze of lights and noise of revelry that awaited them below.

Ten

"But my dears, I do not understand your hurry," said Mrs. Etheridge plaintively. She spoke from her seat beside the drawing room fireplace, where she, Diana, Anne, and Stephen had gathered to rest and refresh themselves with tea and delicacies salvaged from the supper buffet. The party was over; it was some hours past midnight; and both house and hosts were in a state of *déshabille*.

Mrs. Etheridge's plumed toque sat slightly askew atop her gray curls; Diana had kicked off her slippers and was sitting in an upholstered armchair with her feet tucked under her; Anne, on the sofa, had removed her long evening gloves; and Stephen lounged beside her in his shirtsleeves, one arm resting lightly across her shoulders as though to shield her from his mother's disapproval.

The guests had departed nearly an hour before, after drinking a last, loud toast to the newly arrived Christmas. Amy had been discovered not long after, curled up asleep beneath a pier table in the hall. She had been carried off to bed by her nurse, and Lydia had excused herself at the same time to go up to her own room.

Of all the household, only the four of them remained downstairs, their chairs drawn close around the fireplace where the red embers of the dying fire still glowed in the grate.

Mrs. Etheridge surveyed the couple on the sofa with a troubled face as she repeated, "I do not understand your hurry. Of course we are all eager to have you in the family, Miss Compton—or

Anne, as I should say, for as we are so soon to be nearly related, we can surely dispense with the formality of titles. We are all eager to have you in the family, Anne dear, but I see no reason why you and Stephen should not wait a few more months, at least until you are past your first mourning. Then we could have a proper wedding, with a breakfast and a party afterwards—"

"But I've already explained all that to you, Mother," said Stephen patiently. "Anne's affairs were left rather unsettled by the death of her mother, and since then so many complications have arisen that we think it better to marry now so that I may be in a position to manage them for her. I know you regret not having an excuse for a grand show of a party, Mother, but you can make it up later by having a ball after Anne is out of mourning, you know. Indeed, I think this way will be best all around. Our marrying so suddenly may raise a few eyebrows, but given Anne's circumstances I don't think most people will blame us for not waiting. Her mourning naturally means we cannot have a large or public wedding, but there would be no impropriety about our marrying quietly, in a private ceremony."

"No, to be sure there would be no impropriety about it, but still it seems to me a shame to do things in such a hurried, haphazard manner. We could give you such a lovely wedding if you would only wait a few months—"

"I think they are being very sensible about it, Mother," said Diana from the depths of her armchair. "It's their wedding, after all. If they don't want any fuss about it, I don't see why they should be forced into it."

"Oh, but I do not mean to force them into anything, my dear. It is only that it will all be so rushed this way. No wedding party or even a wedding cake—though to be sure Christmas cake is very like wedding cake, and I suppose Cook might put a few flourishes on it to make it more suitable to the occasion. And the chapel is already hung with greenery. If we were to tuck a few flowers here and there, to brighten it up a bit—actually it could all be made very pretty without a great deal of trouble."

"That's the spirit, Mother," said Stephen, smiling at her. "But you'd better start tucking flowers right away, for I intend that we shall be married tomorrow if possible."

"So soon as that? But how will you manage about a clergyman, Stephen? And a license?"

"I already have a license. As for the clergyman, I thought I would speak to Reverend Healy tomorrow after services and see if he might be able to come over sometime during the afternoon. I don't anticipate any difficulty there—it's the settlements that will pose the biggest problem, I suspect. I must send a message over to Briggs first thing in the morning so that he can start drawing up the papers. I'll have to recompense him well for disturbing him on Christmas Day, poor soul."

"You seem to have thought of everything," said Mrs. Etheridge resignedly. "I do hope you know what you're doing, Stephen. When once you get the bit between your teeth, there's no stopping you—you're a great deal like your father that way. I'm afraid you've bullied poor Anne into marrying you in this hurly-burly fashion when she would much rather wait and have a proper wedding."

"Indeed, ma'am, it was my idea as much as his," said Anne earnestly. "I hope you do not mind too much. I know it will all be rather hurried this way, but as Stephen says, it would be of great help in settling my affairs if I were married and settled myself. At the moment it is so difficult, with no home of my own and no one to advise me."

This reference to her orphaned state instantly melted all Mrs. Etheridge's resistance. "Of course, my dear. I quite understand," she said, rising from her chair to embrace first Anne and then her son. "I did not mean to put obstacles in your way. If I seemed reluctant, it was only for your sake—you must know how happy I will be to have you for a daughter-in-law. We will get to work first thing in the morning and plan out your wedding—good heavens, it already *is* morning! You ought to be in bed, my dear. And so ought we all—upstairs to bed, all of you. We've a busy day ahead of us tomorrow!"

* * *

Anne went to bed, but not to sleep. The idea that in a matter of hours she would be a married woman kept running incessantly through her head, making sleep impossible. When at last she did doze off, she was awakened what seemed only minutes later by the sound of church bells and a chorus of lusty voices singing "Christians, Awake" beneath her window. Having risen from her bed and peeped between the curtains at the troop of rustic choristers singing away on the lawn below, she rang for her dressing woman and began to make her toilette for the day— the day that, impossible though it seemed, was destined to be her wedding day.

The news of her wedding had of course to be communicated to Parker, who received it without batting an eye. "We will want to wash your hair then, Miss Anne," she said composedly. "Some time after luncheon would be best, I expect. Have you decided which dress you wish to be married in?"

Anne shook her head with a barely repressed sigh. The question of what she was to do for a wedding dress had been among the thoughts that had troubled her sleep the night before—one of the lesser thoughts, admittedly, but vexatious nevertheless.

"It will have to be black, I suppose, as I have nothing else," she said morosely. "The dress I wore last night would do as well as any."

Parker bowed in acquiescence. "I'll look it over after breakfast and make sure it's clean and in good repair," she said. "And allow me to take this opportunity to say how happy I am for you, Miss Anne. Lord Etheridge seems to be very highly thought of by all the staff here, and in general you can tell a lot about a gentleman from what his servants say about him. I trust the two of you will be very happy."

Somewhat cheered by her servitor's words, Anne left her room and went down to the breakfast parlor. The entire Etheridge family was already gathered there, including Amy, who had been allowed to breakfast with her elders on this special occasion. But it was evident that excitement had entirely done away with her appetite. Her breakfast lay slowly congealing on the plate in front of her while she prattled on happily about the delights that lay in store for her that day.

"First we shall go to church," she told Anne, as Anne took her place at the table beside her. "And then we shall come home and have our presents. I have drawn pictures for you and Uncle Stephen as presents, but that is a surprise. And I have made a pen-wiper for Aunt Diana, and needlebooks for Mama and Grandmother, but those are surprises, too. And then after we have our presents we will have luncheon, and later, after I have had my nap, we will have Christmas dinner with plum pudding. Plum pudding is on fire when it comes to the table, but the fire goes out before you eat it. And then we will play games. And then I will go to bed. And then later you and Mama and Grandmother and Aunt Diana and Uncle Stephen will go to bed, too, and then it will not be Christmas any more. Molly has told me all about it."

"I see that she has," said Stephen. "We seem to have a fairly full day ahead of us, don't we?" His voice was amused, but Anne saw a look of consciousness settle over his face as he spoke. She looked quickly away that she might not meet his eyes.

No more than Amy could she eat her breakfast, and she was on pins and needles throughout the meal, waiting for one of the others to inform Lydia that she and Stephen were to be married that day. The subject never arose, however, and Anne at last concluded that the three of them must have tacitly agreed to postpone telling Lydia until later in the day, perhaps waiting for an occasion when Amy was not present. Anne was heartily grateful for the reprieve, but she could not help wondering a trifle uneasily how Lydia would react to the news when she heard it, and who would be assigned the job of telling her.

She need not have worried, however, for a few minutes later she got a second reprieve even greater than the first. Following Amy's childish recital, Lydia had begun to speak of her own plans for the day, and by a stroke of luck so amazing as to seem positively heaven-sent, it appeared that she would be out of the house while the ceremony was taking place.

"The Shutes are having a masque this afternoon as they always do, and they have very kindly invited me to take part, and to join them for Christmas dinner beforehand. They have their Christmas dinner at midday, you know, so that it need not interfere with your plans, Harriet. I told them I would speak with you first, but I really do not see any reason why I should not go."

"Why, certainly you must go, Lydia," said Mrs. Etheridge, with a cordiality that was positively overwhelming. "Since we wait until evening to have our Christmas dinner, there is no reason why you may not spend all afternoon at the Shutes'."

"Yes, and that way you will be able to have two Christmas dinners instead of one, Lydia," said Diana. Lydia threw her a suspicious look, but Diana's expression was one of angelic innocence.

"You will be here for the presents, Mama?" said Amy anxiously.

Reassured on this point, Amy, too, gave her consent, and as soon as breakfast was over the whole party went out to the carriage that was waiting to take them to church.

The parish church was located in the village that lay about two miles from Etheridge Hall. It was a very small village, comprising only a handful of dwellings in addition to a small general store, a blacksmith's shop, and one or two other businesses.

The church was likewise small, a square gray stone building with a squat belltower at one end, not greatly distinguished in its architecture but beautifully decorated inside with masses of holly, ivy, and rosemary. It also possessed a congregation that made up in enthusiasm whatever they might lack in the way of formal musical training.

As Anne listened to a trio of countrymen perform yet another rendition of "Christians, Awake," she glanced at Stephen sitting beside her in the pew. His eyes were turned toward a large monument that stood on the side wall of the church, not far from where they were sitting. Anne followed his gaze and saw that it was a

funerary monument of a somewhat florid type, featuring a pair
of weeping maidens bearing an urn inscribed with the words
"Requiescat In Pace." Underneath in smaller letters was the inscription, "Sacred to the memory of Marcus Michael Etheridge,
Fourth Viscount Etheridge. 'The souls of the just are in the hands
of God; Lord, grant them eternal peace.' "

Anne read the inscription twice, with an unsettled feeling in
her heart. Once again she looked at Stephen. He was regarding
the monument fixedly, his face grave and impassive; she could
not guess what he might be thinking.

When the service was over, Anne remained in the pew with
Diana, Amy, and Mrs. Etheridge while Stephen went up to speak
with the clergyman. Lydia was in the next pew chatting with
the family seated there, presumably the Shutes; Anne looked
about rather apprehensively to see if the Moorhavens might also
be present, but it appeared that neither they nor Lord Francis
had chosen to attend church that morning. After a few minutes,
Stephen returned from his errand wearing a relieved expression.

"It's all arranged," he told them in a low voice. "Reverend
Healy will come by at four o'clock to perform the ceremony. I
told him I would send the carriage for him at half past three
and take him to the Tarewoods afterwards for Christmas dinner,
and he was satisfied."

"You ought to have invited him to dine with us, Stephen,"
said Mrs. Etheridge reprovingly. "It's really the least you could
do for the poor man, after forcing him out on Christmas Day."

"I did invite him, Mother, but he was already engaged to
take dinner with the Tarewoods," said Stephen mildly. "I will
have to make it up to him some other way—in the form of a
large donation to the poor box, perhaps."

Lydia came up just then, having made her adieux to her
friends in the next pew. With an audacity that astonished Anne,
she went directly to Stephen and took him by the arm, smiling
up at him wistfully. "Oh, Stephen, this brings back memories,
doesn't it?" she said. "I can remember attending Christmas services here years ago, when you were down visiting over the

holidays. It all looks just the same, and sounds the same, too—I think Reverend Healy preached the exact same sermon, and I know we sang the same hymns. It's curious how some things never change through the years."

"Yes, and how much other things do change," said Stephen. There was no animosity in his voice, but Lydia dropped his arm as though it was red-hot. As they filed out of the pew, Diana gave Anne a speaking look, which said as clearly as possible, "I told you so."

In a short time they were back within the walls of Etheridge Hall. Amy ran upstairs to the nursery to fetch her "surprises," while the elder members of the party went to their rooms to retrieve their own Christmas gifts.

Once inside her bedroom, Anne first removed her pelisse and bonnet and then set about gathering up the stack of gold and silver paper-wrapped packages lying ready atop her dressing table.

The largest contained her gift to Mrs. Etheridge, a handsome cashmere shawl which she had worn but once before and which she trusted might pass for new. Beside it was Lydia's gift, a bottle of eau de cologne which had been among the things she had brought back with her from Paris. For Diana she had chosen a handsome volume of Pascal's *Pensées*. The book had been awarded her at school some years before as a prize for penmanship, but since she had never had occasion to peruse it—nor, it must be confessed, inclination—the book still retained its original pristine appearance. As Anne added the package containing the book to the others in her arms, she reflected with satisfaction that it was just the sort of thing Diana ought to enjoy.

Amy's gift had posed more difficulty for Anne. There had been few things among her belongings that would appeal to a small child, and after going through all of her trunks and boxes a couple of times she had decided to sacrifice a trinket box worked in colored wools which a school friend had given her years ago. Parting with the box cost her more regret than parting with Pascal, but of all her possessions it seemed the most suitable

for Amy. Not only would it be a useful receptacle for a child's
trinkets; it also happened to be emblazoned with the letter "A,"
thus making it quite as appropriate to "Amy" as "Anne."

That had left only Stephen, and it was his gift that had given
Anne the most difficulty. Since she was there in the guise of
his fiancée, the others would probably expect her to give him
something rather substantial; yet the only things she possessed
that were at all suitable to the purpose were a few personal
belongings of her long-deceased father's, with which she was
most reluctant to part. There seemed no alternative, however.
Steeling herself to the sacrifice, she had taken them from their
cases, inspected them one by one, and settled at last on a small
ring containing a plaited lock of her own hair.

All this had taken place the afternoon before; and as Anne
had wrapped the box in the gold paper Mrs. Etheridge had provided her, she had debated whether she ought to explain the
matter to Stephen beforehand and ask him to return the ring to
her later on. But this had seemed rather an ungracious request,
and in the end Anne had decided to trust that his own sense of
decency would prompt him to return it to her whenever their
spurious engagement should be dissolved.

Such had been her thoughts previous to the events of the
Christmas Eve party; but now, as she picked up the small gold-
wrapped package, it occurred to her that their engagement was
not going to be dissolved, and that the gift of the ring would in
all likelihood be a permanent one. The thought gave Anne a
long moment's pause. She stood looking down at the package
in her hand until she heard running footsteps and the sound of
Amy's voice echoing excitedly in the hallway. The sound
brought her to herself again; quickly she added the package to
the others in her arms and started for the door.

When Anne got downstairs to the drawing room, she once
again found herself the last to arrive. Amy was prancing impatiently about the room and came rushing over to present her
with her gift as soon as she came in. Anne accepted the crayoned
scribble with suitable words of appreciation, and after the elder

members of the party had received similar scribbles—or, alternately, crudely fashioned pen-wipers and needlebooks—they began to distribute their gifts to each other.

Anne was pleased to see her improvised gifts meet with a universally favorable response. Mrs. Etheridge at once threw her new shawl over her shoulders and declared that nothing could have suited her better. Diana turned over the pages of Pascal with a look of interest, while Amy exclaimed with delight over the "A" box and immediately set about filling it with the toy soldiers Stephen had given her. Even Lydia, who had entered but little into the spirit of the occasion, condescended to thank Anne for the eau de cologne with languid but seemingly genuine pleasure.

In passing out her gifts, Anne had reserved Stephen's till last. It was with a strong feeling of trepidation that she handed him the ring box and sat beside him on the sofa watching him open it.

"How pretty," said Mrs. Etheridge, when the ring lay revealed at last in Stephen's hand. "A lovely token, my dear. Oh, and it has your hair in it, too?—a very pretty idea, upon my word."

Stephen, who had been gravely inspecting the ring, looked up to smile at Anne. "Indeed it is," he said. "Thank you, Anne. I shall always treasure it." Removing the gold signet from his finger, he replaced it with the ring Anne had given him, while Lydia sat looking on with a jealousy she made no attempt to hide.

Besides the drawing Amy had made for her, Anne received several other gifts, including a pretty pearl brooch from Mrs. Etheridge and a set of handkerchiefs from Diana. From Lydia she received a pair of pink kid gloves, their secondhand condition as painfully obvious as their complete unsuitability to her state of mourning.

"So sorry, Miss Compton, but I really had no time to find a proper present for you. If only Stephen had informed us beforehand that you would be spending Christmas with us, I might have done better," said Lydia sweetly, as Anne drew the gloves from their wrappings. Anne gave her a polite smile in reply and mentally resolved not to underestimate the depths of Lydia's malice in the future.

After Anne had laid the gloves aside with the brooch, hand-kerchiefs, and drawing, Stephen presented her with his gift. The others leaned forward curiously to watch as she tore off the paper. Even Amy left off playing with her soldiers and came over to see what was happening.

The size and shape of the package had prepared Anne in some measure for what she would find, but still she was shaken when she saw the diamond ring in its velvet-lined box. "Oh, Stephen," she said, looking up at him with a troubled expression. "Oh, Stephen, it's beautiful, but you needn't have, you know."

"Perhaps not, but I wanted to," he said calmly. "We are en-gaged, after all, and it's only right that you have an engagement ring. This one is in the nature of a family heirloom, but if you would prefer something more modern—"

"Oh, no, indeed, Stephen. If I must have a ring, then I can't imagine a lovelier one than this one. But—" Here Anne caught sight of Mrs. Etheridge's surprised face and Lydia's avid one, and came to an abrupt stop. "But you needn't have gone to so much trouble," she finished, rather lamely.

"I went to very little trouble, I assure you. The ring has been in the family for some years. But I am glad you like it, Anne."

Taking her hand in his, Stephen slipped the ring onto the third finger of her left hand. The touch of his hand on hers affected Anne strangely; she could not bring herself to speak, or even to look at him. But her eyes flew to his face an instant later when he dropped a light kiss on her brow. "Merry Christ-mas, Anne," he said quietly.

In the pause following these words, Lydia arose hastily from her chair. "It's time I got ready to go to the Shutes'," she said. "Amélie, you'd better go upstairs with me and take all these things up to the nursery."

"Indeed, yes," said Mrs. Etheridge, also getting to her feet. "We may have people come to call later, you know, and it won't do to have toy soldiers all over the drawing room. Stephen, whatever possessed you to give her such a thing? A most inappropriate gift for a child her age. Particularly a girl child!"

"I like them," said Amy, carefully laying the soldiers to rest in the trinket box.

"There, you see, Mother? She likes them," said Stephen, laughing. "If there's anything in heredity, it stands to reason that she would. Marcus and I used to play with them by the hour."

"Yes, I remember that you did. This looks exactly like the set you used to have." Mrs. Etheridge picked up a scarlet-coated drummer to examine it more closely. "Why, this *is* your old set, isn't it? Did you send for it from Ash Grove, Stephen?"

"Yes," said Stephen briefly. Anne could not see his face, for he had bent down to help Amy collect a troop of cavalrymen from the drawing room rug, but she thought he sounded rather annoyed.

"And so you gave Amy your soldiers, Stephen! I must say I am surprised. I remember that you were quite adamant about keeping them, even after you returned from Eton—"

"You make too much of it, Mother. I am past the age of playing with soldiers now, I hope." He rose from the sofa to drop the cavalrymen into the box, then returned to the sofa. Anne observed that his color was noticeably higher. From the doorway, Lydia gave him a quick, speculative look but said nothing, and as soon as Amy had gathered up her playthings the two of them left the drawing room.

Eleven

The door had barely closed behind Lydia and Amy when it was opened again by the butler. "I beg your pardon, my lord, but I'm afraid you have a caller," he said apologetically. "A legal person, by the name of Mr. Briggs—he says he is here at your request. I have put him in the small parlor."

Stephen rose to his feet. "My attorney, come about the marriage settlements," he told Anne. "I'll probably be tied up most of the afternoon, right up until the time Reverend Healy arrives. There'll be some things for you to sign, too, I should think, later on. I'll send one of the servants to call you when the papers are ready."

Anne could only nod in reply. He pressed her hand and gave her a quick, reassuring smile before following the butler out of the room. As soon as he was gone, Mrs. Etheridge turned to Anne and Diana.

"Well, my dears, we, too, have a great many things to accomplish this afternoon," she told them. "First is the matter of your dress, Anne. Since the ceremony is to be strictly private, I think you might dispense with mourning, don't you?"

"I suppose I might, but I'm afraid I'm not in a position to do so, ma'am," said Anne. "When Mother died I gave most of my old things away, thinking that they would all be hopelessly outdated anyway by the time I was out of mourning. I haven't a single decent dress that isn't black."

"Oh, but that's no difficulty, my dear. You and Diana aren't too different in size, and one of her dresses might easily be altered to fit you. Mind you, I don't mean to push you into anything you're not comfortable with. You just lost your mother quite recently, I know, and if you have any scruples on that account—"

"No, none on that account, ma'am, but a good many about imposing on you and Miss Etheridge. I'm afraid it would be putting you both to a great deal of trouble."

In a quiet voice, Diana assured Anne that she and her wardrobe were entirely at Anne's disposal. She seemed so in earnest that Anne gratefully gave way, and the two of them went upstairs to look through Miss Etheridge's dresses. These proved to be all very simple, as befitted so young a girl, but Anne felt simplicity was no drawback on this occasion; and between them, she and Diana soon settled on a suitable dress.

Anne then rang for Parker, showed her the dress, and asked if it could be altered in time to serve as her wedding dress at four o'clock that afternoon. Parker looked it over carefully and gave it as her opinion that it could; and with the help of Mrs. Etheridge's dressing woman she at once set about making the necessary alterations.

The rest of the morning passed quickly for Anne. Between fittings she managed to bathe and wash her hair, and the rest of the time she devoted to helping Mrs. Etheridge decorate the chapel.

She saw nothing of Stephen, for throughout the morning and into the afternoon he remained closeted in the parlor with his attorney. He did not even appear at the luncheon that was served in the breakfast parlor at noon, and Mrs. Etheridge ordered some sandwiches sent to the parlor, remarking prosaically that gentlemen always worked better on full stomachs. It was nearly two o'clock when at last Anne was summoned to the parlor to sign the settlement papers.

She came into the room to find Stephen standing in front of a table on which were spread a vast number of closely written documents. Beside him stood a small, bespectacled, not very happy-looking man in an old-fashioned periwig, evidently the long-suffering Mr. Briggs. As Anne stood hesitating in the door-

*A*llow us to proposition you
in a most provocative way.

PRESENTING AN IRRESISTIBLE OFFERING ON YOUR KIND OF ROMANCE.

Receive 4 Zebra Regency Romance Novels (An $18.49 value)
Free

Journey back to the romantic Regent Era with the world's finest romance authors. Zebra Regency Romance novels place you amongst the English *ton* of a distant past with witty dialogue, and stories of courtship so real, you feel that you're living them!

Experience it all through 4 FREE Zebra Regency Romance novels...yours just for the asking. When you join *the only book club dedicated to Regency Romance readers,* additional Regency Romances can be yours to preview FREE each month, with no obligation to buy anything, ever.

Regency Subscribers Get First-Class Savings.

After your initial package of 4 FREE books, you'll begin to receive monthly shipments of new Zebra Regency titles. These all new novels will be delivered direct to your home as soon as they are published...sometimes even before the bookstores get them! Each monthly shipment of 4 books will be yours to examine for 10 days. Then, if you decide to keep the books, you'll pay the preferred subscriber's price of just $3.65 per title. That's $14.60 for all 4 books...a savings of almost $4 off the publisher's price! What's more, $14.60 is your <u>total</u> price...there's no extra charge for shipping and handling.

No Minimum Purchase, a Generous Return Privilege, and FREE Home Delivery! Plus a FREE Monthly Newsletter Filled With Author Interviews, Contests, and More!

We guarantee your satisfaction and you may return any shipment...for any reason...within 10 days and pay nothing that month. And if you want us to stop sending books, just say the word, you're under no obligation.

An $18.49
value.
FREE!
No obligation
to buy
anything, ever.

way, Stephen smiled and beckoned her toward the table of documents.

"Just a few papers to sign, and the thing's done," he said cheerfully. "I've already signed my bits, all except the things that need witnessing. Briggs here will explain to you about the different provisions, and if there's anything that doesn't meet with your approval you must be sure and say so. It's not too late to make changes."

Mr. Briggs confirmed this statement, albeit rather unenthusiastically. He summoned up a brief, dry smile, however, before plunging into a description of the different provisions of the marriage settlements.

Anne's head was soon swimming as she listened to him expound upon the complexities of issue and non-issue, jointures and reversions, but she valiantly read through all the documents he showed her and understood enough to gather that she was to be extremely well-provided for in every possible contingency. When Mr. Briggs had gone through all the documents and presented her with pen and ink, she had no hesitation about signing her name to them.

When the last document had been properly signed, sealed, and dated, with a couple of servants called in to witness, Mr. Briggs' aggrieved expression softened a little. As he gathered up the papers, he observed that it was not so late but that he might get home in time for his Christmas dinner after all.

"I'll have Edmonds harness up my grays and take you there as quickly as possible," said Stephen, reaching for the bellrope. "Your man can take your own carriage home later. And here's a trifle for Mrs. Briggs and the children, to make up for the inconvenience of calling you out on Christmas Day. No, really, Briggs, I must insist. It's hard lines to take you away from your family on such a day, but you may be sure I shan't forget it."

He accompanied the attorney outside to his carriage while Anne went upstairs to see how the wedding dress was progressing. It proved to be nearly finished, and the final fitting was under way when Mrs. Etheridge tapped on the door a few minutes later.

"Upon my word, that looks very well, my dear! I don't think we could have done better if we'd had months to prepare." She watched admiringly as Parker circled around Anne, setting a pin more securely here and there and deftly adjusting the fall of the skirt.

The improvised wedding dress was a simple closed robe of white muslin with short sleeves and a modest round neckline. Parker had shortened the skirt and added a deep ruching of lace around the corsage and hem; from the same lace she had fashioned a bandeau for Anne's head, entwining the lace with a string of pearls and further embellishing it with a length of sheer gauze that hung down in back to a point just below Anne's waist.

"Yes, ma'am, I think we've contrived pretty well, given the time and means within our disposal," agreed Parker, in what was for her an unusual burst of loquacity. She gave a last touch to Anne's headdress and stood back to survey the result with critical satisfaction. "Quite *à la mode* she looks. I saw just such another toilette in the last issue but one of *La Belle Assemblée.*"

Anne contemplated her reflection in the mirror. She could see that she looked very well: quite exceptionally well, in fact, but it was like looking at the portrait of a stranger. The radiant creature in bridal raiment who regarded her from the glass seemed an alien being with no relation to her or her situation.

With a feeling of oppression, she turned away from the glass. Parker was busy gathering up the scraps of lace and other oddments left over from the alterations, and when she left the room presently to dispose of these articles, Mrs. Etheridge came up to where Anne was standing and put her arm around her shoulders.

"I do hope you're not regretting this, my dear," she said, regarding Anne with a worried line between her brows. "I couldn't help seeing that you looked a little distraught just now. You know it's not too late to postpone the ceremony if you're having second thoughts."

Alarmed at having betrayed her feelings, Anne quickly arranged her features into a false bright smile and assured Mrs. Etheridge that she had no wish to postpone the ceremony. Mrs. Etheridge smiled and patted her shoulder sympathetically.

"Poor dear, you're suffering from nerves, I daresay. I remember well enough how it was at my own wedding. But it will all be over very soon now." She hesitated a moment, then went on with an obvious effort. "One's wedding day is a momentous occasion, my dear, as I hardly need tell you. Also one's wedding night—I know you have no mother of your own, and it has occurred to me that you have no one to—ahem—explain your marital duties to you. If you have any questions, I would be more than happy to answer them for you."

Anne, both touched and embarrassed, assured Mrs. Etheridge that she had a reasonably good understanding of the subject. "Such things are more freely discussed abroad than here, I believe. At the school I attended—"

"You studied such things at school?" said Mrs. Etheridge, looking considerably astonished.

Anne laughed. "No, indeed! The good sisters did their best to keep us all in a state of lamblike innocence. But among the pupils there was a very broad range of classes—farmers' daughters, girls from *bourgeois* families, and even a few *aristos* whose parents had chosen to stay and brave out the new order under Napoleon. Some of them were very free in their speech and behavior—really quite astonishingly free."

"Yes, that would be natural, of course," said Mrs. Etheridge with a nod. "Among so many, there would be bound to be a few whose upbringing was not what it should have been. And indeed, it seems to me a trifle unreasonable to take a girl of low background, straight from the farmyard perhaps, and expect her to behave like a lady all at once."

"Oh, but most of the country girls were very well behaved, ma'am. It was the high-born ones whose behavior tended to be the lowest. I think it was that as much as anything that gave me a disgust for the aristocracy. Oh, dear, I didn't mean that!" Anne looked with dismay at Mrs. Etheridge. "On my honor, ma'am,

I didn't mean to insult you and your family. It was the Belgian aristocracy I was speaking of, not the English. I have no fault to find with the English aristocracy—at least, not with *all* the English—"

Mrs. Etheridge broke in briskly upon Anne's confused apologies. "That's quite all right, my dear. I understand perfectly what you mean, and I am sorry to say that the kind of licentious manners you describe are not confined wholly to the Belgians, or even to the aristocracy. My own grandmother was accustomed to discuss the most delicate subjects in her drawing room, but I think that sort of thing is less common now than it used to be. The revolution over in France had something to do with it, of course—"

"Of course," Anne managed to say, but Mrs. Etheridge was already rushing on.

"So very sobering to people over here, seeing noblemen being guillotined left and right, and the whole country in an uproar. I think it made our own upper classes think a little more about the responsibilities of their positions, rather than merely dwelling on the privileges. I'm sure Marcus always took his duties as a landlord very seriously, and Stephen is just the same. Even while he was in Scotland, he made a point of keeping up with the business side of things here, and you can see yourself how busy he's been since he returned."

"Yes, indeed, and I didn't mean to insult him, or you, or Diana, ma'am—"

"Yes, I know you didn't, and you needn't apologize any more, my dear. As I said, I quite understand, and we needn't say any more on the subject—or on the other subject we were discussing, either," Mrs. Etheridge added, with a glimmer of a smile. "You're such a sane, sensible creature, Anne dear. I am quite sure you and Stephen will deal extremely well together. Now if you'll excuse me, I must go down to the kitchen and see if Cook is done with the cake. Reverend Healy ought to be here any time, and I won't have another chance to look in on things before dinner."

So saying, Mrs. Etheridge started for the door, but before she got there she turned back to deliver herself of a hasty addendum. "I've given orders that your things be transferred to the Gold Bedroom," she told Anne. "That's the room traditionally assigned to the lady of the house. The servants will take care of it all while you're downstairs, so you needn't do a thing; just take your time and come down when you're ready. I expect you'd like some time alone before the ceremony, to compose yourself."

A second time Mrs. Etheridge started for the door, but once again she turned back before she reached it, this time to give Anne a hasty hug and kiss.

"You do look lovely, my dear," she said, carefully smoothing the folds of Anne's veil. "Did I say how much I am looking forward to having you as a daughter-in-law? I am, very much indeed. And now I'll take myself off and let you have some time to yourself."

With a warm smile, Mrs. Etheridge once again started for the door, and this time managed to reach it without turning back.

Twelve

After Mrs. Etheridge had left her, Anne remained standing where she was like one frozen. Her mind felt as frozen as her body; she had the sensation of being trapped in a nightmare from which she might awake at any time to find herself back in her lodgings at Harrogate, safe, single, and—in comparison, at least—blessedly free of care.

With a sense of wonder she looked down at her white muslin robes and told herself that it was her wedding day, and that she was about to marry a man who had been a complete stranger to her a week before. But her mind refused to accept the idea: it seemed ridiculous, impossible, too farfetched to be real.

On further reflection, she decided that this might not be altogether a bad thing. Numbed disbelief was perhaps not an ideal state of mind for a bride on her wedding day, but it was infinitely preferable to despair—or panic. As long as her mind remained numb, she was able to preserve an appearance of calm that would not have been hers had she fully grasped the reality of what was happening to her.

Anne felt all this instinctively; she also felt that it would have been a relief to have been sure the calm would continue, but of this she had some doubt. Somewhere beneath the surface tranquillity of her mind lurked an awareness that her situation was both real and serious. The present calm could be no more than transitory; she feared that a single touch, even a single word would be enough to shatter it and throw her into a state of panic.

The word came only a few seconds later. There was a sound

of hurried footsteps in the hall, a scratching on the door, and a pink-cheeked maidservant burst into the room and dropped her a breathless curtsy. "Lord, but you do look lovely, miss," she said, looking Anne up and down with admiration. "Just like a princess. Mrs. Etheridge sent me to say that Reverend Healy's just come, and they're all waiting for you in the chapel. Do you need me to help you with your dress?"

"No, thank you," said Anne, and managed with an effort to summon up her false bright smile once more. The girl bobbed her another curtsy and left the room as abruptly as she had entered it. Anne found herself alone once more, but her former calm had deserted her; she felt a sudden conviction that her knees would not carry her downstairs.

Sinking into a nearby chair, Anne gripped her hands tightly together and gave way to her feeling of panic. Thoughts swirled wildly through her head like leaves in a whirlwind. Escape was her foremost thought: instead of going down to the chapel, she might change her dress, steal down the backstairs, and go—"Go where?" she said aloud. "Wade through the snow, I suppose, and probably freeze to death before ever I reached the village! That *would* be an intelligent thing to do, wouldn't it?"

The idea made Anne smile a little, and suddenly she felt much better. "You're dramatizing yourself, my girl, that's what you're doing," she told herself. "To be sure, it's not the wedding you envisioned in your romantic youth, but it might be far worse. You might be like Virginie back at school, marrying a man old enough to be your grandfather—or you might be yourself, marrying Francis Rowland and never knowing until it was too late that it was your money he was after all along. By marrying Stephen, I will be marrying a man whom I like and trust and respect—and it doesn't seem to me that that's a bad foundation for a marriage."

This was such an indubitable truth that Anne began to feel quite cheerful and to reproach herself for her qualms.

"Indeed, I begin to think you don't deserve him, Anne," she told herself. "How dreadful it would be to back out at this point—

to refuse to marry him, after our engagement has been as good as announced to the whole neighborhood. I know his situation well enough to know that jilting him now would cause a deal of talk, and though I may not be terribly enthusiastic about marrying like this, I hope I'm not low enough to serve him like that odious Lydia. This business has gone so far already that my only honorable course is to go through with it. After all, he was honorable enough to offer me marriage when he was under no obligation to do so; the least I can do is be honorable in return."

With this thought to strengthen her, Anne found it possible to rise from her chair and walk to the door. She caught a glimpse of herself in the cheval glass as she crossed the room, and that glimpse further strengthened her: her mirrored self looked clear-eyed and resolute, a woman fully in command of herself and her destiny. With an approving nod to her reflection, Anne opened the door and began to walk down the hall toward the stairs.

The chapel was located on the ground floor of Etheridge Hall. It was a rectangular room of modest size styled in the classical rather than the Gothic mode. There were a dozen rows of mahogany pews with sky-blue plush cushions for the use of the servants, a small gallery overhead for the family, and on the west wall a row of stained glass windows depicting the story of Abraham and Isaac. The late afternoon sunlight streamed through the colored glass, throwing splashes of color on the wall opposite and casting into insignificance the flickering light of the candles grouped around the altar.

Along with the rest of the house, the chapel had been decorated for the season with wreaths of holly and ropes of greenery. To these, Mrs. Etheridge had added potted plants and masses of white flowers, so that the room now appeared a veritable garden.

Anne's courage almost failed her again at the chapel door, but by calling on the same thoughts that had strengthened her a few minutes ago, she brought herself to enter the room. Once inside, the sight of Stephen standing near the altar drew her on without need for further mental reinforcement. Instead of thinking, "I am marrying a man who was a stranger to me a week ago," she told herself, "I am marrying Stephen Etheridge," and found herself immeasurably comforted.

Stephen was wearing a beautifully tailored topcoat of blue superfine and a pair of dove-colored pantaloons tucked into shining Hessian boots. His dark head was inclined toward the aged clergyman who stood beside him, so that Anne saw him in profile as she came into the room. He turned to look as she approached, however, and his face was illumined by a smile such as Anne recalled seeing there but once or twice before. Without speaking, he took her by the arm and led her toward the altar and the waiting clergyman. Mrs. Etheridge and Diana were already gathered there, and a moment later they were joined by a middle-aged gentleman in a bottle-green coat who came in through the side door of the chapel.

"My steward, John Laughton," explained Stephen, as the gentleman joined them at the altar. "He has kindly consented to act as groomsman for me today." In a lower voice he added, "You look beautiful, Anne."

"Thank you," she said, smiling at him a little shyly. "You look rather beautiful yourself, Stephen."

He smiled back, but any answer he might have made was forestalled by Reverend Healy, who chose that moment to open his prayer book and begin reading the marriage service. Listening to his quavering voice tell over the ancient forms, Anne was once again overcome by a sensation of unreality. As though in a trance she heard his voice droning on and on; she heard herself responding to his questions in a voice that sounded very thin and faraway, and she heard Stephen beside her making the responses with a composure that she would have resented, had her mind been in a state to admit of such an emotion. The hand that held her own was not altogether steady, however, and she remarked with surprise that it trembled slightly as he took the ring the clergyman had blessed and slipped it on her finger.

From that point on, Anne's impressions became increasingly

jumbled. She heard the clergyman pronounce her and Stephen man and wife; she felt his lips touch hers briefly and then found herself being embraced in turn by Mrs. Etheridge and Diana; she received unquestioningly the salute of John Laughton, who took her hand and bowed over it with a good deal of solemn ceremony. "You and Lord Etheridge have my best wishes for your future happiness, my lady," he said.

Anne had been so busy trying to absorb the reality of her newly changed status that she had completely forgotten the change of title that accompanied it. A tiny, surprised gasp escaped her. She looked quickly at Stephen and found he was smiling down at her.

"You must try to get used to it, my dear," he said. "I'm afraid you're one of the cursed race now."

"The cursed race?" repeated Diana, looking curiously from him to Anne. "What race is that, Stephen?"

"The aristocratic race. I don't wish to alarm you, Diana, but I am afraid your new sister-in-law has some rather republican notions. I could hardly persuade her to give me the time of day, once she discovered I was encumbered with a title."

His words made Anne blush, but Diana gave her a look of approval. "And quite right, too," she said. "The class system as it now stands is an absolute disgrace. One need only look at the royal family to see that. If there is to be an aristocracy, it ought to be an aristocracy of talent, as Plato proposes—"

"No, Diana, I will not have you quoting Plato on my wedding day," said her brother with smiling firmness. "He was no proponent of the married state, as I recall. You may kiss me or congratulate me, but let us have no philosophy if you please!" Diana accepted the rebuke good-naturedly and kissed his cheek with a sisterly affection.

From the chapel, the party proceeded to the drawing room. Anne, still in a daze, accepted and drank the glass of champagne that Mrs. Etheridge offered her. She heard John Laughton wish her and Stephen happiness, health, and prosperity in a long and ceremonious speech; she heard Reverend Healy ask Diana if she would be the next to marry, in the jocular tone usual to elderly gentlemen addressing young girls; she saw Diana's polite smile by way of response; and she watched Mrs. Etheridge flit happily about the room pressing further installments of champagne upon her guests.

At last, having drunk two glasses of champagne and exhausted his supply of witticisms upon Miss Etheridge, the aged cleric consulted his watch and announced, rather regretfully, that it was time he started for the Tarewoods. He was just taking a punctilious leave of Mrs. Etheridge when the door opened and Lydia came in.

"Hello, Stephen," she said, singling him out at a glance and making her way directly to his side. It was only after she had bestowed upon him a most fond and particular greeting that she seemed to become aware of the others in the room. Her eyes flickered over Mrs. Etheridge and Diana, rested briefly on John Laughton and Reverend Healy, and finally came to rest on Anne. She regarded the latter for a moment in silence, and it was possible to trace on her features the progress of her thoughts as the significance of Anne's costume gradually dawned upon her. Anne, regarding her in turn, observed that some of the color left her cheeks, but she had to admire the other woman's composure.

"Dear me," drawled Lydia. "It looks as though there's been a wedding in my absence."

Mrs. Etheridge cleared her throat and looked nervously at her son, but it was Diana who spoke first. "As a matter of fact, there has been, Lydia," she said. "You may be the first to congratulate Anne and Stephen upon their marriage."

"Then I do congratulate them," said Lydia. She spoke calmly, but it was obvious that she was struggling to maintain her composure. Anne almost felt sorry for her, but her sympathy evaporated with Lydia's next words. "I must say that you have been very sly about this business, Stephen. I think you might have let an old friend like me in on your secret." Putting her arms around his neck, she gave him a long, intimate kiss.

Mrs. Etheridge cleared her throat again and looked distressed.

Reverend Healy smiled benevolently, while John Laughton's face wore an inscrutable look; Diana's face was likewise inscrutable, and Anne looked down at her left hand and at the wedding ring that gleamed on the third finger.

At last Lydia released Stephen and turned to Anne. "You have all my very best wishes, my dear," she told her. "You are a lucky girl to be marrying Stephen—a very lucky girl." The words were spoken playfully, but the green eyes looking into Anne's were as cold and hard as ice.

Reverend Healy said again that he must be taking his leave. "I'll see you to the Tarewoods, sir," said Stephen. His color was a little higher than usual, but he gave no other sign that Lydia's kiss had affected him. "No, it's no trouble, sir. I can easily drive you there and get back to the Hall in time for dinner."

After he and Reverend Healy had left, Lydia turned to Mrs. Etheridge. "If dinner isn't to be served immediately, I believe I'll go up to my room and lie down for a while," she said. "This has been rather a wearing day."

"But you do plan to join us for dinner, don't you?" said Mrs. Etheridge anxiously. "And for games afterwards? Amy is looking forward to it so much, you know.

"Oh, yes, I'll be there," said Lydia grimly. She shot Anne a malevolent look before turning and leaving the room.

Anne did not change her dress for dinner, but remained in the drawing room while the others went up to change. Her mind still felt rather numb, and she found it very restful to sit on the sofa doing nothing for the half hour or so that everyone else was upstairs. She was still sitting there, idly twisting the wedding ring upon her finger, when Amy came into the room. Molly had her by the hand, but as soon as Amy saw Anne she broke from Molly's hold and ran over to her side.

"Oh, but you do look beautiful, Miss Compton," she exclaimed, reaching up to touch Anne's headdress with a reverent finger. "When I am older, I would like a dress just like this one."

"She's not Miss Compton anymore, Amy; she's Lady Etheridge," said Molly, smiling. "She and your Uncle Stephen were
married today."

The word "married" appeared to mean little to Amy. She
looked puzzled but accepted Molly's statement with a child's
easy credulity. "Lady Etheridge is my mama's name, too," she
told Anne. "But my grandmother is only Mrs. Etheridge. She
is not a ladyship like you and Mama."

"No, darling, and that's how I prefer it," said Mrs. Etheridge,
entering the room in time to hear this speech. "I see you are
admiring your Aunt Anne's wedding finery. Doesn't she look
beautiful?"

"Is she my Aunt Anne?" said Amy, regarding Anne doubt-
fully. "Molly just said she was Lady Etheridge."

"And so she is, but she is also your Aunt Anne—at least, I
suppose she is really your cousin, but since you call me grandmother and Diana and Stephen your aunt and uncle, we may as
well be consistent all around and make her an aunt, too. It will
also be much less confusing than having two Lady Etheridges
in the house, as you yourself just said."

"Aunt Anne," repeated Amy, pronouncing the words with
some difficulty. "Now I have two aunts: an Aunt Anne and an
Aunt Diana."

It was not long after this that the others arrived, and the party
went in to dinner. On this occasion, dinner was served in the
dining room rather than the breakfast parlor. As on the previous
evening, the room wore a festive aspect with its trimmings of
greenery and its chandelier ablaze with candles; Anne blinked
a little at the strong light and stood looking around her until
Stephen took her gently by the arm and led her to her new place
at the foot of the table.

The sense of unreality within her had never been stronger.
Again she looked about the room, telling herself that she now
had a share in all its splendor; that this was her table, and this

her table service, and these her servants bustling about, but i
was of no use: the idea still seemed completely unreal. Evei
the room itself seemed unreal, a fantastic blur of light an
shadow, noise and movement, sights and smells.

In desperation Anne fixed her eyes upon Stephen, the on
wholly solid-seeming object in the room. Yet even he seeme
less solid than usual this evening. As the meal went on, h
demonstrated a flow of spirits that quite astonished his bride
who had seen nothing comparable from him since the day the
had celebrated their safe arrival at the inn in Branwick.

There was soup to begin with, followed by filet of flounde
with shrimp sauce. *"English* shrimps," Stephen told Anne mis
chievously, as he helped her to the dish. "You see, I remembe
your preference."

"You are fond of shrimps?" said Mrs. Etheridge with interes
"I must be sure to tell Cook. But no, I am forgetting, aren't I
You are the lady of the house now and can tell her yourself!
Mrs. Etheridge laughed merrily. Anne gave both her an
Stephen brief, embarrassed smiles before devoting herself t
her plate of fish.

After the fish, the roast was brought forward: a roast of bee
supplemented with horseradish and Yorkshire pudding and accom
panied by dishes of baked celery and parsnip fritters. There wa
also a roast turkey and a haunch of venison with currant jelly, bu
the roast beef had been given the place of honor, and it was wit
roast beef that Stephen insisted on filling Anne's plate.

"You are now in a position to sample, at its best, the hallowe
roast beef of Old England," he said solemnly, as a footman lai
the plate in front of her. "If this does not convert you to m
cause, then I may as well admit defeat at once and retire broke
from the field."

"You don't care for roast beef?" inquired Diana, as sh
helped herself and Amy to Yorkshire pudding.

"Not especially, but your brother has assured me that that i
only because I have never had proper roast beef. I must say tha
this looks very good." Endeavoring to summon some gaiety t

her own manner, Anne sampled a bite and smiled across the table at Stephen. "Yes, very good. You may count me a convert to your cause, Stephen. Never again shall I speak slightingly of English roast beef!"

Though she was sincere in praising the dish, Anne found she had but small appetite for roast beef or anything else that evening. Most of the food Stephen had given her still remained on her plate when the dishes for the first course were removed. The second course was brought on next: this included the ceremonial boar's head, wreathed in rosemary and presented with the traditional garnish of an apple in its jaws. Altogether it made an impressive-looking dish, but as Mrs. Etheridge had said, its function appeared to be more ornamental than edible.

Anne smiled a little to see Amy's dubious look as it was laid on the table in front of her. When Stephen laughingly offered to help her to it, she refused his offer with more haste than courtesy; but a few minutes later, after a swift glance around the table to make sure no one was watching, she put out her hand, quickly removed the apple from the boar's jaws, and bit into it with an air of deep contentment.

Besides the boar's head, the second course included roast pheasant with bread sauce, braised partridge, escalloped oysters, stuffed onions, a turnip gratin, and a large meat-filled pastry which Stephen informed Anne was a Yorkshire Christmas Pie. "You remember me speaking of Christmas pies, I'm sure, on our journey down from Scotland," he added, with a conspiratorial smile.

"It sounds as though you two spent the whole trip talking about nothing but food," said Lydia snappishly.

"It was a subject that happened to interest us both deeply at the time," said Stephen, and gave Anne another smile as he helped her to a slice of the pie.

After the second course was done with, dessert was brought on. This included plum pudding, served aflame with a sprig of holly on top; it also included a couple of mince pies and a large cake decorated with marzipan and sugary frosting.

"Your wedding cake," Mrs. Etheridge told Anne and Stephen

proudly. "Of course it should really be served by itself, but this being Christmas, I was afraid some people might be disap pointed if we left out plum pudding." She cast a smiling glance at Amy, who was regarding the blazing pudding with a look o rapturous delight.

When the flames had subsided, the company began to help themselves to the Christmas desserts. Anne observed that Lydia took a small sliver of mince pie and a morsel of pudding, bu emphatically rejected the cake, which she herself had been called on to distribute. Amy vibrated uncertainly between the different desserts and finally settled the matter by demanding portions of all three.

"It *is* Christmas, after all, and I don't suppose it will hurt her to eat so many sweets just this once," Mrs. Etheridge told Lydia as she put servings of mince pie and plum pudding on Amy's plate. When Anne had added to it a slice of cake, Mrs. Etheridge turned to Diana and urged her to take a slice of cake, too. "And Anne must put a piece of it through her wedding ring, so tha you can put it under your pillow tonight and dream of you future husband," she told her daughter. Diana rolled her eyes but accepted the cake and its auguries with a resigned smile.

After dessert, the party retired to the drawing room, where a tray of apples, oranges, nuts, and dried fruits awaited them along with the tea tray. Amy, her appetite nothing impaired by three desserts, immediately plopped down in front of the table and began stuffing herself with raisins, figs, and Spanish plums Stephen seated Anne on the sofa beside him and set about crack ing filberts and walnuts for her to eat, while the others took their places in chairs around the fireplace. Mrs. Etheridge set tled into her chair with a contented sigh.

"I really believe that was the best Christmas dinner yet," she told the others. "But I do wish Reverend Healy might have stayed to eat it with us. I'm sure the Tarewoods won't give him nearly such a good dinner. Mrs. Tarewood is dreadfully close they say, and never serves more than two courses even for com pany. I think he would have liked to stay, poor man, only he was afraid of hurting her feelings. Such a dear old gentleman he is, and so completely unselfish; it was very good of him to come out on Christmas Day just to oblige you, Stephen. I hope you gave him something handsome for his trouble."

Lydia moved impatiently in her chair. "Really, it has been an exhausting day," she said. "If you don't mind, I think I will retire early tonight."

At these words, Amy left off eating plums and turned to her mother with a look of consternation. "But we haven't played any games, Mama," she cried. "You said you would be here to play games with us. You will stay just a little while longer, won't you?"

Lydia hesitated, then nodded reluctantly. Amy at once set about drawing the party into a circle around the fire. The games of which she spoke proved to be of a rather juvenile nature, but all the elder members of the party, not excepting Lydia and the dignified Diana, took part in them with good grace.

It was very entertaining to watch Amy's small face as she stood in the center of the circle, trying to determine which of her relatives was concealing a slipper behind his or her back. At forfeits Diana reigned supreme and sentenced the rest of the party to a variety of imaginative penalties; at jackstraws it was Lydia who triumphed, and some of her sullenness was lost as she deftly plucked straw after straw from the heap.

Last of all, the candles were extinguished, a dish of brandy was set alight, and the party settled down to play at snapdragon. In this sport Amy chose to be only a spectator. In spite of her repeated denials to the contrary, it was obvious that she was dropping with fatigue; and when the clock struck ten, Molly came and carried her off to bed, still protesting sleepily and clutching a bunch of figs and raisins in one sticky hand.

Her exit caused Lydia to relapse into her former sullen humor. She excused herself a few minutes later, wishing Stephen, Diana, and Mrs. Etheridge a merry Christmas and pointedly excluding Anne. After she had left, a deep silence settled over the drawing room. It was so quiet Anne could hear snatches of song and bursts of laughter drifting up from the servants' hall, where the servants were having their own Christmas celebration. At one point she could even distinguish the song being sung: the inevitable "Christians, Awake," performed by a whole chorus of rather maudlin-sounding voices. But her companions in the drawing room seemed content to sit quietly around the hearth, watching the fire slowly dwindle in the grate.

Mrs. Etheridge was the first to break the silence. "It is so nice to have all of us together again," she said, looking contentedly around the fireside. "Of course, Amy is a dear child, and having a child about does make Christmas seem more like Christmas, but having Lydia here, too . . . not that I mean to find fault with her behavior, for I'm sure this is all very trying to her, but I must confess that I enjoy having just our family by ourselves for a little while. You see that I count you as one of the family already," she told Anne with a smile. "I trust this will be only the first of many Christmases we spend together. Is your first Christmas back in England all you had hoped for?"

There being no possible answer to this question but a polite assent, Anne politely assented, but to herself she reflected that in some ways it was a Christmas a good deal more than she had hoped for. Stephen on the sofa beside her stirred a little at his mother's words, as though they had awakened some uncomfortable reflection. Mrs. Etheridge went on talking for some time, recalling past Christmases and speculating on those to come; at last she glanced at the clock on the mantelpiece and rose to her feet.

"I think it is time we were all getting upstairs," she said. She managed to sound casual, but it was noticeable that she carefully avoided looking at either her son or daughter-in-law as she spoke. "Diana, where's that piece of wedding cake we put aside for you?"

Diana, with the air of one humoring a small child, said she supposed it was still in the dining room unless the servants had cleared it away. She wished Anne and Stephen a polite good night before leaving the room with her mother to collect the portentous fragment of cake. As soon as the door shut behind them, Anne got quickly to her feet. "I think I'll go up now, too," she said, and escaped before Stephen could say anything in reply.

Thirteen

Anne lingered in the downstairs hall until she heard Mrs. Etheridge and Diana going up the main staircase. As soon as the sound of their voices had died away, she followed after them, reaching the upstairs gallery just as the longcase clock on the landing struck eleven. Diana's tour on the previous day had acquainted her with the location of the principal bedchambers, so that she had no difficulty in locating the Gold Bedroom, but she hesitated a moment on the threshold before stepping inside.

The Gold Bedroom was both larger and grander than the one she had quitted a few hours before. It was really a suite of rooms, encompassing a private sitting room, dressing room, and closet as well as the bedroom itself. All four rooms were decorated in a style that might best have been described as light-hearted Gothic. The bed was a four-poster, to be sure, large and square and festooned with heavy draperies, but still there was nothing gloomy or forbidding about it; rather it was a fanciful pavilion of rosewood generously inlaid with ormolu and further lightened with hangings of ivory damask embroidered in gold.

The windows were also hung with ivory damask, elaborately embroidered and fringed with gold, and the floor was covered with a flowered Aubusson carpet. Even the caryatids that supported the mantelpiece seemed to regard Anne with a benevolent air as she stood looking around her.

In the time she had been downstairs, the room had been made ready for her occupancy. A cheerful fire burned in the grate, and through the door to the dressing room she could see her own brushes and toilet articles laid out upon the dressing table. It remained only to ring for Parker to help her undress. Anne went to the bellrope, but once again she hesitated a moment before taking the rope in her hand and pulling it twice or thrice in quick succession.

Parker appeared so quickly that it was clear she must have been waiting for the summons. With her usual quiet efficiency she set about getting Anne ready for bed. There was nothing in her manner to show that this night was different from any other night, yet her actions showed an awareness that her manner did not. Instead of arraying Anne in an ordinary cambric nightdress, she produced a fine French peignoir of silk and lace, and when she had finished brushing Anne's hair she left it loose instead of arranging it into plaits for the night. All this she accomplished in near silence, speaking only when it was necessary to direct her mistress to sit, stand, or turn her head. When she had finished, she bade Anne a quiet good night and left the Gold Bedroom without a backward glance.

Left to herself, Anne went about extinguishing the candles one by one until the room was illuminated only by the glow from the fireplace. When this was done, she went resolutely over to the bed and lay down upon it, drawing the bedclothes over her and arranging the pillow comfortably beneath her head.

As she lay staring up at the gold-embroidered canopy above her, she was conscious of a nervous flutter in the pit of her stomach. With a touch of wry amusement, she reflected to herself that this was positively the last ordeal she would be expected to endure that day. It was an ordeal she would have been very glad to have behind her. She lay in bed, looking up at the gold-embroidered canopy and listening for the sounds in the next room that would herald Stephen's arrival.

Downstairs in the drawing room, Stephen remained on the sofa in front of the fireplace, trying to get up courage enough to go upstairs to his bride. Her abrupt departure had raised in him a number of doubts, not least of which was the fear that she had taken this way to show him that she wanted no part of his company that night. Although she had consented to marry him, it might be that she considered their marriage to be a marriage in name only and would hotly resent any attempt to force the usual marital attentions on her. He wished very much now that he had discussed the matter with her beforehand.

Rising from the sofa, he went into the dining room, filled a glass with port from the decanter, and returned to the drawing room to continue his meditations in front of the fire. One glass brought him no nearer a resolution than before. He rose again, refilled his glass, and returned to his seat.

Just as he was arising a third time, his butler came into the room. He looked at first rather surprised to find his master there; then his eyes fell on the glass in Stephen's hand, and Stephen could have sworn he saw a flicker of a smile cross the butler's austere face.

"Good night, Elliot," said Stephen, with as much dignity as he could muster. "I was just going up." He set down the empty glass on the mantelpiece and left the drawing room hastily.

Fearing further embarrassment, he elected not to ring for his valet when he reached his bedroom. He undressed quickly and wrapped himself in his dressing gown, all the while debating whether or not he ought to venture into the room next door. He even went to the door and listened for a moment, trying to judge by the sounds within whether or not he was expected. But he could hear nothing in the next room, although a cautious trial of the doorknob revealed that it was not locked. This seemed a favorable omen, but he could not forget the way Anne had left the drawing room after dinner—fled it, really, in the manner of a frightened deer. But perhaps that was only shyness. She had let him kiss her only the evening before without making any objection to the business—but there was, after all, a great deal of difference between a simple kiss and what might be expected to take place on one's wedding night.

Stephen left the door, went over to the fireplace, and began pacing back and forth in front of it, trying to make up his mind. He told himself that he had no wish to force upon her attentions that were unwelcome. If he could have been sure they were unwelcome, he would have been—not glad, exactly, but willing to leave her in peace, trusting that time and better acquaintance would bring about a change in her feelings. On the other hand, what if she was even now waiting for him and wondering why he did not come? The thought brought him up short. He looked at his reflection in the glass over the mantel and castigated himself as a fool and a coward.

"Enough of this," he told his reflection. "You're a man, aren't you? At least go over there and see if she wants you. If she doesn't—well, the worst she can do is throw you out again!" Squaring his shoulders beneath the dressing gown, he walked over to the door again and opened it.

In the meantime, Anne, having waited nearly an hour for her errant bridegroom, had given up waiting and had fallen asleep. The strain of the past few days had taken its toll on her, as had her sleepless night the night before, and even a flourishing case of wedding night nerves had not been enough to keep her awake. She stirred now as Stephen seated himself gingerly on the edge of the bed and began rather fearfully to draw back the bedclothes. "Stephen?" she said.

Her voice sounded drowsy and a little shy, but it was definitely not a "get-out-of-my-room-this-minute" voice. Stephen let out his breath in a long sigh. "Anne," he said, and drew her into his arms.

Anne did not return his embrace, but neither did she make any attempt to resist it. She lay passively in his arms with her eyes closed, awaiting whatever might come next. Her mind was in that curious state between sleeping and waking where real events are indistinguishable from dreams. When Stephen kissed he, she found the sensation agreeable and allowed him to kiss her again; by the time he had kissed her three or four times she had roused sufficiently to return his kiss; and before long she found herself kissing and being kissed with an ardor that seemed to meld their mouths into one.

It was as strange and intimate a sensation as it had been the night before, but this time Anne responded to it with an abandon unfettered by the restraints of her conscious mind. While he was kissing her so passionately it seemed natural to put her arms around him, to touch his back and shoulders and run her fingers through his hair; to exult in the hard muscularity of the one and the smooth silken feel of the other. When at length she discovered that her nightdress and his dressing gown had somehow melted away, she felt only pleasure in the increased warmth and intimacy of his skin next to hers. Even the hard pressure that bespoke his own state of arousal gave her no alarm, immersed as she was in her dreamlike state of pleasure.

His lips had strayed from hers now and begun to touch her ear, her hair, and her neck with light little kisses. Anne sighed, then drew in her breath sharply as they strayed lower. When at last his mouth touched her breast she caught her breath again and then again, running her fingers through his hair and arching her back in an ecstasy of pleasure. She felt as though she were melting inside; her body ached for him with a hunger that grew stronger and stronger as his mouth continued to tease and fondle her breast.

It seemed not enough to embrace him with her arms, so she put her legs around him, too, and held him tightly, seeking by this means to draw him nearer, to somehow relieve the ache of desire within her that had grown to nearly unbearable proportions. In some faraway corner of her mind, she was aware that she was behaving in an extremely wanton and undignified manner, but that awareness was nothing compared to the immediacy of his mouth on her breast, the warmth of his body against hers, and the fierce ache of her own desire.

When at last one of his hands stole down to touch the secret places between her legs, it was not an embarrassment but an overwhelming relief. She clung to him tighter still, her breath coming faster as his hands grew bolder. At one point a small cry escaped her, but it was instantly muffled by Stephen's mouth, which came down hard on hers in a kiss even more demanding than before. Between the hard urgency of his kiss and the insinuating touch of his hands, Anne was soon in a state beyond protest. She was so engrossed by the different sensations he was arousing in her that it came as a shock to her when she felt the pressure of him seeking to enter her.

The shock was only fleeting, however. She must have been ignorant indeed if she could have failed to see the direction things were taking, and for some time now the desire mounting within her had been focusing itself more and more in that one part of her body. Of their own accord, her hips rose to receive him, but he in turn drew back so that the surcease she sought was denied her. She turned her head aside with a sob of sheer frustration. Once more he began to ease himself into her with what seemed a tantalizing deliberation. She lay still this time, catching her breath a little with each minute accession; then it seemed as though he encountered resistance, for he paused.

Throughout all this Anne had kept her eyes tightly shut, even after it had become very apparent to her that she was not dreaming. Now she ventured to open them and found his eyes only inches away, burning into her own. Anne found herself unable to look away. She stared back at him, her breath coming fast and her heart pounding with a mixture of fear and excitement. He seemed to gather himself for a moment, then drove himself deep within her.

The pain that accompanied this movement came as an unpleasant surprise to Anne. She gripped his shoulders tightly and made a small, hurt noise as tears filled her eyes. Once more his mouth came down on hers, but this time his kiss was gentle, as though seeking to make amends for the hurt he had caused her. His hands, too, were gentle, and for several minutes he did nothing more than kiss her and stroke her shoulders, giving her time to adjust herself to the feel of him inside her. At last he ventured to withdraw a little, then repeat the thrusting motion, slowly at first and then faster.

The first few minutes were more pain than pleasure to Anne. Before long the pain began to ease, however, and she was able to bear each thrust without gripping his shoulders in an agony of apprehension. This in itself was quite as much as Anne would have bargained for, but once she had begun to relax she was amazed to find that there was actually a degree of pleasure in it. As the pain receded, the pleasure began to predominate more and more, until it had attained a pitch at once exquisite and unbearable. It came at last to a point where Anne could bear it no longer in silence and found it necessary to give vent to her feelings in speech. Words spilled out of her, both in English and in French: entreaties mixed with endearments, shamelessly urging him on to greater efforts.

Her lover's response was inarticulate but enthusiastic. He became almost savage in his thrusts, but it was a savagery which Anne, in her present state, found wildly exciting. Just when it seemed as though her pleasure could reach no higher, the unthinkable happened, and she found herself caught in a flood of sensation that swept her higher still, to a truly dizzying height, then brought her low to a state of gasping, shuddering fulfillment.

She had hardly recovered from the shock when Stephen achieved his own climax. He did this much more quietly than she had, but still there was no mistaking his pleasure in the performance. Although Anne was by now thoroughly exhausted and beginning to be rather sore as well, she found herself becoming excited all over again. It was strange to see a man usually so quiet and self-controlled in the grip of uncontrolled passion, and she felt it no small compliment that this particular display of passion had been inspired by her.

When he had exhausted himself at last and was lying motionless on top of her, she reached up to stroke his back with a timid hand. He drew a deep sigh and buried his face in her hair, kissing her with a tenderness far removed from the urgency of his previous caresses. Anne shut her eyes again, feeling the warmth of his breath on her skin and the beat of his heart next to hers, very strong and rapid first but gradually slowing as they lay in each other's arms. For a long time she was content merely to be and to feel, but eventually her mind began to stir and then grow anxious. At last she could bear the silence no longer.

"Stephen, what are you thinking?" she said in a small voice.

He was quiet a moment or two, apparently considering the question. "Well, to tell the truth, I don't know that I *am* thinking," he said at last. "I think I'm still reeling in shock more than anything."

His voice was warm with laughter, but Anne was only partially reassured. The longer she thought, the greater grew her conviction that her recent behavior had been exceedingly undignified, and unladylike in the extreme. She cringed to think of it, an action which made her aware that Stephen still occupied his former position of intimacy and embarrassed her even more.

"Oh, dear," she said weakly. "I don't know what you must think of me, Stephen."

He raised himself on his elbows to look at her. His eyes dwelt in turn upon her face, her shoulders, the gentle swell of her breasts and the slim curve of her hips and waist. "I think you are beautiful," he said. "And I think that I am a man most fortunately situated."

The smile that accompanied these words left Anne in no doubt as to his meaning. She blushed, and blushed all the more as he continued mischievously, "I can see being married to you is going to be very educational. I never had Diana's passion for languages, but the prospect of improving my French in such a painless manner is enough to make a philologist of me, too. I must confess, however, that I wasn't entirely sure if I was doing what you were telling me to . . . I hope I got the main points right?"

Anne covered her face with her hands. Stephen laughed and kissed them, and she parted her fingers to smile at him. "Oh, dear! Indeed, Stephen, I don't know what came over me. But I have never felt anything like that before." Suddenly serious, she lowered her hands and looked at him searchingly. *"You* have."

The words were a statement, not a question. "Yes," he said honestly. "I am older than you, you know—and society does generally grant bachelors a certain leeway in these matters. I don't pretend to be better than most men of my age and—"

"And position?" said Anne, with an edge to her voice. But he only smiled and stroked her cheek with one finger.

"You've still got it fixed in your head that any man with a title's bound to be a complete blackguard, don't you?" he said softly. "I suppose that's natural in light of recent events, but you really mustn't judge all of us by Lord Francis Rowland, you know. For myself, I can say truthfully that I've never been so circumspect in my life as in the two years that've passed since I inherited the title. About the worst debauchery I've indulged in was drinking whiskey around a turf-fire with Rob and his cronies!"

In a more serious tone he continued, "As I said, I don't pretend to be better than most men my age, but I'm pretty sure I haven't been any worse—and whatever my indiscretions in the past, I can assure you, Anne, that they *are* past. It is a genuine relief to me to be able to put all that behind me. I know there are men who can indulge in those sort of affairs without doing any apparent damage to their consciences, but I was never one of them. I won't pretend there is no pleasure in it—there is, of course, as you can see for yourself—but what pleasure there was, was for me always a pleasure mixed with guilt. I had a decent upbringing, and it has always been very difficult for me to reconcile that kind of behavior with what I was taught to believe was right. Indeed, I don't think I ever was able to reconcile it. The best I could do was to shut up the different parts of my life in separate compartments, so to speak, and try to pretend the one didn't exist while I was living the other. But I was never completely easy in my mind about it. Perhaps it's because of my upbringing, as I said— or perhaps it's only that I was born with an overdeveloped sense of responsibility, as various people have told me over the years. In any case, it is a relief to be married and have that particular moral dilemma behind me."

Anne digested this speech in silence for several minutes. On the whole she found it satisfactory, but she could not help wondering if his recent turn for "circumspection" had been inspired by his disappointment with Lydia. "If your conscience has been troubling you as much as that, I don't see why you didn't get married years ago," she said, and watched sharply to observe his reaction.

His reaction was to laugh and kiss her on the tip of her nose. "Perhaps I should have," he said, smiling down at her. "Perhaps I should have—but I am very glad I did not, Anne." And he kissed her again in a manner that, for the moment at least, satisfied her entirely.

Fourteen

Sunlight was filtering through the curtains of the Gold Bedroom when Stephen awoke the next morning. Even before he opened his eyes, he was conscious of Anne lying in the bed beside him. She lay on her side with her head cushioned on her arm and her face turned away from him, but by raising himself on one elbow he could see her hair fanned out on the pillow, the curve of her cheek, and the steady rise and fall of her breast beneath the bedclothes. Taking infinite pains not to wake her, he put out his arm and drew her a little closer. She made a small contented noise and snuggled against him quite willingly, with her back against his chest and her head nestled beneath his chin.

As he lay with her in his arms, he was struck by the realization that he was, at that moment, perfectly happy. He was in his own home, among his own family, and married to the woman he loved; and even if his new wife did not fully return his feelings, as he hardly dared hope, at least he now had positive proof that she did not regard him with loathing.

He told himself hopefully that if he were patient and did not force the issue, love might come with time. After what had happened the night before, anything seemed possible; he felt ready to conquer the world at a moment's notice, or perform any other trifling task of a like nature that might be required of him.

So potent was his euphoria that he found it almost frightening. A superstitious voice within him whispered that it was dangerous to be so happy. At best, it was inviting future disappointment; at worst, it was a kind of tempting fate, liable to bring disaster in its train. At any moment his happiness might be wrenched away from him, leaving him with a sorrow all the deeper for what had preceded it. Unconsciously his arm tightened around Anne, as though defying fate to take her away from him. She made another small noise, this time of protest, and opened her eyes.

"Good morning," he said.

"Good morning," she responded, pushing the hair out of her eyes and giving him a quick, shy, sleepy smile. "It wasn't all a dream, then?"

"If it was, then I dreamed the same dream," he said, smiling back at her. As he raised himself again on one elbow, the bedclothes fell back from his shoulders. Anne looked at him, and her eyes widened. "Oh, Stephen, did I do that?" she exclaimed.

Stephen craned his neck around to inspect his shoulder. It was marked with half-a-dozen superficial scratches, and when he inspected his other shoulder he found it similarly marked. "Yes, I believe you did," he said, running a hand gingerly over the scratches. "I seem to recall the circumstance now, though at the time it scarcely registered upon me. I was thinking of something else, I suppose."

This won him another quick, shy smile, but Anne's expression was worried as she reached out to touch the injured shoulder. "I am so sorry, Stephen," she said. "I cannot think how I came to—that's to say, I certainly did not *mean* to do such a thing. Truly I am very sorry."

"You needn't be," said Stephen. "I did worse to you, you know. I imagine the state of the sheets will bear me out."

Anne stole a quick look beneath the bedclothes and emerged with her cheeks bright pink. "How *horribly* embarrassing," she said fervently. "I suppose the servants will see all this when they change the sheets and know that we—how horribly embarrassing."

"You may think yourself fortunate that they don't fly them out the window anymore," he said, laughing. "There's a good old English custom for you—one that's fallen into disuse, I am happy to say."

Anne shuddered; but, recovering her spirit, said that it sounded more like Old English barbarism to her. Stephen smiled, pushed back the bedclothes, and swung his legs over the side of the bed. Anne looked at him and then looked quickly away with an even deeper blush staining her cheeks.

"I'm sorry," he said, observing her embarrassment. "I don't usually sleep in a nightshirt, but if it disturbs you I can certainly do so from now on."

Anne, still averting her face, said that she did not expect him to change his habits because of her. "I daresay I will become used to it in time, Stephen. Yes, and it will be a good opportunity for me to put into practice your sister's teachings about self-discipline. Diana says the best way to conquer a thing that disturbs you is to force yourself to face it over and over again, until it doesn't disturb you anymore. So—here I go."

Folding her arms over her chest, Anne looked at him determinedly. She made a pretty picture as she sat there with rosy cheeks and tousled hair, her bare shoulders white against the golden counterpane. The sight of her affected Stephen powerfully: so powerfully that he had to turn hastily away to hide his own immediate physical reaction.

"Not to disparage Diana's teachings, but I'm not sure how well they apply in this kind of situation," he said, speaking over his shoulder as he put on his dressing gown. "If you keep looking at me like that, I'm going to forget all about the work that's waiting for me downstairs and get back in bed with you. And if once I do that—well, I won't be answerable for the consequences."

Anne, with rather a provocative smile, suggested that he, too, might profit from a course of self-discipline. "In any case, don't think your threats frighten me, my lord. I'm not afraid of anything you can do to me now!"

"Is that so?" Stephen made a move toward her, then stopped himself with an effort. "Tonight," he told her, and went into his own room followed by the sound of her delighted laughter.

After he had left, Anne remained in bed for some time smiling to herself over the interview just past. She had already found that she was rather sore in one or two places, but overall she felt very well—"Quite remarkably well, in fact," she said aloud, and stretched luxuriously before getting out of bed. Having put on her dressing gown and arranged her face into an expression not too revealingly cheerful, she rang the bell for her dressing woman.

As soon as Stephen had dressed and eaten a hasty breakfast, he set about the day's business. It was Boxing Day, entailing interviews with all his servants and tenants as well as calls upon the local tradespeople. Stephen conscientiously discharged all these duties, but he had difficulty keeping his mind on the business at hand. Several times during the day he caught himself rubbing his shoulder with a foolish smile on his face; and it was all he could do to keep from blushing when his steward, observing the gesture, solicitously inquired whether he had suffered an injury.

His business made him absent at the luncheon table, where the female members of the household gathered at mid-day to partake of cold meat, cheese, and fruit. Lydia arrived rather late for the meal, having paid an early call at Moorhaven Manor, and as she sat down at the table, Anne observed that her eyes were sparkling maliciously. The reason for her malice became clear with the first words out of her mouth.

"I was speaking with Lord Francis Rowland this morning," she said, looking directly at Anne as she spoke. "He was very surprised to hear of your marriage, Anne. I didn't realize you and Francis had been acquainted before you came here."

Anne, with tolerable composure, said she had known Lord Francis for nearly a year. "I met him while I was staying in Bath with my mother."

"Yes, that's what he told me. He also told me several other things—very interesting things, some of them. He had a most intriguing story to tell about an incident that took place last week up by the Scottish border. It seems that a mailcoach got caught in a snowstorm, and the passengers had to spend the night in the coach—there were only two passengers, a lady and a gentleman, and not a married lady and gentleman either. According to Francis, they were complete strangers to each other before they got in the mailcoach. Can you imagine how that poor woman must have felt, being forced to spend the night with a man she'd never seen before? Of course her reputation would have been quite ruined afterwards."

"I don't see why," said Diana, eyeing Lydia with contempt. "After all, it was only an accident that put them in the same coach on that particular day. It might as easily have been two men or two women who got stranded overnight, and then nobody would have thought anything about it."

"Indeed, I think Diana is quite right," said Mrs. Etheridge. "Why should the poor woman bear a stigma all her life only because she happened to be in the wrong place at the wrong time? It seems to me ridiculous to apply ordinary moral standards in a situation like that."

"Yes, but she was traveling alone in the first place, you know, which would indicate that her morals couldn't have been terribly good to start with. Anne, you haven't spoken—how would *you* feel if you were forced to spend the night in a mailcoach with a gentleman you didn't know?"

Anne felt her hackles rise, but she forced herself to take a bite of bread and butter, chew it, and swallow before answering. "Why, it would depend on the gentleman, I suppose," she said coolly. "To be trapped in a mailcoach with a rattle like Lord Francis Rowland would be a heavy penance, but with the right gentleman I think it might be very romantic." She smiled sweetly at Lydia and took another bite of bread and butter.

Lydia's eyes snapped dangerously, but she said nothing more on the subject of snowbound mailcoaches. As soon as she had finished her own scanty luncheon of tea and unbuttered bread, she announced she was going for a walk and left the table precipitately.

Diana watched her go, then turned to Anne and asked if she had time that afternoon to help her with her French. Perturbed by Lydia's behavior but trying not to show it, Anne said that she did; and she spent the next couple of hours in the library helping Diana with the finer points of French grammar. But when at last her rather demanding pupil had released her from service, she left the library and hurried downstairs to see if Stephen had returned.

She told herself that she needed to inform him of Lord Francis's latest counter-maneuver, but in reality this was only a pretext; she had been thinking of little besides Stephen all that day, and though she would not admit it to herself, it was for his own sake that she wanted to see him.

Stephen finished his errands in the village late that afternoon and got back to Etheridge Hall just before five o'clock. That left him barely time to change his clothes before dinner, but he spared a few minutes to go first to his study on the ground floor to collect some papers he needed for his next day's business. He had just located them and was preparing to leave when the study door opened and Lydia came in.

His principal emotion was one of annoyance. He had been hoping to get upstairs in time to have minute or two alone with Anne before dinner, but now the chances of that looked exceedingly slim; whatever Lydia's business, it was certain to delay him long enough to make a *tête-à-tête* impossible.

In all this, he had no curiosity to know what Lydia's business might be. His former relations with Lydia he had long considered to be a closed chapter in his life, and recent events had so overshadowed them that he found it hard now to remember that they had ever been more to each other than cousins by marriage. He was perfectly willing to forget the past and be on friendly terms with her, but not now, when he was eager to get upstairs and see Anne.

"Hello, Lydia," he said, masking his impatience as best he could.

Although he was willing to forget the past, it seemed that Lydia was not. She caught him by the arm and held him with all her strength, so that he was forced to either shake her off or turn and face her. Chivalry forbade the first alternative, but he found it harder than ever to hide his annoyance as he turned to look at her.

"Oh, Stephen, how can you?" she said tragically. "To speak to me as though I was a mere acquaintance, when we were once so much to each other. Don't tell me you've forgotten the past, Stephen?"

"I can't say I remember it as well as all that, Lydia, but I do remember that you chose to marry my cousin instead of me," he said, rather dryly.

"Oh, but you mustn't hold that against me, Stephen. I know you thought I married Marcus only for his position, but it truly wasn't like that at all. I loved him, I really did—not as much as I loved you, of course, but I didn't find that out until it was too late. If I made a mistake, God knows I've suffered for it, Stephen. I simply cannot bear to have you hate me." With a sob, she threw herself into his arms.

Anne, quietly opening the door of the study, found herself suddenly confronted by the sight of Lydia in Stephen's arms. His back was to her, so that he did not see her standing there, but Lydia's eyes met hers over his shoulder with an expression at once malicious and triumphant. Anne stood stock still for an instant, then turned and left the study, closing the door noiselessly behind her.

Stephen, unaware of her presence, had stoically endured Lydia's embrace, but as soon as it slackened he set about gently detaching himself from her hold. Again, his emotion was principally one of annoyance. He found the incident unpleasant but not particularly upsetting, for Lydia had no power to move him anymore; as he drew away from her he found himself thinking how different she was from Anne, not merely in the way she looked and acted, but also in a more physical way, from the scent and texture of her hair to the way she felt in his arms. The thought made him even more eager to get upstairs.

He began to edge toward the door, but Lydia followed after him, stretching out her arms in entreaty. "Stephen, don't go. I know I hurt you badly when I married Marcus instead of you, but all that was years ago. Cannot we at least be friends?"

"I don't see why not," he said, rubbing his shoulder rather absently. "Consider us friends, Lydia. And now, if you'll excuse me, I must go up and change for dinner." Congratulating himself on having cut short a most tedious and disagreeable interview, he left the study and went upstairs to his bedroom.

After leaving the study, Anne had gone upstairs to her own room and turned the key in the lock. This done, she sank down into a chair in front of the window and gazed out at the snow-covered lawn below and at the thin sliver of new moon that hung in the fast-darkening western sky. Neither moon nor snowy landscape registered upon her consciousness, however; in her mind's eye, she was again seeing Lydia in Stephen's arms, looking over his shoulder with a triumphant smile. The remembrance made Anne feel a little sick, but it also made her angry with an anger that was new to her: a fierce, primitive anger that had unmistakably a strong tinge of jealousy about it.

With an effort, she damped down her anger and forced herself to consider the situation calmly. It was quite possible that the scene she had witnessed had an innocent explanation, if it were not actually some machination on the part of Lydia. She reminded herself that she had already witnessed one or two other incidents of that lady's malice since her arrival at Etheridge Hall. The more she considered this explanation, the more likely it seemed, and her anger began to subside of its own accord. She regretted now that she had not stayed and made her presence known instead of quitting the room in such a hurry. By doing so, she had probably played right into Lydia's hands, but the situation was fortunately not irremediable. She resolved to ask Stephen about it as soon as she had a moment alone with him and find out the truth of the matter.

That he would tell her the truth she never doubted. She could more easily believe him guilty of embracing Lydia of his own volition than of telling her a deliberate lie, but she had hopes of absolving him of that charge, too. If she had been called on to choose one word to describe the man who was now her husband, that word would have been honorable; she found it impossible to believe he could be guilty of any mean or sordid behavior.

"I do trust him," she said aloud. "He risked his life to save mine and was willing to marry me, only to save my reputation. In everything he has done, he has shown himself worthy of my trust. I will not believe him guilty until I hear it from his own lips."

It was at that moment that Anne realized she loved him. The realization came as a shock to her, yet at the same time it was not a shock; it was more as though she were at last recognizing a truth that had been evident for some time. "I love him," she told herself with amazement. "I don't know how it happened, but I do. I love him, and he loves Lydia—or does he? It certainly looked like it this afternoon."

The thought of Lydia continued to oppress her as she rang for Parker and set about changing her dress for dinner. She completed her toilette very quickly and was ready to go downstairs long before she had reached any conclusion about how she ought to approach Stephen regarding the scene she had witnessed in the study. In view of her own newly discovered feelings, she felt it behooved her to tread carefully; she had no wish to betray herself before she learned if there were a possibility of those feelings being returned. "Though after last night, he must be blind not to see how I feel about him," she told herself ruefully.

Although some minutes remained until the dinner hour, she decided to go on down to the drawing room anyway. She left her room and was already halfway down the main staircase when Stephen tapped on her bedroom door.

Fifteen

Stephen was disappointed not to find Anne in her room. He dressed quickly, but even so it was several minutes past the dinner hour by the time he had finished tying his neckcloth and had shrugged himself into his topcoat. As he hurried down the stairs, he once again cursed Lydia for delaying him in the study. But then he reflected that it was probably as well that she had. "If I had got upstairs earlier and found Anne in her room, there's no saying but I might have made us both late for dinner," he told himself with a smile, as he went into the drawing room.

The ladies were already assembled there waiting for him. He greeted them all civilly, then extended his arm to Anne, who took it with a hesitant air. He smiled at her as they walked decorously into the dining room together. She smiled back, but it struck him that her smile seemed rather forced. He had little time to analyze it, however, for scarcely had they taken their places at the table when there was a sound of loud and excited voices in the hall outside.

The butler, who had been standing at the sideboard pouring wine and water, put down the decanters and went to the door. They could hear him remonstrating with some person or persons outside; Stephen laid down the soup plate he had been about to fill with *potage à la Condé* and listened, trying to make out what was being said. A moment later the butler appeared in the doorway wearing a disturbed expression.

"I'm very sorry to disturb you, my lord, but there's a gentleman just arrived who says he needs to see you very urgently," he told Stephen. "A Mr. Connor, from Ash Grove. He says he is one of your tenants."

Stephen pushed his chair away from the table, but before he could get to his feet Mr. Connor himself had shouldered his way past the butler and come into the room.

"I'm truly sorry to disturb you, my lord, my ladies," he said, bestowing a perfunctory bow upon the latter. "I wouldn't have interrupted you at your dinner if it hadn't been a very urgent business. I nearly killed my poor horse getting here. I'll have to borrow one of yours to get back, my lord, or perhaps it'd be as quick if we both went in your carriage."

"First you'd better tell me what the problem is, Connor," said Stephen. Although he managed to speak calmly, he felt a premonition of disaster as he regarded his tenant's soot-stained jacket and small-clothes.

Mr. Connor's next words confirmed his worst fears. "It's fire," he said. "Up at Ash Grove—the whole place may be in flames by now, though the men was working hard to put it out when I left."

"A fire? At Ash Grove?" Mrs. Etheridge half rose from her chair with a look of consternation. "What a dreadful thing, Mr. Connor! Is the house completely destroyed?"

Mr. Connor said that it had thus far escaped damage, but added depressingly that it had looked to be only a matter of time before it, too, was ablaze.

"It was the cottages where it started, ma'am. That whole row of 'em down by the spinney was on fire when I left, and the men was trying to soak down the stables in hopes of keeping the fire from spreading on to them and the house. But it's been a problem getting enough water to do the job, seeing as it's winter and the beck's pretty nearly all frozen over. And since we haven't had as much snow up that way as you have down here, there's nothing to stop it—once it got started, everything went up like tinder."

Before he had finished speaking, Stephen was on his feet and moving toward the door. "I'll go change out of these clothes and be with you in a trice, Connor," he said. "The curricle and grays would be fastest, I think. I'll order them round immediately and send word to John Laughton what's happening. He can see about mustering some of our men down here to come up and help fight the fire. I hope no one's been injured?"

"No, no one so far, but there'll be a deal of folks left homeless before it's over. In this weather, too—it couldn't have happened at a worse time."

Mrs. Etheridge shook her head. "This has been quite the winter of disasters for Ash Grove," she said. "I just got a letter from the housekeeper telling me that we lost half our avenue in that bad ice storm last month. First ice and now fire—it really does seem as though we've been dreadfully unlucky, doesn't it? I can only be thankful that you're here to see to things, Stephen. So you plan to leave immediately?"

"Yes, I'm afraid so," said Stephen. His eyes were on Anne as he spoke, and he saw a fleeting look of dismay cross her face. Although genuinely sorry to be called away at such a time and for such a reason, he could not help feeling a little glad to see that she apparently felt some small distress to see him go.

"I'll be back as soon as I can, but I don't know when that will be," he said, addressing her directly. "I must see about getting the fire out first of all, and then make some provision for my tenants who were left homeless."

Anne nodded. "Of course you must go," she said in a constrained voice. "Is there anything I can do to help?"

"Nothing now, but I suppose you might see about collecting clothes and household goods for the people who lost their homes. There must be some things up in the attics that would do to begin with. Mother will show you where everything is stored. Take what you need and order anything else you think might be useful; I give you *carte blanche.*" He came around the table as he spoke to drop a kiss on her brow. "I'll write you," he said, looking down at her. "I hate like anything to rush off and leave you like this, but you see how it is."

"Yes, I see," she said, and even managed a brief smile. "You needn't worry on my account, Stephen. I will miss you, of course, but your first duty must be to your tenants."

"Yes, we will miss you, Stephen," said Lydia in an unctuous voice. "Write and tell us as soon as possible when you plan to return."

After he had left, blank silence settled over the dining room. The butler, who had been hovering near the doorway while Mr. Connor was delivering his message, came forward now and quietly took over the task of serving the soup.

The meal progressed through its several courses with almost no conversation, save for an occasional remark from Mrs. Etheridge lamenting this latest disaster to her former home. When dinner was over, the ladies retired to the drawing room, but there, too, conversation languished. By mutual accord, they retired early to their beds.

Anne, lying alone that night in her rosewood and ormolu pavilion, experienced great difficulty in falling asleep. She tossed and turned, prey to the thoughts that came crowding in upon her as soon as she closed her eyes. Stephen had been called away so suddenly that she had had no opportunity to ask him about the scene she had witnessed earlier in the study between him and Lydia. Despite her resolution to trust him until she could hear his side of the story, she found herself dwelling upon it now; over and over she asked herself the same question: did he or did he not still care for Lydia?

Judging solely from his behavior that evening, she was inclined to say he did not. He had barely glanced at Lydia when she had greeted him in the drawing room before dinner; and later, when he had been called away from the table by Mr. Connor, his regrets had been addressed to her, not Lydia, whom he had distinguished with only the most cursory farewell. But though this seemed like indifference, Anne was forced to admit that it might equally well be an attempt to distance himself from a person still capable of causing him pain—a person, in other words, for whom he cherished feelings the very reverse of indifference.

The idea was very depressing to Anne. She could not forget that he had abandoned his home and family and spent the last few years in virtual exile, all because of Lydia. It must have been a strong passion that could prompt such a man, seemingly so calm and level-headed, to such a drastic action. Anne's fear was that some trace of that passion still lingered, making it impossible for him to care for any other woman. She was not naive enough to think that what had taken place the night before was any indication of his real feelings. On the positive side, however, it did seem to show that his allegiance to Lydia was not so complete as it might have been, which was something, at least.

Despite her worries, Anne felt a surge of exultation at the recollection of that night. "And he did say, or at least imply, that he was glad he married me," she reminded herself. "He is a sensible man, after all. He must know that Lydia is unworthy of him, even if he has not entirely ceased to care for her. That must be my consolation."

It was indeed some consolation, but still Anne continued to toss and turn long into the night as she pondered the uncertainties of her position. When she slept at last, her sleep was haunted by dreams in which familiar persons and places took on strange and disturbing aspects. She was relieved when she awoke and found it was morning, with Parker moving silently about the room laying out her clothing for the day. She rose, made her toilette with the dresser's help, and went downstairs to the breakfast parlor.

After breakfast, she and Mrs. Etheridge went upstairs to the attics to search out such furniture and household goods as might be useful to those left homeless by the fire. At her mother-in-law's suggestion, Anne also sent a message to Reverend Healy proposing that a subscription be set up to provide the displaced tenants with new clothing. This work took most of the morning, but when afternoon came, Anne found herself at something of a loss. Diana had retired to the library to study; Mrs. Etheridge had driven into the village to do some shopping; and though she knew Lydia to be in the drawing room, Anne had no great desire to be in her company. She finally decided to go for a walk and explore a little more of Etheridge Hall's grounds and gardens, of which she had seen only a small part thus far.

It took Anne only a few minutes to put on her pelisse, gloves, and bonnet. As she was on her way downstairs, however, it occurred to her that this was the day Lord Francis had set for their assignation down by the river. Since Lydia had already informed him of her marriage, it did not seem likely that he would be waiting for her at the pavilion, but Anne felt Lord Francis might be expected to do the unexpected, and she had no wish to encounter him by accident. To be on the safe side, she chose the opposite direction for her walk, setting out from the rear terrace of the house toward the tower that stood on the hill behind.

The hill was neither steep nor especially lofty, and was traversed by a graveled path that made it easy to climb even in spite of slush and snow. Ten minutes' brisk walking brought Anne to its summit, where she paused to rest and cool herself before undertaking to climb the tower itself.

The tower was a cylindrical structure some sixty feet high, built of the same pinkish-gray stone as the house below. There was a doorway cut in the side of the tower that gave access to a central spiral staircase, which in turn gave access to a roofed and railed gallery overhead. As soon as Anne had recovered from climbing the hill, she set about climbing the hundred or so steps that led to this vantage point.

When she reached it, she found her efforts well rewarded. From the gallery she could see the whole of the surrounding countryside, from the house nestled in the valley immediately below, past the wood surrounding the entrance gates, and on to the village in the far distance.

It was a beautiful bright afternoon, warm enough to finish off the little snow that still remained from the storm of the previous week. For a long time Anne stood looking down at the landscape spread before her. It was upon the near landscape rather than the farther that her eyes chiefly dwelt: upon the cluster of roofs, railings, and chimneys that was Etheridge Hall. She noted the stables and stableyards that lay behind the house; the kitchen gardens and orchards farther on, bounded by stone walls; and still farther on the open expanse of fields marked here and there with traces of white where a patch of snow lay unmelted.

Most of all she studied the house itself, serene and symmetrical in its setting of formal gardens and terraces. With amazement, Anne told herself that she herself now possessed a share in all this magnificence. It still seemed impossible to believe; impulsively she pressed the wedding ring beneath her glove, in much the same spirit that she might have pinched herself to make sure she was truly awake.

"This is my home now," she said aloud. "And I think I could be happy here, if only I were here under different circumstances. If only I had come as a regular guest, instead of being forced into all this intrigue and deception—and if only Stephen hadn't been forced into marrying me as he did, on such short acquaintance—and if only Lydia weren't here, to complicate things even further, who knows what might have happened? Our acquaintance would have had a chance to develop naturally, and possibly—just possibly—he might have come to care for me as I care for him. And possibly he still might, but my being married to him already makes things so much more complicated. No, be honest with yourself, Anne: it isn't that it makes things more complicated, but rather that it makes *you* so much more vulnerable. If you don't take care, you'll end up having your heart broken, I'm afraid."

Turning away from the railing, Anne was about to start down the stairs when a moving figure in the landscape caught her eye. She turned back to study it and before long had satisfied herself that it was Lydia, toiling her way slowly up the slope of the hill toward the tower. Anne stood watching her with a feeling of surprise. Although Lydia had showed signs of becoming less sedentary lately, it seemed strange that she would voluntarily undertake such a strenuous exercise as this.

So Anne reflected, but then it flashed into her mind that perhaps Lydia was coming to see her. If she could recognize Lydia's figure from a distance, it stood to reason that Lydia could recognize hers, especially since she was the only one in the household likely to be wearing black.

For a moment Anne hesitated, uncertain whether to stay where she was and meet Lydia, or to quit the tower in haste and endeavor to avoid her. This last course seemed rather craven, however, and in the end Anne decided to stand her ground. She had a curiosity to hear what Lydia might say, and she felt also a certain satisfaction, ignoble but real, in the thought that the other woman would be forced to climb the hill and all that long flight of stairs in order to reach her.

It was a considerable time before Lydia finally arrived at the top of the stairs. Her face was beaded with perspiration, and she was so out of breath that for several minutes she was unable to speak. Sinking down on one of the stone benches that encircled the gallery, she sat there, breathing hard, while Anne stood watching her unsympathetically. At length she recovered her breath and looked up, fixing Anne with a long, steady, assessing gaze.

"You missed seeing Lord Francis," were her first words, spoken in a tone of significance. "He came to call this afternoon with the Moorhavens. I think he was disappointed to find you out."

"I'm sorry to hear that," said Anne coolly. Her heart sank to think of what further indiscretions Lord Francis might have been betrayed into, but she tried to look indifferent as she waited to hear what Lydia might say next.

Lydia continued to eye her with the same steady, assessing air. "Lord Francis is quite an amusing gentleman," she said. "Very amusing, and very handsome, too. But of course he can't compare to Stephen. There is no one like Stephen, I truly do believe. We were in love, you know, once upon a time."

"Yes, I know," said Anne.

"We were in love and planned to marry—and then Stephen's cousin came between us. He had fallen madly in love with me when I was down with Stephen to attend a party, and he wanted to marry me himself. It was a source of a great deal of contention between him and Stephen. Of course I was sorry—for myself, I cared nothing for wealth and title, but unfortunately my parents were ambitious. Pressure was brought to bear on me—I was told it was my duty to better myself if I could, and since I was only a girl and not used to defying my parents in anything, in the end I gave way. I accepted Marcus's suit rather than Stephen's."

For a moment Lydia was silent, gazing ahead of her now as though she no longer saw Anne. "Marcus and I were married, but it wasn't long before I knew I had made a great mistake. Our marriage was a charade, a farce—it was no more a real marriage than yours and Stephen's."

Anne moved impatiently and made as though to turn away. Lydia raised her head to smile at her sadly. "Yes, it was a great mistake. Marcus was always jealous of Stephen, and especially so after Amèlie's birth. You knew, did you not, that she was Stephen's child?"

These words, dulcetly spoken, burst upon Anne's ears like a veritable bombshell. For an instant the world around her swam sickeningly out of focus, and she grasped at the gallery railing to support herself as her mind grappled with the enormity of what Lydia had just told her.

Appalling though it was, she could not long doubt the truth of it. Corroboration was soon forthcoming, and corroboration of a most damning kind: the corroboration of her own mind and heart. She recalled Stephen's curious reticence on the subject of his past; of his words, "It's a long and rather sordid tale." Indeed, as she thought back over all he had said and done during the past week, she thought she must have been blind to have missed so many obvious clues. His restraint when speaking of his cousin, his avoidance of the whole subject of his cousin's wife, and his treatment of that wife and her child since returning to Etheridge Hall: all might have shown her some part of the truth, if she had only had eyes to see it.

Having reached this conclusion after what seemed long and

painful cogitation, though in reality only a minute or two could have passed, Anne became aware that Lydia was still looking at her, still waiting for an answer to her question. "No," she said through dry lips. "No, I did not know that."

"So Stephen did not tell you? I would have thought he must have said *something*—but of course, he hasn't known you very long, and it wouldn't be an easy thing to discuss with a stranger. Not many people do know about it, apart from ourselves. In the normal way that's how I prefer it, for it doesn't reflect very well on me, as you can probably imagine. But I did think you ought to know, Anne, now that you're married to Stephen and living here at Etheridge Hall."

Again Lydia paused, looking at Anne expectantly.

"Yes," was all Anne could bring herself to say, and even that single word cost her an effort. It was sufficient for Lydia, however, who began to speak again in the same sad, reflective voice she had used before.

"It's really quite ironic the way things have turned out. You know that Marcus banished Stephen from the house when he found out?—oh, yes, that's why Stephen went off to Scotland in the first place, and why he hasn't been home since. It was a truly dreadful scene. I blamed myself, of course, but there was really nothing I could do about it. To have tried to intercede for Stephen would have only made things worse. Thank heavens he is home at last. It is quite touching to see how fond he is of Amèlie, and she of him. I could weep when I think that he has never had a chance to see her before now."

Lydia's eyes were indeed brimming with tears as she spoke. She sniffed and put her handkerchief to her eyes as she continued. "I hope you won't blame me too much for telling you all this, Anne dear. I can see you think I am dreadful, but truly it was a situation beyond my control—beyond both our control. Love has a way of carrying everything else before it. If you had ever been in love yourself, you would understand."

Anne said nothing. She was, at that moment, beyond speech; she could only look at Lydia and wait helplessly for whatever blow she might inflict next. Lydia applied her handkerchief to her eyes again and gave her a tragic smile.

"As you can imagine, the situation between Marcus and me grew even more impossible after Amèlie's birth," she told Anne. "I don't blame him, of course; it was an impossible situation for all of us. It's a terrible thing to say, but when he died I felt as though a burden had been lifted from my shoulders. I was free again, and there was nothing to stop Stephen and me from marrying; we need only observe a decent period of mourning, and then we could be together at last. He was actually on his way back to me when you and he were thrown together—and of course we all know what happened after that."

Anne made an inarticulate noise of assent. Lydia gave her another tragic smile. "Oh, you mustn't think I blame you for what you did, Anne dear. You couldn't know what Stephen and I were to each other, and I can quite understand your grasping at the chance to marry him once you had come to know him. But you must admit that your presence in that mailcoach was untimely, to say the least. Were it not for you, Stephen and I would probably be married by now—however, there's no use crying over spilt milk. It's a difficult situation for all of us, and we must all try to be very civilized about it."

At the moment, Anne felt anything but civilized. She wanted to weep, to shout, to rail at the heavens with unbounded fury; and more than anything she wanted to strike out at the woman who sat before her, regarding her with teary eyes and a tragic smile. But Anne did none of these things. She only gave Lydia a look of disbelief, then turned and ran down the stairs. Lydia made no move to follow her or call her back. As Anne made her way back to the house, however, she turned once and saw the other woman silently regarding her from atop the tower. The handkerchief was no longer in evidence, and neither was the tragic smile; in every line of Lydia's face and figure there was reflected now nothing but pure, savage triumph.

Anne felt fortunate when she got back to the house, inasmuch as she encountered no one on her way upstairs. She did not think she could have spoken to Mrs. Etheridge or Diana or even a servant without bursting into tears. As it was, she was barely able to make it to her room without breaking down.

The tears were already flowing as she shut the door behind her, and the sight of the bed with its fanciful peaked canopy and flowing curtains made them flow even faster. She felt betrayed: betrayed by her own feelings and betrayed by the man she had trusted, who had turned out to be no better than her former suitor, Lord Francis Rowland. Lord Francis's offenses had perhaps been the more serious, but Stephen's had cut deeper, for her opinion of him had been higher to begin with; it was devastating to learn how grossly she had been deceived in his character.

"How could he?" she said aloud, looking at the bed through a blur of tears. "It was inexcusable of him not to tell me. To talk about honor and responsibility, when all the while he and Lydia—oh, I can never forgive him. He must have known I would never have married him if I had known the truth."

It occurred to her then to wonder just why he *had* married her. After Lydia's revelation, she was prepared to believe the worst of him, and her imagination was not slow to come up with a suitably villainous motive.

Undoubtedly he had married her for her money, just as Lord Francis had tried to do. To be sure, Lydia had said nothing of such a possibility, but perhaps Lydia was unaware of it, or perhaps she, too, had been deceived in him. He might well have been traveling home to marry Lydia and then, when Anne had crossed his path, the chance of securing an easy fortune had seemed too good to pass up. It seemed likely enough, in view of what she had just learned of his past conduct. A man who did not scruple to make love to his cousin's wife would have no scruples in passing over that same cousin's wife when it came time for him to marry, if he thought he could better himself by marrying someone else.

And he had done so, as Anne reflected bitterly to herself. He had married her and made love to her, and now he was expecting her to tamely share living quarters with his mistress and illegitimate daughter. Anne marveled at the conceit that could fancy itself capable of reconciling her to such a situation.

"Did he suppose I would never find out?" she soliloquized aloud. "He must have known I would learn the truth eventually. Perhaps he simply doesn't care. He has control of my money now, and that is probably all he cares about. It had better be all he cares about, for it's certain he'll get nothing else from me!"

This thought held Anne fulminating for some minutes, but eventually a more practical spirit began to assert itself. "As Lydia says, there's no use in crying over spilt milk," she told herself grimly. "There are some things that are past recovering, but my freedom isn't one of them, and it might be that my money isn't, either. Surely there must be some way of setting a marriage aside under such circumstances. I will have to consult a lawyer and see what can be done. One thing is certain, I cannot go on living here after what I have learned today."

Rising from her chair, Anne moved purposefully toward the bellrope, but her steps slowed as she approached it. It had just occurred to her that if she left now, she would have to give some kind of explanation for her departure to Mrs. Etheridge. To tell her the truth was out of the question; even if Mrs. Etheridge was already aware of Amy's paternity, Anne did not feel equal to discussing the subject with that good lady.

After considering the matter for a few minutes, Anne reluctantly reached the conclusion that it might be better to remain at Etheridge Hall until Stephen returned. In the back of her mind lurked a hope, all the stronger for being unacknowledged, that he would somehow be able to refute Lydia's story. It might be that he could not, of course, in which case she would have to leave immediately, but before she did, she made up her mind that she would tell him exactly what she thought of him before shaking the dust of Etheridge Hall from her feet forever.

Anne had reached this point in her meditations when the sound of the dressing bell rang out below. Again she turned toward the bellrope, but when Parker arrived in answer to her summons Anne sent her off again with a message to Mrs. Etheridge, informing her that she was feeling unwell and had decided to keep to her room that evening. After Parker had left, Anne sank down again into her chair to continue her meditations.

"I'm glad Mother isn't here to see what a mess I've made of things," she said aloud. "For the first time I find myself almost glad she died when she did. First I let Francis abduct me like a simpleton in a storybook—but I don't blame myself so much for that. Mother trusted Francis, too, and neither of us could have known he would turn out to be such a villain. No, I can't blame myself for trusting Francis.

"But this business with Stephen—yes, I can and do blame myself there. How could I have been mad enough to think of marrying a man I had known only a few days? I should have done anything rather than that—but then, if I hadn't, Francis would have told the world about our spending the night together, and that would have been nearly as bad. I don't know what I ought to have done. In any case, worrying about what I should have done isn't going to do me much good; I ought to be worrying about what I'm going to do, once I finally get free of this horrible, sordid mess. I must have it all settled in my mind so I can be ready to leave as soon as Stephen gets back."

Obedient to her own behest, she tried to think, to make some kind of plans for the future once she had left Etheridge Hall. But her mind was still numb from the shock of Lydia's disclosure. She could only think of Stephen and how he had betrayed her. Finally she gave up and went to bed, though not, she feared, to sleep.

"It doesn't matter where I go once I leave here, just so long as I do go," she told herself. "And perhaps once I've put all this behind me, I will be able to think of the future and make some plans."

Sixteen

It was three days before Stephen was able to return to Etheridge Hall. He had hoped to be away no more than one day, or two at the most, but though the fire at Ash Grove was extinguished shortly after his arrival, the chaos it left behind took rather longer to settle.

In addition to destroying nearly a dozen cottages, the fire had leveled the dairy and wash house and had heavily damaged the stables. This was not so bad as it might have been, for the servants had fortunately had time to remove all the horses prior to the conflagration, but it meant that Stephen had to find temporary accommodation for them as well as for the tenants who had lost their homes in the fire, no easy task in late December.

Even after he had found shelter for his cattle in the barn of a generous neighbor and had seen his tenants installed in Ash Grove's manor house, his difficulties were far from over. The household staff at Ash Grove greatly resented being asked to wait on those whom they regarded as their social inferiors, and for the first day or two there were constant clashes, which only his own presence served to mediate. In addition to all this, he had also to meet with builders and architects and make countless decisions related to the business of rebuilding, so that he was tired both physically and mentally when at last he drove his curricle and grays into the stableyard at Etheridge Hall.

In spite of his fatigue, his mood was cheerful, even buoyant. He was happy to be home, and happier still at the prospect of being reunited with his new wife, whom he had missed with a true loverlike fervor.

As he swung himself down from his curricle, he reflected that he would be seeing her now within a matter of minutes; within a few hours he might even be holding her in his arms, though he feared that would be about the extent of his capabilities that night. He consoled himself with the thought that there was always tomorrow night—or it might be, tomorrow morning. He was smiling as he gave orders to his groom for the care of the grays, and as he strode toward the house he found himself rubbing his shoulder in a manner that was fast becoming talismanic with him.

Once inside the house, he went first to the drawing room. To his disappointment, Anne was not there: only his mother and sister, both of whom were sewing. Diana merely looked up and nodded at his entrance, but his mother rose to greet him with an exclamation of pleasure. "Where's Anne?" he asked, dropping a hasty kiss on her cheek.

Mrs. Etheridge shook her head in mock reproach. "That's a fine greeting for your family, Stephen. Only a 'Where's Anne?' and never a word for the rest of us! I will tell you where she is, but only on the condition that you tell us first the news from Ash Grove. Are the stables repairable, or must they be rebuilt? And have you settled yet on a plan for the new cottages?"

Restraining his impatience as well as he could, Stephen gave her and Diana an account of his travails at Ash Grove. Mrs. Etheridge asked a question or two and then smilingly bade him be off to his wife.

"You will find her in her bedroom, I think. She went up just a few minutes ago, when we heard your carriage in the drive. I don't want to worry you, Stephen, but she has been looking rather peaked lately. She's taken to spending a great deal of time alone in her room, and at dinner she hasn't been eating enough to keep a bird alive. Truth to tell, I wondered if she might be increasing. It's early days yet, I know, but such things do happen, and if she is, you must tell her not to be embarrassed about it. I became *enceinte* with you only weeks after marrying your father, so I know exactly how she feels."

Stephen muttered something indistinguishable under his breath and left the drawing room hurriedly. He ran upstairs, taking the steps two at a time in his haste, and arrived in a remarkably short time outside Anne's bedroom door. Once there, he took a deep breath, tapped lightly on the door, and let himself in.

Anne was awaiting his arrival. At the first sound of his carriage in the drive, she had excused herself to Mrs. Etheridge and Diana and come upstairs so that she might be alone with him during this critical interview.

As she stood by the window waiting for him, she was conscious of a nervous flutter in the pit of her stomach, not unlike what she had felt while waiting for him to come to her on their wedding night. When the comparison occurred to her, she pushed it angrily aside. But when at last the door opened and he was standing before her, smiling down at her with a warm glow in his eyes, she was assailed by emotions more difficult to push aside. It would have been so easy to return his smile, fall into his arms, and pretend nothing had happened since he had left for Ash Grove. By contrast, it took every ounce of resolution she possessed to remain standing where she was, regarding him silently and unsmilingly.

He knew immediately that something was wrong. "What is it, Anne?" he asked, tossing his hat and coat on a chair and coming toward her anxiously.

She took a couple of steps backward but continued to regard him unsmilingly. "I have just learned the truth about you and Lydia," she said.

Stephen felt suddenly weak in the knees. It struck him forcefully that he had been a fool not to tell her long ago about his engagement to Lydia. Living in the same house with Lydia, she was bound to find out about it, and it was not unnatural that she would resent having to learn of it from someone other than himself.

"Anne, I'm sorry," he said contritely. "I did mean to tell you, only somehow I never got around to it. It's not a chapter in my life that I particularly enjoy talking about——"

"I should think not indeed!" Anne's voice was scathing. Up till that moment she had been hoping against hope that he would be able to refute Lydia's charges, but his words, coupled with his guilty expression, had effectively laid her last hopes to rest. She was sick with disappointment, and her voice was bitter as she continued, "I'm not surprised you don't care to talk about it, Stephen. It must be a heavy burden on your conscience——always assuming you have a conscience. After what I've learned this week, I'm beginning to doubt it."

"Anne, you must hear me out," said Stephen, astonished by her vehemence. "I know I ought to have told you before. I was on the verge of it a hundred times, but——"

"But what, Stephen? Did you think I wouldn't have married you if I had known the truth? You were quite right, I wouldn't have——and now that I do know, I don't intend to stay in this house another day."

Stephen felt as though his world was falling to pieces around him. "Anne, I can understand your being angry," he went on, a little desperately. "It was unforgivable of me not to tell you beforehand about my former——er——attachment to Lydia. Was it my mother who told you?"

"It was Lydia herself, Stephen. She told me all about it—— boasted of it, if you please." Anne found herself perilously close to the brink of tears. She blinked them back and went on angrily, "I cannot believe you would have put me in such a position, Stephen."

"Oh, Anne, I am sorry," he said, and the words were heartfelt. "I don't think it ever occurred to me what an uncomfortable situation it would be for you. But surely we can resolve the situation in some other way than your leaving! I would rather leave Etheridge Hall myself than go on living here without you. We might move up to Ash Grove, perhaps. It would be easier if we could simply move Lydia there, but unfortunately she is entitled to stay at Etheridge Hall as long as she pleases under the terms of Marcus's will. Would you like to live at Ash Grove, Anne?"

He came a step closer as he spoke and tried to take her by the hand. She put both hands behind her, however, and took a step backwards, regarding him all the while with a cold-eyed, inscrutable stare.

"No doubt that would be very convenient for you, Stephen," she said. "With me at Ash Grove and Lydia here, you could divide your time between us and—how did you put it the other night?—oh, yes, 'keep the different parts of your life in separate compartments.' Or is it possible that you're trying to tell me you're tired of Lydia?"

By this time Stephen was beginning to be rather angry himself. It was not pleasant to have his own words thrown back in his face—words that had been spoken in intimacy and trust.

"Tired? Yes, I *am* tired of Lydia, God knows. She can be very tiresome, as I'm sure you've already discovered for yourself. But if, as I think, what you're really asking is if I still have feelings for Lydia, then the answer is an unequivocal no. Any feelings I had for her died a long time ago. I wouldn't care now if I never saw her again."

This answer, far from soothing Anne, made her lose her temper entirely. "Just the answer I would have expected from a man in your *position,* my lord," she said in a shaking voice. "And you talk of having an overdeveloped sense of responsibility! Well, you may not think you have any responsibility to Lydia, but I do, and after what you've just told me I wouldn't stay another day in your company if you were to beg me on bended knee. Indeed, I'd rather not be within a hundred miles of you. Out of respect for your mother and sister, I don't wish to cause a scene, but I *will* go, even if I have to sell the clothes off my back to get coach fare."

"That won't be necessary," said Stephen. He was deeply hurt by her words, and it was a struggle to keep the reproach out of his voice as he continued. "If you are really set on leaving me, Anne, then of course I shall make over your own fortune to you, just as soon as it can be arranged. But—don't you think you're reacting to this thing a little drastically? I'll admit that it was remiss of me not to tell you about Lydia and me beforehand, but I give you my word that everything between us was over a long time ago. There is no woman I care for now but you. And I do care for you, Anne—even if our marriage was rather a hasty affair, I still thought we had a decent chance of being happy together. Our wedding night—"

"If there is anything that *could* make me think less of you after what Lydia told me, then it would be that. How could you, Stephen? With that woman actually in the house—" Anne's voice broke, and she turned away, trying without success to blink away her tears. "If you will send for your carriage, I'll see about removing myself and my baggage to the nearest inn. I'll let you know in a few days what my plans will be, so that you will know what to do about my money."

Stephen was as upset as she was, but he tried to remain calm and think quickly. Incredible though it seemed, he could not doubt that she meant what she said and would leave that minute unless he could hit on some means to keep her there. And it did seem incredible: though he did not blame her for being angry, he thought her anger a trifle disproportionate to the offense and hoped she might be more amenable to reason once she had had a chance to cool down. His most urgent duty seemed to be to delay her long enough for the cooling-down process to take place. He felt instinctively that if she were to leave Etheridge Hall now, she would never return.

"If you are set on going, then I will not try to stop you," he said finally. "But my mother will be very sorry to see you go. Diana, too—I know she has grown very fond of you in the time you've been here. Your leaving this way will come as a great shock to them both."

Watching her closely, he saw a shadow of indecision cross her face. It passed quickly, however, and when she spoke, it was to repeat her intention of leaving immediately. "I am sorry to leave like this with no word to your mother and sister, but there's

no help for it. Please make my excuses to them and tell them
how sorry I am that it ended this way. And Stephen—you don't
have to tell them the real reason I'm leaving. I don't care if you
put the blame for our separation on me if that will make it easier
for you, and them."

"Nothing will make it easier, for me *or* them," he said flatly.
"But I don't ask your consideration for myself, Anne. It is Diana
and my mother I am concerned about, more especially my
mother. By now you must know how much store she sets by
the holidays and having the family together. This business is
going to hit her very hard. I realize I'm in no position to ask
favors of you, but I do wish you would consider staying at least
through the holidays. Please, Anne? Only until Twelfth Night—
only a little more than a week. If you would stay that long, I
give you my word I would not trouble you in any way, and I
would do my best to see that Lydia didn't trouble you either."

Anne hesitated. On one hand, she was eager to be gone; on
the other, it did seem a poor return to Mrs. Etheridge's hospitality to ruin her holidays for her.

"Very well," she said reluctantly. "I will stay through Twelfth
Night for your mother's sake, but the very next day I shall leave.
And I give you warning, Stephen, that once I do leave, I mean
to set immediately about obtaining an annulment. I don't know
enough about English law to know if that's possible, but an
annulment would certainly be the least painful solution. But
even if I have to sue for divorce, I mean to have my freedom
again, as soon as I can."

"I see," said Stephen, trying not to look as shocked as he
felt by this speech. "But even an annulment would not be a
painless solution, Anne. As for divorce—I don't need to tell
you how painful that would be for both of us. Don't you think
it might be worth it to give our marriage another try—to stay
and try to make things work?"

The look she gave him was so full of scorn that he wished
he had held his tongue. "Certainly not," she said. "I should
think it would be obvious by now that there never were two

people with less in common than you and I. I shall stay until Twelfth Night out of consideration for your mother, but it won't do a bit of good to try to persuade me to stay longer. My decision is irrevocable."

Stephen bowed. "I understand," he said. "I will say no more about it." Picking up his hat and coat, he left the room, pulling the door quietly shut behind him.

Seventeen

Anne soon found Stephen to be as good as his word. In the days that followed, she saw almost nothing of him except at dinnertime, when it was necessary for them to meet and exchange a few civilities to keep up the pretense of being happily married. He was equally careful to keep Lydia away from her and spent many hours daily in Lydia's company, walking or driving or simply sitting with her in the drawing room. Although Anne had agreed to this in theory, she found she objected to it in practice; it hurt every time she caught a glimpse of him seated beside Lydia on the sofa or strolling arm in arm with her in the wintry gardens.

To spare herself these painful sights, Anne took to spending most of her free time in the library with Diana. Mrs. Etheridge was busy making preparations for a large party on New Year's Eve; and though she had suggested rather diffidently that since Anne was now mistress of Etheridge Hall, she might like to take charge of the preparations herself, this was a suggestion Anne had had no hesitation about rejecting. Mrs. Etheridge therefore went happily on with her work of supervising, decorating, and arranging, while Anne tried to lose herself in reading Pascal and Montaigne aloud, or in elucidating the mysteries of French grammar to Diana.

One person whose company she would have been glad to have been spared, if she could, was Amy. Although Stephen and Mrs. Etheridge were unquestionably Amy's favorites in the household, she had unfortunately conceived a great fondness for Anne as well. Nearly every day she found an excuse to visit Anne's room, where her favorite pastime was to seat herself at Anne's dressing table and ritually examine the contents of its drawers, besieging Anne all the while with questions about the use and purpose of curling tongs, pomatum, Denmark lotion, etc. Anne bore with these visits as well as she could, but she was always glad when they were over. It was difficult to look at Amy's vivid little face and reflect that something so innocent could be the cause of so much dissension.

New Year's Eve arrived at last, the occasion of another of Mrs. Etheridge's celebrated parties. This was a smaller, more exclusive gathering than the Christmas Eve party and was attended only by those local gentry who formed the Etheridge's own social set. Anne felt sure that Lord Francis would attend with the Moorhavens, and her expectations were not disappointed. The Moorhaven party arrived rather late in the evening, just as they had on Christmas Eve, and as on Christmas Eve Lord Francis immediately singled Anne out as she stood beside Mrs. Etheridge greeting guests.

"If you have a few minutes free this evening, Anne, I wish you would spend them with me," he said, gracefully bowing over her hand. "Perhaps you could show me the conservatory. Miss Moorhaven has told me you have a lovely conservatory here at the Hall."

Mrs. Etheridge, overhearing this remark, at once urged Anne to show Lord Francis the conservatory. "There's no reason why you shouldn't, for nearly everyone has arrived now, and I don't think we need stand here any longer. No, indeed, it's quite all right, my dear—you go on with Lord Francis."

Anne took Lord Francis's arm with a show of reluctance, but in truth she was rather curious to hear what he had to say. Now that she was married, she judged she ought to be safe in his company—safe at least until he learned of her annulment, she added bitterly to herself.

Together she and Lord Francis went along the hall until they came to the doors that led to the conservatory. Lord Francis stepped forward to open the door for Anne and was greeted by a blast of warm, humid, flower-scented air. He recoiled and shut the door again with a look of ludicrous dismay.

"Dear me, it's like a jungle in there, isn't it? On second thought, I think we'd better forget the conservatory. The humidity would undoubtedly take all the starch out of my neckcloth, and I would not for the world appear before company in a sodden neckcloth. In any case, the conservatory was only a pretext, as you have probably already guessed. My real intention was to get you alone so that I might speak to you privately."

"And what did you wish to speak to me about?" inquired Anne, watching with contemptuous amusement as Lord Francis anxiously examined his neckcloth in the nearest pier glass. "To apologize, perhaps?"

"That's it," said Lord Francis with disarming candor. "It seems I did Etheridge an injustice. Obviously he *was* willing to marry you, just as you said, and now it only remains for me to make my apologies and remove myself gracefully from the scene. I would consider it a personal favor if the two of you would refrain from telling anyone about my—ahem—role in bringing you together. It reflects so badly on my credit, you know, and when one exists so exclusively on one's credit as I do, one takes great pains to preserve it from damage. To figure as an abductor, and an unsuccessful abductor at that, is unlikely to enhance my reputation in the eyes of the world."

"Why should I care about preserving your reputation, Francis? You've been doing your best to destroy mine ever since you got here," said Anne hotly.

Lord Francis eyed her in a nervous way and prudently put himself beyond arm's reach before replying. "Not so," he protested. "Taken all in all, I have been the soul of discretion. I'll admit I was a trifle indiscreet when I was talking to the fair Lydia the other day—well, actually I suppose I was quite hideously indiscreet, considering how ill my own part in this business can bear scrutiny. I really had no intention of telling her as much as I did, but she somehow wormed it out of me. I am always as putty in the hands of a pretty woman, I'm afraid."

"Are you indeed? From my own observations, I would have said that money rather than women was your weakness, Francis."

Lord Francis ignored this sarcasm, being still intent on the subject of Lydia. "She is really quite lovely, you know," he told Anne seriously. "Large but luscious, and very rich, too, I understand. Tom Moorhaven was telling me the other day that the previous Lord Etheridge left everything that wasn't entailed to her rather than his successor. Perhaps that's part of the reason Etheridge was so eager to marry you—not that I mean to denigrate your personal charms, my dear. I know you have reason to think my earlier praises not exactly disinterested, but surely I may be acquitted of any low motive now when I say that I have always admired you most sincerely, quite apart from your delightful fortune. Just for my own satisfaction, would you mind telling me if it was thirty or forty thousand pounds? I was never able to obtain any precise information on that point."

"As a matter of fact, it was fifty thousand, Francis," said Anne, smiling at him mockingly.

Lord Francis flinched a little, but otherwise bore the news philosophically. "Was it indeed? If I had only known—but I don't suppose it would have made much difference in the long run. There is a fate in these things, I do honestly believe. It simply was not fated that you and I should be together. And that being the case, I think we should make every effort to bury the events of the past week in a decent obscurity, don't you? God knows neither of us has anything to gain from making them public."

"I couldn't agree more, Francis. Let us bury them, by all means!"

"Very well, then. You must try and forget all that unfortunate business at Gretna last week, and in return I shall refrain from making public the more titillating details of you and Etheridge's courtship. By the by, I hope you will tell him that, Anne, at your earliest opportunity. It will save him the trouble of calling me out, as I can see he is positively itching to do. He was looking daggers at me when you and I left the hall together just now."

"Was he?" said Anne. She herself had seen almost nothing of Stephen that evening. Once or twice she had caught a glimpse of him at the far end of the hall, but in general he had taken great pains to avoid being even in the same room with her. It was Lydia who had been at his side the few times she had seen him: a Lydia glowing and vivacious, with her hand resting possessively on his arm. "I hadn't realized Stephen had seen us leave."

"Indeed, yes; he's been scowling at me ever since I walked through the door. You must be very flattered, Anne. Jealousy is such an infallible test of devotion, don't you think? And indeed, I think he is quite *épris* of you. 'Love and a cough cannot be hid', as the poet says."

Anne said nothing. After waiting a minute or two for a response, Lord Francis went on, with a touch of anxiety. "I hope you won't waste any time setting Etheridge's mind at ease about my future conduct, Anne dear. To speak truth, it would do a great deal toward setting *my* mind at ease. There's no telling what these large, laconic Corinthian types will do when they become riled. It will be quite unnecessary for him to put a bullet through me— unnecessary, yes, and very ungrateful, too. After all, if it hadn't been for me, he would likely not have met you at all. A curious instance of the workings of fate, don't you think?"

"Oh, yes," said Anne, in an ironic voice. Lord Francis was too busy developing his theme to notice her lack of enthusiasm, however.

"Yes, you might almost say that my role was that of minister of Hymen—a minister of Hymen, bringing the pair of you together in one of His Majesty's mailcoaches. A pretty conceit, don't you think? Almost I feel I ought to be rewarded for my services. Perhaps you might just hint as much to Etheridge when you speak to him—no, on second thought, perhaps you'd better not. I think on the whole it would be better not to allude to my part in the affair at all."

"You may be sure I won't, Francis," said. Anne. Once again there was a touch of irony in her voice, but Lord Francis took her words at face value and looked relieved.

"That's right, my dear. Just tell Etheridge that I wish him well as one man to another and assure him that he may depend on my discretion in the future. As for my indiscretion in the past—well, I'll see what I can do about it. Telling Lydia was certainly a slip on my part, but I fancy I am not entirely without influence in that quarter. I'll do my best to see she doesn't spread the word any further abroad. And now I think that is all, Anne dear—all I have to say to you at the moment, anyway. I'd better be getting you back to the party before your husband orders out his duelling pistols and comes looking for me."

Stephen had indeed observed Anne leaving the hall on Lord Francis's arm. He watched them, unconscious of the scowl on his face, until he was called to order by Lydia.

"What is it, Stephen?" she asked.

Following his gaze, she caught sight of Anne and Lord Francis just exiting the hall. Her eyebrows rose.

"Your wife seems to have a fondness for Lord Francis's company, Stephen," she observed dryly. "Of course, you knew they were acquainted before? From one of two things Francis let drop, I gather there was a time when she didn't scruple to set her cap for him."

Stephen gave a short laugh and turned away. "Hardly," he said.

Lydia gave him a curious look but did not pursue the subject. Instead, she linked her arm with his and smiled up at him beseechingly. "Do listen to that lovely music, Stephen," she said. "Won't you come and dance with me? It would be quite like old times, us dancing together—though of course we never got to waltz in the old days. We had nothing more exciting than country dances back then."

Stephen did not want to waltz, but the prospect of waltzing

with Lydia was marginally less distasteful than the task of trying to smile and make pleasant conversation with his neighbors
while he was feeling so thoroughly unsociable. He took Lydia's
arm and accompanied her onto the floor.

Anne returned to the hall with Lord Francis just in time to
see the two of them sweep past in each other's arms. The sight
made her heart swell, but she told herself sternly that it was
nothing to her whom Stephen danced with. If it had not been
for her mourning, she would have found a partner and taken to
the floor herself, just to show him that she was as capable as
he of amusing herself with someone else. As it was, she was
forced to sit beside Mrs. Etheridge and watch with feigned un-
concern as he and Lydia waltzed airily about the room in time
to the lilting music.

As she watched, she thought back over the conversation she
had just had with Lord Francis. In spite of her low spirits, she
could not help smiling a little at the remembrance; it was difficult to stay angry with a gentleman who acknowledged his
transgressions with so much candor. Her smile faded a little as
she recalled the remark he had made about Stephen marrying
her for her money. It was a remark that tended to confirm her
own suspicions, although Francis had mentioned in the same
breath that Lydia, too, was a considerable heiress. Perhaps
Stephen's motives in marrying her had not been wholly mercenary, as she had thought. Perhaps he had been telling the truth
when he said he was tired of Lydia; though admittedly a liber-
tine, he need not necessarily be a liar as well, she supposed.

Indeed, as she thought over their various conversations in the
past, she had to admit that he had been singularly truthful in
all he had told her, insofar as it went. Finding however that this
train of thought tended to soften her feelings toward him alarm-
ingly, she reminded herself that telling half-truths was every bit
as bad as outright lying. By suppressing a part of the truth and
misleading her about his character and past conduct, he had
shown himself to be utterly unworthy of her love and trust.

Her trust she had therefore withdrawn, but she found it harder to withdraw her love. She knew perfectly well that the sight of him waltzing with Lydia would not have bothered her in the least if her feelings had been in the state of indifference she was trying so hard to counterfeit. In a burst of self-honesty, she even admitted that she had felt a thrill of pleasure when Francis had spoken of his apparent devotion to her. Such feelings were very bad; they showed that she was still vulnerable, still capable of being moved by him, even now that she knew the truth about him.

Anne told herself firmly that she must simply fight all the harder to overcome such feelings during her remaining stay at Etheridge Hall. But she felt inadequate to the battle tonight; there was a lump in her throat as she watched Lydia sweep radiantly past in Stephen's arms. She averted her face and wished fervently that tonight was Twelfth Night and she were leaving Etheridge Hall tomorrow.

The waltz was the last dance before supper. Only a few minutes remained until midnight, and the servants were already circulating through the hall with glasses of champagne so that the guests might drink a last toast to the old year before welcoming in the new. Stephen was called on to propose the toast and did so with quiet composure, expressing his pleasure at being back in the neighborhood and even making humorous reference to the change the past year had wrought in his marital status. Anne flushed at the smiling glances that were cast her way and wondered that he could joke on such a subject.

When Stephen had finished speaking, the guests lifted their glasses and drank enthusiastically to the year that was almost past. Anne raised her glass with the others, then took a small sip, thinking to herself what a strange year it had been. So much had happened, most of it bad: the vain search for a cure for her mother's illness; the months of traipsing from watering place to watering place with growing fears and dwindling hopes; her mother's final illness and death, closely followed by the revelation of Lord Francis's treachery. Last but not least, there had been the strange series of events that had brought her to Etheridge Hall, wed her to a man she hardly knew, brought her a brief happiness and then destroyed it again, all within the space of a few days. With all her heart Anne hoped she would never live through another such year.

Carefully she took another sip of champagne, trying not to look at Stephen as she drank. She had been obliged to stand beside him while the toast was being drunk, and she found herself beside him again as they crowded into the drawing room to watch the clock there tick off the minutes till midnight.

Such a large party in one moderate-sized room made for an exceedingly close and noisy atmosphere. Gentlemen talked farming and politics and tugged at their starched collars while their ladies laughed, chatted, and waved fans; several young gentlemen in a mild state of intoxication were shouting hilariously to one another across the room, and servants struggled through the crowd with trays, distributing fresh glasses of champagne and refilling old ones.

At last the clock gave a wheezy gasp and began to strike twelve, tolling off the hours in a low, melancholy tone. All fell silent, but when the last stroke had sounded the room resounded with cheers and clapping. The guests turned to each other and began to exchange handshakes, embraces, and best wishes for the coming year.

"A very happy new year to you, my lord," said a smiling gentleman, clasping Stephen warmly by the hand. "And to you, too, my lady," he told Anne, as he bestowed a similar salute on her.

"I hope it will be a happy year for us both," said Stephen soberly, and took a deep draught of champagne. Another gentleman who had been lurching his way past on unsteady legs paused to regard him owlishly.

"Lord, Etheridge, you oughtn't to have any doubts about that," he said, nudging Stephen familiarly in the ribs. "Mean to say, with the two of you just married and all, it stands to reason *your* new year'll be a good one! Yes, by Jove, and that reminds me—we haven't yet drunk to your bride. A toast to the lovely Lady Etheridge," he shouted, swaying slightly as he lifted his glass on high. "And to her lucky dog of a husband, too—to

Lord and Lady Etheridge. May they have—hic—great happiness in the year ahead."

This proposal was greeted with more cheers and applause and drunk to readily. Anne felt she would have given all she possessed if the floor had opened that moment and swallowed her up. She cast a suffering glance at Stephen, but he was standing quietly with his champagne glass in his hand, looking as gravely composed as ever.

Just then, another gentleman standing nearby let out a snort of laughter. "Demmed if they ain't standing beneath the kissing ball," he said, pointing toward the ivy-covered sphere that hung over their heads. "Better look sharp and claim your privilege, Etheridge, or somebody else'll beat you to it. I wouldn't mind doing it myself," he added, with a friendly leer toward Anne. "Don't be bashful, you two. It's past midnight now, and you know what they say—if you want your New Year's business to prosper, now's the time to make a start of it!"

"Aye, go on and kiss her, Etheridge," called the gentleman who had proposed the toast. There was a murmur of approbation from the other guests. Stephen looked around the circle of laughing, expectant faces that surrounded him and Anne and smiled rather grimly.

"I don't seem to have much choice, do I?" he said. Turning to Anne, he took her in his arms and kissed her long and deliberately.

His action was greeted by more cheers and applause, and a few noisy catcalls. Almost immediately a scuffle broke out in the vicinity of the kissing bush, as several enterprising gentlemen tried to maneuver ladies of their acquaintance into a position to be kissed. There was loud laughter from the spectators as this was accomplished, or not accomplished.

Under cover of the confusion, Stephen looked down at Anne rather apprehensively. He expected to find her spitting sparks of fury over the liberty he had taken, but the look he surprised on her face was more desolate than angry. He could have sworn he saw tears glittering in her eyes. "Anne?" he said uncertainly.

She shook her head and turned away. He was debating whether or not to follow her when Lydia appeared at his side, breathless and a little disheveled from pushing her way through the crowd.

"There you are, Stephen," she said. "Such a squeeze in here, isn't it? Your mother stopped me on the way in to tell me that the supper is ready in the next room. You'll take me in to supper, won't you, Stephen? Lord Francis said something earlier about doing it, but I told him I had to speak with you first—and now it looks as though he's found another partner." She looked significantly at Anne, who was smiling and talking to Lord Francis with determined gaiety.

"Certainly I will take you in to supper, Lydia," said Stephen, forcing a gaiety of his own. Taking Lydia's arm, he led her into the dining room.

Eighteen

The next few days passed without much incident, though with plenty of heart-burnings for Anne. Stephen continued to avoid her company and to absent himself from Etheridge Hall as much as possible. Lydia, too, was absent a great deal; Anne assumed they were together and took bitter satisfaction in seeing her suspicions realized.

In an effort to distract herself from Stephen's behavior, she took to spending more and more time with Diana. She never had to worry about Diana remarking with surprise on Stephen's frequent absences, as Mrs. Etheridge sometimes did, and the younger girl's calm, quiet manner was very soothing to nerves worn thin by the strain of keeping up a continual pretense.

To Diana she went, therefore, whenever her spirits grew low and she felt the need for sympathetic companionship. Diana always received her kindly, and it was not long before a real friendship had sprung up between them. Anne accompanied Diana on long walks about the estate and watched her at her archery; together they studied French, read aloud from improving books, and practiced the pianoforte. Anne was amazed and a little humbled to see how advanced Diana was in her studies, far beyond what she herself had been at the same age. Diana clearly possessed a plenitude of her favorite quality of self discipline, in addition to a very powerful and discerning native intelligence. The two in combination were formidable indeed, so that Anne had sometimes the impression that their roles were reversed and that she, rather than Diana, was the younger and less worldly-wise. If it had not been for her proficiency at French, she feared Diana could never have respected her at all. In general the younger girl paid her a most flattering deference, however, and their friendship grew ever closer until there was hardly a subject that remained undiscussed between them.

It was natural, then, that the subject of Anne's relations with Stephen should one day arise, and arise it did, one fateful afternoon only two days before Twelfth Night.

Anne had come into the library to discover Diana frowning over the pages of a morocco-bound quarto volume. "Oh, hullo, Anne, I'm glad you're here," she said, laying down her book and taking up a sheet of paper lying beside it. "I've been trying to make sense of this book, but it's in French, and there are some words in it I'm not familiar with. They don't seem to be in the dictionary, either. I wondered if you might just look over this list I've made and translate them for me?"

Anne took the list willingly enough, but after one glance she hastily laid it down again. "Good heavens, Diana," she exclaimed. "Whatever kind of book are you reading?"

Diana displayed the covers of a lurid French novel. "It's called *Les Liaisons de Madame L.,* author anonymous. I think it must be Lydia's. She's the only one in the house who would buy such ridiculous stuff."

"Ridiculous or not, it is not at all the type of book you should be reading," said Anne with conviction.

Diana gave her a patronizing smile. "Don't be silly," she said. "I've read Apuleius and Ovid and Petronius, after all. I doubt there's anything in here that's going to shock me!"

"As to that, I can't say, for I've never read any of those authors. But I do know that my mother would have been very upset if she had caught me reading a fast French novel when *I* was sixteen!"

"Would she have? But you see, my mother doesn't censor my reading. She trusts me to regulate myself, and really that's quite sensible, I think, for at sixteen one is quite old enough to decide what one ought or ought not to read. Don't you agree, Anne?"

"Well . . . actually, no, I don't think I do agree. I don't say there's anything wrong with *you* reading what you like, but then I don't believe there are too many sixteen-year-old girls like you, Diana. Most girls your age are a good deal more . . . impressionable."

"I don't think anybody could be impressed by such stuff as this," said Diana, looking amused. "It really is the most ridiculous book, although I must own that it manages to hold one's interest pretty well even in spite of that! But I shouldn't think anyone in their right mind would think of behaving like Madame L. Of course, she's supposed to be in love with one gentleman or other throughout the whole book, and people in love do tend to behave rather irrationally, from what I have observed."

There was a speculative light in Diana's dark eyes as she looked at Anne. "It must be a very strange experience, being in love. You're in love with Stephen, aren't you, Anne?"

Anne felt her cheeks grow warm with embarrassment. "Yes," she said helplessly. "But really, Diana—"

"How did you know it was real love? Did it strike you all at once, as it did Madame L. when she first looked into her *chevalier's* eyes?"

"No . . . no, it was more gradual than that. When we first met, I thought him a very civil, pleasant-spoken gentleman, but it wasn't until after I had known him for a while that I came to—well, to fall in love with him, if you will."

"More like Madame L. and the marquis," said Diana, nodding her head in a satisfied manner. "It seems to me that that is a much more sensible and realistic way to go about it—although nothing Madame L. does is very sensible and realistic, when you come right down to it! I wonder if I will ever fall in love? I must say that it doesn't seem very likely."

"I don't see why not," said Anne, glad to encourage the conversation in this less personal turn. "Does your mother plan to present you this spring?"

"Yes," said Diana without enthusiasm. "But I'm afraid she will be wasting her time."

"Why ever would you say that? I don't wish to turn your

head, Diana, but surely it cannot have escaped your notice that you are a very pretty girl—quite beautiful, in fact. I'm sure you will make a great sensation when you come out."

Diana shook her head dubiously. "I am very blue, you know," she said. "I shall probably frighten all the gentlemen away. Of course, I might find a gentleman who liked me in spite of my being intelligent—but then, there's no saying that I would like him in return. I might have the misfortune to fall in love with a man who preferred silly women, and then what would I do?"

Anne could hardly forbear smiling at Diana's serious voice. "Yes, that would be quite a tragedy," she said.

"It would, wouldn't it? Of course, I could always pretend to be hen-witted as long as I was being courted, but I couldn't keep up such a pretense forever—indeed, I wouldn't want to, even if I could. In my opinion, it's downright immoral to represent yourself as something you are not, merely to get married. That would be behaving like Lydia, you know, and to behave like her is something I trust I will never lower myself to do. And then, just imagine the strain of playing a role, day in and day out! I can't imagine anything more stultifying than that, can you?"

Anne's "no" was barely audible. Diana did not seem to notice, however, but continued speaking in a serious, reflective voice.

"In any case, I am by no means certain that I want to be married at all. I will have some money of my own when I am of age, and sometimes I think I would rather spend my life seeing the world and perhaps writing books about my experiences, something like Lady Mary Wortley Montagu did, you know. I would like to see France and Italy and Switzerland, as you have, and perhaps go even farther abroad—to Russia, or even the Orient."

"Would you indeed? That's quite an ambition, Diana, but I'm sure you could do it if anyone could, as clever as you are about learning languages. But what does your mother think about the idea?"

Diana made a face. "All she says is to wait until I've had a Season or two before making up my mind. Of course she is hoping that I will fall in love and get married and forget all about wanting to see the world—and perhaps I shall, or perhaps I might be fortunate enough to marry a gentleman who would want to see it along with me. But I think it much more likely that at the end of one or two Seasons I shall return to Etheridge Hall a confirmed spinster and settle down to wait until I am twenty-one and can set off on my own. Would you mind very much if you and Stephen were saddled with me for a few more years, Anne?"

Anne assured her she would not mind at all, even were the years to stretch into decades, but her heart was heavy as she spoke. In the Gold Bedroom most of her bags and boxes were already packed, and her trunk stood locked and corded, ready for her departure three days hence. When the time of which Diana spoke finally came to pass, she would be long gone from Etheridge Hall, and Lydia would probably be presiding as mistress in her place. It was such a painful reflection that several minutes passed before Anne became aware that Diana was regarding her curiously.

"I'm sorry," she said, attempting a smile. "I was wool-gathering, I'm afraid—a bad habit of mine. Did you say something, Diana?"

Diana ignored the question and continued to survey Anne thoughtfully. At last she spoke, with a diffidence that was in striking contrast to her usual self-assured manner.

"It isn't my intention to pry, Anne, but I am, I think, a fairly observant person, and one or two things I have observed these last few days have made me wonder if you and Stephen might be experiencing . . . difficulties. As I said, I don't wish to pry. You need not talk about it if you don't want to, but if you do, I am very willing to listen. His being my brother need not deter you, you know. I am quite capable of maintaining my impartiality, even if we are related."

Greatly flustered by this speech, Anne said confusedly that she did not wish to burden Diana with her problems.

"You mean it's none of my business, I expect," said Diana calmly. "I know it's not, and you needn't scruple to say so if that's how you feel, Anne. You know I always prefer plain speaking. I had thought perhaps you might like to talk, but if you don't—"

"Oh, but I do, Diana—I'm just not sure that I can. It is such a difficult thing to talk about, especially with you."

Diana gave her another thoughtful look. "If I had to hazard a guess, I would say it had something to do with Lydia," she said. "Oh, you needn't look surprised, Anne. Even Mother has commented on how much time Stephen's been spending with her lately. Has Lydia been making things difficult for you?"

"You could say that, yes," admitted Anne.

Diana nodded, looking grim. "I'm not in the least surprised. She's been making life difficult for Mother and me ever since we moved down here from Ash Grove. More for Mother than for me, I'm afraid. If Lydia steps on my toes, I make a point of stepping right back, but Mother always feels obliged to be polite no matter how badly Lydia behaves."

"Yes, I'm sure your mother has had a great deal to endure these past few years."

"Indeed she has. Not just from Lydia, either—it has been very difficult for her with Stephen being gone and so much of the household business falling on her shoulders. There have been times when I was quite angry with him for staying away so long, but Mother always said it was better than having him here where Lydia could get her clutches on him again."

Anne could only nod her assent. Diana's eyes rested on her thoughtfully as she continued, "Don't misunderstand me, Anne. I love Stephen very much, but sometimes I find his behavior perfectly incomprehensible. It's not so much that he went off to Scotland in the first place—I can understand his pride being hurt by Lydia's breaking their engagement and wanting to get away for a while until all the talk had had a chance to die down. But I simply cannot believe that anything more than his pride was involved. After all, he knew when he went away that Lydia was a faithless, mercenary liar. Why should it have taken him almost four years to get over her? I'm sure if a man treated me the way Lydia treated him, I would make it a point to put him out of my mind and get on with my life as soon as possible. And I certainly would not be walking and driving out with him every day, as Stephen is doing now!"

Anne paid no attention to this last acerbic statement. She was staring at Diana with wide eyes. "Four years," she said breathlessly. "You said it took him almost four years to get over Lydia. But surely—but surely you don't mean to say he was in Scotland all that time?"

"Yes, indeed I do. He left the night before Lydia and Marcus's wedding and hasn't been back until just a few days ago, when he came with you."

"Yes, but—oh, but that's impossible. Surely he didn't spend all that time at Sir Robert's castle?"

"No, I believe he spent some time in Edinburgh as well, but I oughtn't to have to tell *you* that, Anne. That's where you met him, after all! He was in Edinburgh and I think also in Aberdeen for a while, but I am quite certain he never came south into England until now."

"Diana, there must be some mistake," said Anne distractedly. "I am sure that Lydia told me that—oh, there must be some mistake. Did perhaps Lydia and her husband make a visit to Scotland while he was there?"

"Never," said Diana with finality. "They spent their honeymoon in Brighton and then went on to London, because Lydia wanted to be presented at court. But I am positive they never went to Scotland."

"There must be some mistake," said Anne again. "I am quite sure Lydia told me Stephen did not leave for Scotland until *after* she and Marcus were married."

Diana gave her a look of amazement not unmixed with contempt. "But surely you know better than believe anything *she* says, Anne! I told you when you first came here how unscrupulous she was. And you must remember, too, that she's insanely jealous of you right now. I think she would say anything if she thought it would hurt you. Has she been trying to make trouble between you and Stephen?"

"Yes, and succeeding very well. But I still cannot believe she would have lied about such a thing. And then Stephen himself confirmed it, when I asked him about it later. Or did he?" Feverishly Anne thought back over that fateful interview, trying to remember what she had said and what Stephen had said in return. She could remember enough to convince her that his seeming admission of guilt might have been a different kind of admission altogether.

Anne sat down abruptly on the edge of the library table. "Oh, Diana, I have done a foolish thing—a wicked thing," she said. "I hardly know what I ought to do."

Diana gave her another amazed look and shook her head sadly, as though pitying an intellect so patently disordered. "Why, tell Stephen, of course," she said. "That would seem to me the logical first step, anyway. I expect he'll understand, Anne. One more instance of Lydia's perfidy ought not to come as any great shock to him."

"Oh, but the things I said—the things I said! I don't see how he *can* forgive me. But at least I can explain why I said them, and beg his pardon for speaking as I did."

Sliding off the table, Anne turned again to Diana. "Thank you for telling me all this, Diana," she said. "I think I understand the situation now—most of it, anyway. There are still some things I can't explain, but I'm beginning to suspect there's more to this business than either one of us knows. How I wish I had talked to you sooner!"

"I'm glad I could help. And if there's anything else I can do, please don't hesitate to ask, Anne. It's the least I can do, in return for all the time you've spent helping me with my French."

"I will," said Anne. Impulsively she put her arms around Diana and kissed her. "You are very good, Diana."

"No, but at least I'm honest," said Diana, returning the embrace with unexpected fervor. "Now you'd better go find Stephen and kiss *him*."

"I'm afraid it won't be as easy as that," said Anne with a sigh. "But I shall try." Bidding Diana an affectionate farewell, she left the library and went in search of Stephen.

Nineteen

In the days following the New Year's Eve party, Stephen's spirits sank deeper and deeper into melancholy. At first he had tried to struggle against his depression, making strenuous efforts to rouse himself by means of those stratagems common to disappointed lovers. He told himself that Anne was hardhearted, unreasonable, and bad-tempered: that he ought to be glad to be rid of her rather than sorry to see her go. All such arguments proved unavailing, however. Bad-tempered or not, he wanted her, and the prospect of losing her was like a black cloud that threatened to cast a shadow over his entire future.

After a day or two of this kind of struggle, Stephen gave up the struggle and surrendered himself to melancholy. He was as miserable as possible and sometimes more than he thought possible, but his misery was not without utility, for it gave him a powerful incentive for keeping to the agreement he had made with Anne. The mere sight of her reminded him so bitterly of what he had lost that he willingly did all he could to avoid being in her company.

If Anne's company was a misery to him at this period, Lydia's by contrast was almost soothing. His warmer feelings for his former fiancée had long ago given way to a kind of angry contempt; now even contempt had faded, and he was able to regard her with an indifference that had in it no feeling at all. There were times when he found himself forgetting all about their former relations and treating her exactly as if she was, what she was in fact, his cousin by marriage.

This being the case, he was perfectly willing to walk or drive out with Lydia whenever she wished. It was true that he took no pleasure in these outings, but at least there was no pain in them, except when some chance remark happened to remind him of Anne.

As might be expected, this occurred much more often than Stephen would have liked, but it never happened on purpose; Lydia was scrupulous about avoiding any mention of Anne's name, and it was this as much as anything that recommended her company to him. He would have been grateful had his mother shown a similar forbearance, but she, knowing nothing of the circumstances, had no scruples at all about bringing Anne's name into the conversation. She often gave him a great deal of pain by expressing her satisfaction with his marriage and by speculating fondly about his and Anne's future together.

He could not bring himself to disillusion her. To do so, indeed, would have been contrary to the agreement he had made with Anne, but his mother's happiness was so great that he felt obliged to give her some hint that it might not be of long duration.

"You must not be assuming that Anne and I will spend all our time here at the Hall, Mother," he said, in a voice he strove to make light and cheerful. "She has led rather a Gypsy existence for the past decade or two, you know. I doubt she will be content to stay in one place for long."

"Well, naturally I did not suppose you would spend *all* of your time here, Stephen. You will want to spend some time in London, I daresay, and of course you will have to run up to Ash Grove now and then, but I do hope the two of you will not be jaunting off immediately. I don't mean to lecture you about your duties, Stephen, for you know them as well as I do, but it does seem as though you ought to spend a little time here at Etheridge Hall after being absent so long."

"I had intended to, but—I do not think the situation at Etheridge Hall completely agrees with Anne."

"I had always thought the situation hereabouts 23exceedingly healthy," said Mrs. Etheridge, regarding him with astonishment.

"Here in the uplands we have such fine, fresh air, not at all like the atmosphere around Leeds or Manchester. Or is it the situation with Lydia you're referring to, Stephen? I will admit that it is very awkward having her here in the same house with you, but I haven't noticed that Anne much minds—in fact, she seems to me quite remarkably forbearing. I haven't wanted to mention it, Stephen, but I couldn't help noticing how much time you've been spending with Lydia lately. Do you think that is quite wise, my dear? You must know that people are still inclined to talk about that old business with you and her years ago, and there is no need to give them more food for gossip. You were out with her yesterday all morning, and then again for most of the afternoon."

"No, you're mistaken there, Mother. I spent all yesterday morning with John Laughton. I don't know where Lydia was— over at the Moorhavens', I suppose. She said something about calling on Miss Moorhaven after breakfast, as I recall. We did go for a drive together in the afternoon, but I don't see why you or anyone else should object to that if Anne did not—and I assure you she did not."

Mrs. Etheridge looked doubtful but said only that in her opinion it was a very peculiar way to run a marriage. Stephen silently agreed and left her room wearing an expression more than usually grim.

As he rounded a corner in the hallway, he came suddenly upon Anne standing near the door to his room. She started slightly at his appearance, but then recovered herself and came toward him. "Stephen, I must speak with you," she said.

He could see that she was very agitated. Her face was pale and set, and her accent much more noticeable than usual, always a sign with her of strong emotion. Stephen supposed she must want to discuss with him some detail of her departure, which was now only a few days away. The thought stung him to the core, but it was her manner that hurt him most: it was obvious that she was finding it difficult, even painful to speak to him. His sensitivities had already been rubbed raw by his recent interview with his mother, and now he felt suddenly as though he could bear no more.

"Later, Anne," he said brusquely, and went into his room, shutting the door behind him with a bang.

In the face of such a snub, Anne had no heart to persevere. She went into her own room, rang the bell for Parker, and began to change her dress for dinner. Tears kept springing to her eyes as she dressed, but she brushed them away and kept on, trying to keep her face averted from Parker as much as possible.

When her toilette was finished and Parker had gone away again, she went to the glass and surveyed herself unhappily. Her eyes were reddened from weeping and her cheeks unbecomingly flushed; if she had not had a strong object in going downstairs, she would have chosen to forgo dinner and spend the evening in her room.

"Naturally he is angry," she told herself. "I don't wonder that he doesn't want to talk to me. But I must make him listen—I cannot leave here without at least apologizing for the things I said before. Perhaps there will be an opportunity to speak to him downstairs before dinner. If I hurry and get down before Lydia does, I might be able to catch him alone for a few minutes in the drawing room."

With this resolve strong in her mind, Anne wasted no more time brooding in front of the glass but hurried on downstairs. When she got to the drawing room, however, she found that her hurrying had been in vain: Lydia had got there before her, robbing her of any opportunity of speaking to Stephen before dinner. It would have been easy to have become thoroughly disheartened by this second setback, but Anne swallowed back her disappointment and pinned her hopes on finding a moment alone with him after dinner instead.

But here, too, her hopes were disappointed. When dinner was over, the ladies adjourned to the drawing room as usual to talk and drink tea, but on this evening they were not joined by Stephen immediately afterwards, and when Anne finally nerved herself to question the butler, she learned that he had gone out.

"To Moorhaven Manor, my lady. A matter of some business with Sir Thomas, I believe it was," said the butler.

Anne was disappointed, but found comfort in reflecting that on this occasion, at least, it was not Lydia who was depriving her of his company. Later that evening, when she had made herself ready for bed with Parker's help, she lay in her curtained four-poster listening for the sounds that would signal Stephen's arrival in the next room.

It was some time after midnight when she finally heard his step in the hall and the creak of his door opening and closing. Pushing aside the bedclothes, Anne rose quietly from her bed and went to the door that gave communication between his rooms and her own. When she went to open the door, however, she found that it was locked. The logical course would have been to knock for admittance, but Anne had not quite courage for that; it seemed probable that he would only reject her a second time, and a rejection under such circumstances would have more of a sting to it than Anne, at that moment, felt very well able to bear. The spirit of cowardice, never lacking on such occasions, whispered that it would be much better to wait and approach him tomorrow, by daylight, on some more neutral ground. On this occasion, cowardice won out; Anne returned to bed and lay listening to the movements in the next room until she finally fell asleep.

When daylight came, however, she found her hopes frustrated once again. In spite of his having gone to bed so late, Stephen managed to be up before her and had already breakfasted and gone out by the time she got downstairs. It was Lydia who gave her this information, further adding to her chagrin, and Lydia also made a point of telling her that the two of them were engaged to drive out again that afternoon.

Anne had to struggle hard to accept this unwelcome news with the appearance of complaisance. Although she was on the watch all that day, no opportunity presented itself for private speech with Stephen; it seemed almost as though Lydia had divined her intentions and was taking great delight in thwarting them. At all events, she managed to remain close by Stephen's side every minute he was home that day, as well as accompanying him when he went out that afternoon. Anne went to bed that night no closer to achieving her purpose than before.

By this time she was growing desperate. Twelfth Night was now less than twenty-four hours away, and unless she managed to speak with Stephen sometime during the following day, she might find herself obliged to leave Etheridge Hall without ever having spoken to him at all. It was urgent that she obtain an interview with him tomorrow, whatever the outcome, and in truth Anne was not cherishing too many hopes in that regard. She thought it quite probable that he had been so offended by her behavior that he would not hear her explanation, or (worse yet) that he was so much in love with Lydia that it would make no difference if he did. Anne made herself face both possibilities, but still she was determined to speak to him.

"At the very least, he shall know how Lydia misled me," she vowed to herself. "And if he can still love her and want to marry her after that—well, then, I shall not stand in his way."

For much of the night Anne lay awake pondering these and other matters, and she arose the next morning with the conviction that drastic measures were called for. When she got downstairs, she was not much surprised to learn that Stephen had already breakfasted and gone out, but instead of hanging about the house waiting for his return, she went in search of Diana.

From a passing maid, she learned that Diana was outside practicing her archery. Anne threw on her bonnet and pelisse and went out to join her at the range. Her face must have revealed something of her state of mind, for Diana put down her bow as soon as she saw her and hurried over to meet her.

"Diana, you told me a few days ago that you would help me if you could," said Anne, coming directly to the point. "I don't know if you can or not, but I do need help most desperately."

In general terms she outlined her situation to Diana, not mentioning the exact cause of her quarrel with Stephen but describing its outcome with great frankness. "After talking to you the other day, I came to realize that perhaps I was unjust to him, and I have been trying to apologize ever since. But it seems that he is either occupied with business, or else Lydia is with him, and I simply cannot bring myself to speak in front of her. The one time I did manage to speak to him alone, he brushed me aside with hardly a word. I am afraid he is still very angry with me. Of course he has every right to be angry, after the way I spoke to him, but you can see what an impossible situation it leaves me in. What shall I do, Diana?"

"It's an awkward situation, certainly, but I shouldn't call it impossible," said Diana, after a moment's consideration. "Possibly Stephen *is* angry with you, Anne, but I should say myself that he was more upset than angry. By now he ought to be in a more reasonable frame of mind. I do not think he would refuse to hear you if you went to him and told him frankly just what you've told me."

Anne made a despairing gesture. "I would, but I don't know where he is. He had already gone out when I got downstairs. I suppose he is with Lydia again."

Diana shook her head decidedly. "No, I know he is not, for I saw him myself only a little while ago. He was walking up the path that leads to the tower on the hill. The tower has always been one of his favorite places here at the Hall—I know that he and Marcus used often to play there when they were boys, and when he was older it was always the place he went when he wanted to be alone. You can probably catch him there if you hurry."

Anne was already tying on her bonnet and tucking up her skirts in a businesslike manner, but her expression was rueful. "I daresay Lydia is there, too," she said with a sigh. "Or something else will happen to hinder me."

Diana looked at her sternly. "If you take that kind of attitude about it, Anne, then something probably will! But I can tell you with absolute certainty that Lydia isn't with him this morning. He was by himself when I saw him, and I would have seen if anyone had gone up after him. Now's your chance, and you'd better make the most of it. It would be just like Lydia to be spying on us from the windows. If she guesses what you mean to do, you can be sure she'll try to put a spoke in your wheel somehow—she must be in a perfect fever lest you and Stephen compare notes and discover what she's been up to. Go on now, and hurry!"

Anne needed no urging. At a near run she set off along the path that led to the tower on the hill. The sun had just risen above the hill and was in her eyes as she climbed, but when she neared the top she could discern a lone figure in the tower, a figure she had no difficulty recognizing as Stephen's.

Rejoicing to find him alone and in a place that did not admit of easy retreat, she entered the tower and ran up the stairs, emerging at last breathless onto the gallery overhead.

Stephen was standing quietly at the far end of the gallery. He was leaning against the stone railing, looking out over the house and gardens below. As Anne came toward him, he turned his head to regard her briefly, then resumed his study of the landscape.

"Stephen," she said, between gasps for breath. "Stephen, I must talk to you."

Once again he turned to regard her, and the look on his face smote her more painfully than any words he could have said. When he did speak, however, his voice was calm and perfectly emotionless. "You are leaving tomorrow?" he said.

Anne took a deep breath. "Only if you want me to, Stephen," she said. "And indeed, I would not blame you if you did. I think— I am almost sure—that I have done you a great injustice."

Without waiting for a reply, she launched into her explanation. The words came haltingly at first but soon were tumbling out faster and faster as she told him all that had happened during his stay at Ash Grove.

"So you can see what Lydia led me to believe, but now it seems from what Diana says that there was some mistake about it—that Lydia lied, in fact. Stephen, tell me truly: are you Amy's father?"

The stunned look on his face was all the answer she needed,

even had his next words not confirmed it. "I, Amy's father?" he repeated. "Good God, no. After what Lydia did to me—and to Marcus—I wouldn't have touched her for any consideration. Not if I'd been offered half the kingdom."

"I knew it," said Anne, letting out her breath in a rush. "Or rather, I should have known it. How could I have been such a fool? Only when I asked you about it before, it seemed as though you were admitting to it. You said you had meant to tell me the truth earlier. . . ."

Stephen shook his head with a dazed air. "I was talking about my being engaged to Lydia, years ago," he said. "You said you had learned the truth about me and Lydia, and I naturally assumed that's what you were talking about. And I should have told you the truth, way back when we first became engaged and certainly before I ever brought you here. None of this misunderstanding would have arisen if I'd made a clean breast of it at the start."

"I suppose it was rather a painful subject," said Anne hesitantly. "It must have been, to have made you leave your home and family and hide away in Scotland all those years. To lose your fiancée in such a way must have been very upsetting."

Again Stephen shook his head. "But you see, it wasn't losing Lydia that upset me. Mind you, I don't mean to say I was happy about being jilted. I was pretty bitter about it at the time, but it didn't take me long to get over it. It was so obvious that she was marrying Marcus only for his title and money. I simply told myself she wasn't worth it and did my best to put the whole business out of my mind."

"But why then did you go to Scotland?" said Anne. "If it wasn't because of Lydia, why was it?"

"It was because of Marcus," said Stephen simply. "He couldn't seem to leave the subject alone. We had always been very close growing up, and even after he became engaged to Lydia, when anyone might have thought there was sufficient reason for us to avoid each other's company, he still insisted on our being together as much as ever. It was as though he were trying to convince me, or himself, that what he had done hadn't changed anything between us. If you can believe it, he even asked me to be groomsman at his and Lydia's wedding."

"And you agreed?"

"Yes, I did. Naturally I wasn't very enthusiastic about the idea, but I didn't like to refuse when it was obvious he was trying to conciliate me. I suppose, too, that there was a certain amount of pride involved. It seemed to me that it would be better to put a good face on it and stand groomsman than to refuse and have it be known I was off sulking somewhere in the role of rejected lover.

"So I agreed to be groomsman, and the plans for the wedding went forward. It came down at last to the night before the wedding. Marcus had been drinking pretty heavily all that day for one reason or another, and after dinner he went on drinking until I began to be alarmed. It seemed to me I ought to try to stop him, and so I did—I did my best to make a joke of it, telling him he wouldn't be able to stagger to the altar if he drank much more. He turned on me, saying something to the effect that he supposed that would suit me very well. I protested, naturally, but he went on and on, growing more offensive with every word.

"I can see now what must have been in his mind. Marcus wasn't a stupid fellow; he must have known as well as I did why Lydia was marrying him, but to himself he tried to pretend it wasn't like that at all. He said some truly unforgivable things—and I'm afraid I said some pretty unforgivable things in return. The upshot was that I packed my bags and left the house that night, swearing never to return. Somebody else had to be found at the last minute to be groomsman at the wedding next day; it all caused quite a scandal at the time, I believe.

"After leaving the Hall, I posted up north and took refuge with Rob. I had already gotten over the worst of my anger by then, and I didn't intend to stay in Scotland long; only until things cooled down and I got an apology from Marcus. He'd always had a pretty hot temper, but as a rule it never stayed hot for very long. We'd quarreled countless times as boys, but our quarrels always blew over after a day or two, and I assumed this one would, too, if I only waited long enough.

"So I settled down to wait. It wasn't unpleasant staying with Rob, but as the weeks went by, I began to be anxious to hear from Marcus. The weeks stretched into months, and finally into a whole year, and still I had never heard a word from him. I began to think at last that perhaps he was waiting for *me* to apologize. But by that time I was feeling doubly offended by his long silence and was more determined than ever to let him make the first move toward apologizing. I considered that I'd been the injured party, you see, and I couldn't quite bring myself to come slinking home with my tail between my legs. And then the next thing I heard was that he was dead. . . ."

"Oh, Stephen, I'm so sorry," said Anne, shocked by the depth of suffering in his voice. "How terrible to hear about it like that."

"It *was* terrible. We grew up together, went to school together—he was like a brother to me, and then suddenly he was dead without my ever having had a chance to be reconciled to him. Nothing has ever tortured me so much as the memory of that last evening we were together. I ought to have taken into consideration his situation, made allowance for his jealousy—I ought to have done anything rather than run off to Scotland in a fit of pique. It made it even worse that I came into his title and estate after he died. I couldn't bring myself to return to the Hall and step into his shoes, after everything that had happened. And then in his will he made such a point of leaving me nothing he wasn't absolutely obliged to—it was obvious he hadn't relented, though Mother says he did ask for me when he was actually dying. It's a poor consolation, but it's all I've got."

"Oh, Stephen," said Anne, greatly moved. She came a step closer and laid her hand on his shoulder. "Stephen, you don't have to say another word. I understand enough now to know why you acted as you did, and it isn't necessary that you say any more. I know how painful it must be to talk about it."

He smiled tiredly, lifted her hand from his shoulder, and kissed it. "As a matter of fact, it's rather a relief to talk about it with someone," he said. "In all this time, I've never said a word to anyone, not even to Rob. It is an indulgence to have you as a listener, Anne. But I won't ask you to indulge me much longer; it's a sad and sordid tale, but there really isn't much more of it to tell. After Marcus's death I stayed on in Scotland, putting off returning to England week by week and month by month, until I received that fateful letter from my mother urging me to come home for Christmas. So I packed up my things, booked a seat on the southgoing mail—and the rest of the story you know." Stephen paused and looked down at Anne. There was a half smile on his lips, but his eyes were grave and searching. "So you truly believed Amy was my child, not Marcus's? No wonder you were so angry with me."

"I was a fool to believe Lydia," said Anne passionately. "I ought to have known you would never do such a thing. But Lydia made it sound so convincing—and then, you seemed so fond of Amy. You gave her your own toy soldiers at Christmas. . . ."

"Ah, the soldiers! That's another story, but in a way it all goes back to Marcus and me, too—way back to when we were both boys. Even when we were very small, Marcus had always an eye for those soldiers. He had soldiers of his own, of course, but mine were a very fine set that a family friend had brought me from Germany. You couldn't buy anything half so fine around here. Marcus was quite frantically jealous of them, and some of our most memorable battles were waged over possession of those wretched soldiers. It sounds foolish, I know, but by giving them to his daughter I felt as though I was making some amends for the past—laying to rest what had been at least one source of contention between us. It doesn't make much sense, does it?"

"On the contrary, it makes perfect sense," said Anne. "Oh, Stephen, how I wish you had told me all this before."

"I wish I had, too. Unfortunately, 'too little, too late' seems to be a regular motto of mine—though I hope that in this case, I may not be irretrievably too late." Putting his hands on Anne's shoulders, Stephen looked down at her searchingly. "You said a few minutes ago that you would not leave unless I wanted you to. Does that mean that your decision to leave Etheridge Hall is not, after all, irrevocable?"

"I revoke it here and now," said Anne, smiling up at him rather tremulously. "But you would be quite within your rights to wash your hands of me, Stephen, after the horrible things I said to you the other day. At the very least you ought to be cool and standoffish for a week or two, to pay me back."

Stephen's response was to fold her tightly in his arms. "No, indeed," he said roughly. "I consider that we've already wasted entirely too much time with *that* sort of thing! Oh, Anne, I have missed you. I don't know what I would have done if you had really left me."

"I don't know what I would have done, either," said Anne, laying her face against his chest and closing her eyes. "I've never been so miserable in my life as I have these past few days."

"Not half so miserable as I was. The thing is, you see . . ." Stephen hesitated, then went on resolutely: "The thing is that I love you, Anne. I think I've loved you almost from the first moment I saw you."

"Oh, Stephen," said Anne in amazement. She tilted back her head to look at him. "Have you, indeed? I never would have guessed it. At least, there were times when I did wonder—but most of the time you were so cool and calm about it."

"I wasn't feeling cool and calm, I assure you! After this last week or so, I think I could teach Diana a thing or two about self-discipline. There've been a hundred times when I wanted to tell you how I felt, but I was so afraid of doing the wrong thing. I didn't want to frighten you away."

Anne gave him a look of amusement mingled with incredulity. "Really, Stephen, we *are* married, you know. I think you might have trusted me to stand the shock! It so happens that I love you, too, but I'm afraid it took me a little longer to recognize your excellencies as a husband than it did you mine as a wife. It wasn't until after we were actually married—sometime around the morning after, I believe it was."

A blush and a rather mischievous smile accompanied her words, but their meaning was lost upon Stephen. He was gazing down at her with an amazement even greater than her own had been a moment before. "God, what a fool I have been," were his next words, spoken in a voice of abject humility. "Can you ever forgive me, Anne? It seems to me I've conducted myself like a perfect imbecile from start to finish."

"I've just told you I love you," she reminded him gaily. "That presupposes a measure of forgiveness, I should think!" More seriously, she added, "Don't let us talk any more of forgiveness, Stephen. If you have been at fault, then so have I, and I think the best thing we can do is put all this behind us and make a fresh start."

"You're right, of course. It's the same thing you said that night in the mailcoach, and if it was true then, it's doubly true now. All we really have is the present—and from now on, I intend to make the most of it." Putting one hand under Anne's chin, he tilted up her face and kissed her.

From somewhere in the vale below a piercing shriek rang out. A tremor went through Stephen's body, but he did not loose his hold on Anne. "I'm not even going to look," he told her. "Whatever it is, there are plenty of other responsible people down there who can handle it just as well as I could. *My* responsibility lies *here*—" and he kissed her again.

It was some time before either of them had occasion for further speech. Anne was reluctant to put an end to an interlude so thoroughly satisfactory, but the sun's progress overhead had reminded her that she, too, had responsibilities, at least one of which was awaiting her below. When her husband's ardor showed signs of progressing beyond the kissing stage, she spoke apologetically.

"Stephen, I'm afraid I must be getting back to the house now. Your mother was wanting me to look over the household accounts with her this morning, and if I don't go immediately there won't be any morning left. By the looks of the sun, it must be eleven or later."

Stephen had paid scant heed to the first part of this speech, but the second produced a very sudden and dramatic effect. His arms dropped limply down to his sides, and a comical look of dismay spread over his face. "Good lord, and I was supposed to meet with a group of my tenants at half past ten this morning! I suppose I'll have to be leaving, too, if I don't want a riot on my hands. But I will look forward to seeing you later, sometime this afternoon, perhaps—no, damn it, that won't work, either. I told Sir Thomas Moorhaven I'd be at home this afternoon to discuss the Parish work fund with him. Well, then, may I hope we can get together this evening to—ahem—celebrate our reconciliation?"

"That won't work, either, Stephen," said Anne regretfully. "It's Twelfth Night, remember? Your mother is holding a Twelfth Night party tonight for Amy."

Stephen swore mildly and ran his hand through his hair in a frustrated manner. "Mother and her parties," he grumbled. "At least this one is only a family party. I hope it will break up early."

He gave Anne a look that brought the color to her cheeks, but she only laughed and turned toward the stairs, advising him over her shoulder to make haste if he did not want to be left behind. This challenge brought him after her post-haste, of course, and they went down the stairs arm in arm.

As they came out of the tower onto the hill, they saw far away below them a horse-drawn gig bowling along the drive leading to the house. Stephen shaded his eyes with his hand and regarded it with a frown.

"I don't recognize the carriage, but whoever it is seems to be in a deuce of a hurry," he said. "God forbid it's not more bad news from Ash Grove."

Anne's heart sank within her, but she forced herself to respond cheerfully. "If it is, we will simply have to make the best of it, Stephen," she said. "We both know you must go if you're called away again. But with luck, you needn't be gone very long, and when you return home I can guarantee that your reception will be more cordial than it was last time!"

Stephen laughed and enveloped her in a crushing embrace. "There's not going to be any more separations, my lady," he told her. "If I find I must go to Ash Grove again, then you're coming with me. Even if I have to abduct you!"

Laughing, Anne returned his embrace, and then they set off down the hill again arm in arm. They reached the terrace in a matter of minutes, but as they rounded the hedge that enclosed the terrace walk, they were brought up short by a scene of confusion.

Half-a-dozen servants were milling about in a distracted manner, while Mrs. Etheridge stood upon the terrace talking excitedly to a grave-faced gentleman carrying a black valise. At the far end of the terrace, some way apart from the others, stood Diana, still clad in her Lincoln green archery dress with her quiver slung over her shoulder. On her face was a most peculiar expression, a mixture of defiance, penitence, and a kind of guilty amusement. Anne, looking at her, was suddenly reminded of the shriek she and Stephen had heard earlier, and a strange premonitory conviction swept over her. She came to an abrupt stop, but Stephen quickened his steps to join his mother on the terrace.

"What's the problem, Mother?" he said, looking from her to Diana to the gentleman with the black valise.

Mrs. Etheridge threw up her hands. "Ask your sister," she said with asperity. "She can tell you better than I can."

Stephen turned an inquiring eye toward his sister. "Diana?" he said.

Diana returned his gaze limpidly, but there was still a trace of guilty amusement lurking in her eyes. "I was practicing my archery," she said. "And Lydia came out of the house—I think she must have been going to join you two up at the tower. And I can't think how it happened, but I'm afraid one of my shots went wide, and I—er—wounded her slightly."

"Wounded her? Is she badly hurt?"

"Oh, no, it was only a very small wound. The arrow only just grazed her. But you would have thought it had killed her, from all the fuss she made—"

"Diana, you are being unfair," said Mrs. Etheridge warmly. "She had every right to be upset, and you ought to be ashamed of yourself for making light of it. It might easily have been quite a serious injury. Dr. Esmond has just been examining Lydia," she continued, nodding to the gentleman beside her, who smiled and bowed at Stephen and Anne before resuming his air of professional gravity. "He says the wound is a minor one, and that, barring any complication, Lydia ought to be up and around in a few days."

"Of course, she may have some difficulty *sitting,* just at first," added Diana in an innocent voice.

Stephen had to chew his lower lip to keep from smiling. "I see," he said. "So your shot went wide, did it, Diana?"

"Yes, I cannot think how such a thing came to happen. I suppose a gust of wind must have carried it from the target." Her brother said nothing but looked expressively at a nearby group of evergreens, their branches standing motionless in the bright morning sunshine. Diana's eyes flickered, acknowledging a hit, but still she held her ground. "A very *sudden* gust of wind," she said earnestly.

"It must have been," agreed Stephen. "Quite a freak of nature, in fact. Let's hope it doesn't happen again. It would be a shame to have to curtail your archery practice on that account."

He held his sister's gaze for a long moment. Anne, who had been standing a little way back listening to this exchange with great amusement, thought it a proper moment to intervene.

"I'm sure it won't happen again, Stephen," she said. "Why don't you go on to your tenants' meeting? I know you said you were already late for it. . . ."

Stephen, with a glance at his watch, confirmed this and took leave of them all with a final word of admonition to his sister and a final, rueful smile at Anne. His departure was a signal for the rest of the group to disperse. Mrs. Etheridge accompanied the doctor to his gig to receive some further instructions on Lydia's care; the servants began to drift back to the house; and Anne and Diana were left standing by themselves on the terrace. Anne waited until the others had moved beyond earshot, then leaned over to whisper in Diana's ear. "Nice shot, Diana," she said.

Diana smiled modestly, but her eyes were aglow with laughter. "It was an easy target," she whispered back.

Twenty

So it was that Anne made her preparations for Twelfth Night in a very different spirit than she had anticipated a few days before. Since the party that evening was to be only a family party, she had no excuse to make herself very fine, but she bathed, washed her hair, and chose her dress and ornaments with the same care she might have bestowed upon the grandest ball.

As she dabbed perfume behind her ears and touched her lips with salve, she laughed at herself for her pains, but pains she took nevertheless; and when Parker had put the last touches on her hair and had fastened her necklace around her neck, she took a last, critical look at herself in the glass. Unrelieved black could never look really festive, but it could and did look elegant, and Anne reflected with satisfaction that tonight there would be no Lydia to make her look drab by comparison.

"Really, Diana's 'accident' was providential in more ways than one," she told herself, as she turned away from the glass. "I would have had trouble being civil to Lydia tonight, after everything that's happened. As it is, I'm afraid it will be at least a week before I can look at her without wanting to reach for the fire-irons!"

The idea brought a mischievous smile to Anne's lips, and she was still smiling as she went out into the hall. The first thing she saw there was Stephen, gravely inspecting an engraving of the ruins of Athens that hung on the wall outside her door. As soon as he saw her, he left off his study of Athens and came over to take her by the arm. "I was waiting for you," he said.

"You didn't need to do that, Stephen," said Anne. Something about the way he was looking at her made her feel almost shy; to cover her confusion, she assumed a flippant tone. "I've lived in this house almost two weeks, Stephen. You must have a poor opinion of my powers if you think I can't find my way downstairs by now. Or is this merely another instance of your famous chivalry?"

"My motives were more selfish than chivalrous, I'm afraid. After everything that's happened this past week, I've become rather wary of long separations! By personally accompanying you downstairs, I can make sure you don't go slipping away from me again between here and the dining room—and I can also take a moment to tell you how beautiful you look, before we have to join the others."

"Thank you, Stephen—but I would rather you told me a little about what I'm going down to. I'm sure I must have attended one or two Twelfth Night parties when I was a child, but I don't remember a thing about them. What old English customs may I look forward to tonight?"

"Well, to begin with, we have dinner. In honor of the occasion it's a fancier dinner than usual, much like Christmas dinner—"

"With roast beef as the *pièce de résistance,* no doubt?" said Anne teasingly.

"No doubt," agreed Stephen solemnly. "But it's dessert that really makes Twelfth Night dinner special. In addition to mince pies and the usual things, we have Twelfth cake."

"And what is so special about that? We had cake on Twelfth Night in France and Belgium, too. Twelfth Night is called *le jour des rois* there—kings' day, you know—and the cake is called *gateau de roi,* or king's cake. It's more of a flat pastry tart, really, and before it's baked, the cook marks it into pieces and puts a bean in one. Whoever gets the piece with the bean in it gets to be master or mistress of ceremonies for the evening."

"The custom here is much the same, but our cake really is a cake, and instead of just a bean in it, we have a pea *and* a bean. The man and woman who find them get to be King and Queen for the evening. Ideally it's a man who finds the bean and a woman the pea, though mishaps have been known to occur. And there've been years when we had to draw straws, because someone inadvertently swallowed one or the other of them!"

"And what do the King and Queen do, once they've assumed their thrones?"

"That's the fun of it—they can do whatever they like. They can order the party to play games, or dance, or perform recitations, or anything else they might choose. I remember one year when Diana was Queen, and she saw fit to make me construe Latin verse, as a punishment for having spoken slightingly of Virgil earlier in the day. With a large party and an imaginative King and Queen, it can make for quite an entertaining evening."

"Yes, I imagine that it could," said Anne with a smile.

"Of course, it will be quieter this year with just the family participating. Mother is getting older, and she felt two large parties were enough for this holiday season, but she didn't want to let the custom lapse altogether because of Amy. I find it hard to believe that a child that young can remember anything that happened a year ago, but Mother tells me she's been looking forward to Twelfth Night and Twelfth cake all year long. I gather the pea fell to her lot last year and that she had a wonderful time ordering her elders about!"

"Indeed, it sounds very diverting," said Anne. "I must be thinking up some suitable commands to issue, just in case I should be fortunate enough to be Queen for the evening."

They had reached the drawing room door by now, but Stephen hung back a moment before opening it. "Kisses are a usual request," he said, eyeing her hopefully. "Perhaps we ought to put in some practice now, just so I'll be all ready when the time comes."

Anne laughed and kissed him lightly on the lips. "No, I think we put in quite enough practice this morning, sir," she said. "If you want more, you must await the Queen's pleasure!" Nimbly evading his outstretched arms, she whisked past him into the drawing room.

Mrs. Etheridge was already there, together with Amy, but neither of them was looking very festive. Amy, indeed, appeared to be on the verge of tears, and Mrs. Etheridge was speaking to her in a sympathetic voice.

"It is very disappointing, I know, but you mustn't be selfish about it, Amy. Your mother had a little accident this morning and isn't feeling very well. If she doesn't feel equal to coming downstairs, then we must simply accept her decision and make the best of it."

Amy sniffed and made a valiant effort to blink back her tears. "I don't mean to be selfish, but I did so want Mama to be at the party," she said pathetically. "Could she not come down for just a little while?"

"I'm afraid not, dear. I know it's a disappointment to you, but it wouldn't be fair to ask her to come down when she is feeling so unwell. The doctor says she is not badly hurt, however, and perhaps you can go up later and take her a piece of Twelfth cake so she will not feel completely left out. Would you like that?"

"Yes," said Amy, looking more cheerful. "I would like that very much. Oh, and I have another idea, Grandmother!" In sudden excitement she bounced off the sofa and put her hand on Mrs. Etheridge's knee. "Since Mama can't come down for the party tonight, could Molly come down instead? She would like to very much, I know, and that would be even better than having Mama there. Molly likes playing with me much more than Mama does, and she is never cross."

"Why, yes, I suppose Molly could come down for a while, if you like—"

"To eat dinner with us, and play games, too?"

"Yes, I don't see why not. You run up and invite her, and the rest of us will wait here until you get back."

Amy immediately dashed off to tell her nurse the joyous news. Mrs. Etheridge watched her go, then shook her head and looked ruefully at Anne and Stephen. " 'Out of the mouths of babes!' " she murmured. "It seems Lydia isn't well enough to come down this evening. I told her we could probably have some of the footmen carry her down on a sofa, but she was quite adamant about staying upstairs."

"I'm not surprised," said Stephen, smiling rather grimly. "Let's hope her recuperation doesn't take too long. I am looking forward to having a talk with Lydia in the very near future."

"Oh, yes?" said Mrs. Etheridge, eyeing him in a doubtful way. Anne squeezed his arm and gave him a warning look. His expression at once softened into a more natural smile, and he returned her squeeze with one meant to convey reassurance.

The drawing room door opened just then, admitting Diana; she was followed by Amy, who was leading by the hand a shy-looking Molly clad in a beribboned cap and gay print dress that showed signs of having been donned in haste.

"Here she is," said Amy triumphantly. "It's all right, Molly; there's nothing to be afraid of. You can sit right here on the sofa with me until Elliot tells us the dinner is served. When that happens we will go into the dining room, but you must go in ahead of the rest of us with Uncle Stephen, because *you* are the guest of honor."

Poor Molly looked appalled by this speech, but everyone else laughed; and when presently the butler appeared to make his announcement, Stephen turned to Molly and solemnly offered her his arm. With a blush and a shy curtsy, she took it, and they all went in to dinner.

As Stephen had predicted, the meal was much on the order of Christmas dinner. There was soup, baked fish, roast beef, and an assortment of side dishes for the first course; roast goose, a brace of pheasants, and sundry other viands for the second. For the dessert course, plum pudding put in another appearance, as did the ubiquitous mince pies, but the central attraction on this occasion was without question the elaborate Twelfth cake. Anne, as hostess, was appointed the job of cutting and distributing this confection, a dense fruit cake covered with marzipan and swirls of snowy white frosting.

"I want the piece with the pea in it," announced Amy, as

Anne began to divide the cake into slices. "Whoever gets the pea gets to be Queen, and that's what I want to be."

"When you ask for something, you've got to say 'please,' Miss Amy," said Molly, with an apologetic look around the table. "You know I've told you that many and many a time."

"And you can't just *ask* for the pea, darling," added Mrs. Etheridge. "It's entirely a matter of luck who gets it. I've already explained to you that just because you got it last year doesn't mean you will again this year."

Amy accepted this statement in silence, but it was obvious she was not convinced by it. She watched eagle-eyed as Anne placed slices of cake on the dessert plates, and as soon as her own slice was laid in front of her, she immediately set about reducing it to crumbs in quest of the pea.

"I've got the bean," said Stephen, triumphantly holding this object aloft.

"We don't care about that," said Diana crushingly. "You would have been King by default anyway, since you're the only gentleman here. The real question is, who's got the pea? I don't."

"Thank heaven for that," returned her brother. "You may profess yourself a republican, Di, but in practice you're the worst kind of tyrant. I still haven't forgotten the dose of Virgil you put me through five years ago!"

Everyone laughed except Amy, whose lower lip was quivering ominously. "I don't have it," she wailed. "I've looked and looked, but the pea isn't there. I did so want to be Queen!"

Anne, who had just discovered the pea in her own slice of cake, smiled sympathetically at the little girl. "Perhaps you ought to look a little more, just to be sure," she suggested. "It might have rolled under your plate, or even into your lap." While Amy was anxiously shaking out the folds of her skirt, Anne swiftly deposited the pea behind a cluster of raisins that decorated the margin of Amy's plate. "Not there, either? Well, perhaps it wouldn't hurt to check your plate just one more time. . . ."

Amy spotted the pea almost immediately. "Oh, it *is* here," she cried, reaching out to pluck it from its place of concealment.

"I am the Queen, I am, I am! Oh, thank you, Aunt Anne, for helping me look."

No one said anything, but a ripple of communication appeared to go around the table all the same. Mrs. Etheridge coughed slightly, Molly smothered a chuckle, Diana smiled knowingly at her plate, and Stephen gave Anne a look that made her feel amply repaid for her small sacrifice.

When dessert was over, the party retired to the drawing room, and the Twelfth Night King and Queen commenced their reign. It might have been more accurate to say that the Queen alone commenced her reign, for Stephen sat back and let Amy take charge of ordering the evening's festivities. It was an office she was not at all backward about exercising.

To begin with, the party was called on to play a vast number of the same juvenile games they had played on Christmas evening. This by itself might have comprised the whole evening's program if the King had not finally stepped in, taken his consort aside, and strongly suggested to her the propriety of introducing a few other diversions which would, he said, be at least as amusing as playing jackstraws or hunt-the-slipper.

Amy, to do her credit, was very willing to fall in with Stephen's suggestion. The two of them then retired to the far end of the room to hold a whispered conference, punctuated by bursts of giggles from Amy. When they returned, the King settled back on the sofa with an anticipatory grin, while the Queen called the others forward one by one and informed them of the part they were to play in the evening's entertainment.

The royal couple had shown considerable imagination in devising appropriate tasks for their subjects. Mrs. Etheridge, no singer by her own admission, was called on to warble operatic arias for the company. When she had done her best and been applauded roundly for her efforts, Molly was called forward, presented with two oranges and an apple, and ordered to demonstrate her skill in juggling—a skill which she proved really to possess, as the Queen had confidently asserted.

Finally, in what was agreed to be the evening's grand climax,

Anne was blindfolded and set to play a piece at the pianoforte, to which accompaniment Diana was ordered to dance upon one leg. When the two of them had stumbled through this task, the Queen pronounced herself satisfied; and the King, grinning from ear to ear, told his flushed and breathless sister that he now considered himself avenged for the humiliation he had suffered at her hands five years before.

The whole party being badly in need of refreshment at this point, Molly was sent to the kitchen to fetch the tea-tray. Amy went along with her to demand of the cook a supply of those sweetmeats most suited to the tastes of an infant monarch. While the two of them were absent on this errand, Mrs. Etheridge confided to Anne that it was a fortunate thing Twelfth Night came only once a year.

"That was a kind thing you did, dear, letting her be Queen instead of you. Next year I really shall have to put my foot down, however. She must understand she can't be Queen every year, no matter how badly she wants it. Children are so easily spoiled by over-indulgence. But she really did deserve a treat tonight, I think, to make up for the disappointment of not having her mother here. I must remember to have her take a piece of cake to Lydia when she goes up to bed tonight."

That time soon arrived, in spite of Amy's attempts to assert her royal authority in the matter. She departed from the drawing room at last, under protest, accompanied by Molly and carrying in both hands a plate containing a slice of Twelfth cake for her mother. After she had gone, Mrs. Etheridge turned to Stephen. "Well, dear, have you any more commands for us?" she asked.

He smiled and shook his head. "No, I think not. I've had enough games for one evening. I'd just as soon sit and talk now."

"The King has spoken," said Diana in an oracular voice, and moved from her chair to one closer to the fire.

Stephen was already seated on the sofa; he looked at Anne, raised one brow, and jerked his head toward the vacant place beside him. She gave him a reproachful look, but came over to sit beside him nonetheless. He put his arm around her shoulders and drew her closer, stroking the back of her neck with his hand and letting his fingers toy with the jet beads on the collar of her dress.

From beside the fireplace Mrs. Etheridge drew a contented sigh. "It has been a lovely evening," she said. "I'm not sure family parties aren't the best kind, when all's said and done."

"You know you don't mean that, Mother," said Diana. "It's only that you've had your fill of large ones these past few weeks. Next Christmas you'll be as eager as ever to roll up the rugs and fill the house with company."

Mrs. Etheridge smiled rather sadly. "No, the fact is that I'm getting old," she said. "Don't shake your head, Diana. It *is* a fact, and there's never any point in refusing to face facts, as you're always saying yourself. Next year I shall be glad enough to stand back and let Anne give the parties."

She turned her head to smile at Anne. "It's a fortunate thing Stephen found you when he did, my dear," she said. "Fortunate in every way. You seem quite like one of the family already, and I can only thank the lucky star that brought the two of you together."

"More like a lucky snowstorm," said Stephen, in a voice too low for anyone but Anne to hear. She smiled and shook her head at him before expressing herself honored by her mother-in-law's good opinion.

The four of them talked for some time, now dwelling on the holidays just past, now turning their thoughts toward the future, discussing subjects as diverse as the new cottages Stephen was having built at Ash Grove, the plans Mrs. Etheridge had made to have Diana presented that spring, and that young lady's own equally determined plans to carry on her studies with Dr. Schultz even in spite of balls and court presentations. Finally Mrs. Etheridge rose from her chair with an ill-concealed yawn.

"I do not know about the rest of you, but I feel completely exhausted," she said. "I can't remember the last time I was tired so early. But then, it's been a day of unusual excitement, what with one thing and another." She looked pointedly at Diana. Diana ducked her head in a shamed manner, but the expression on her face looked more like a grin. "And I never will believe that that arrow of yours went wide by accident, Diana, whatever you may say about sudden gusts of wind! You shall have to make Lydia a formal apology as soon as possible."

"I may as well do it now, then, and get it over with," said Diana philosophically. Rising from her chair, she accompanied her mother out of the room to pay a call on the invalid.

When they had gone, Stephen turned to look at Anne. "Is this your cue to jump up and run after them?" he said. "Or have you finally reached the conclusion that you may remain alone with me in perfect safety?"

The look Anne gave him held a hint of mischief as well as a hint of challenge. "I told you once before that I'm not afraid of anything you can do, my lord," she said. "I don't plan to run away."

Stephen's response was to draw her into his arms and kiss her. Being taken by surprise, she was a little stiff with him at first, but soon had relaxed sufficiently to participate willingly in a second and lengthier kiss. "I *have* missed you," he murmured in her ear. "More than you can imagine. Have you missed me, too?"

The sensation of his mouth on her ear was a peculiarly intimate one. Anne shivered and closed her eyes. It seemed to her that the room had suddenly grown much warmer. "Yes," she said faintly. "Quite a bit, actually."

" 'Quite a bit, actually,' " he mimicked, letting his lips stray to her neck. "You sound exceedingly cool about it, Lady Etheridge. I personally have found it very difficult to pass the evening in the same room with you, knowing I could only look and not touch. I've felt something like a starving man must feel, confronted by a baker's window."

Anne laughed, a little shakily. "Ah, you laugh," he said darkly. "You don't know your peril, my lady. I'm half inclined to dispense with the formalities and ravish you right here on the sofa."

"Think of the servants," said Anne. She shivered again as his lips trailed down her neck. "You ought at least to wait until we're upstairs."

"Is that an invitation? Very well, then: I accept." In a movement that caught Anne off her guard a second time, he stood up, swept her up in his arms, and started for the door.

"Stephen, really, I can walk," said Anne, affecting to protest, though in fact she was not ill-pleased by her lover's eagerness. She reached up to stroke his face with one hand. "And I ought to go upstairs before you anyway. I must ring for my maid to help me out of my dress—"

"No, indeed, my lady! I intend to have that pleasure myself."

"Oh," said Anne weakly. "Well, then, you must at least allow me to put my jewelry away. After that—I suppose you may do as you please."

"Yes, I know," said Stephen, and laughed at her indignant look. "I know I may do as I please," he continued, looking down at her with a noticeable glint in his eye. "After all, I *am* king for the evening, remember?"

In the end he did not carry her upstairs, for Anne felt such a proceeding must appear rather singular to the servants. Stephen gave it as his opinion that the servants had better things to think about, but he consented to set her on her feet again, and they went up the stairs together. At her bedroom door he took her in his arms and kissed her with an ardor that left her breathless. "Only the jewelry, and mind that you hurry," he said. "I will expect you in my room in five minutes."

Anne had neither the strength nor the inclination to defy this autocratic speech, but it was not in her nature to let it pass without remark. "The King has spoken," she said with exaggerated humility, and dropped him a mocking curtsy before disappearing into her room.

Rather less than five minutes had elapsed when she reappeared in the doorway to Stephen's room. Her entrance was so quiet that he did not hear her, and for a moment she stood looking around his bedchamber.

It was a room she had not previously had an opportunity to view: a large rectangular apartment, equal in size and elegance to her own bedchamber but a good deal more somber in its appointments. The bed and window hangings were of dark green velvet rather than ivory brocade; the furniture was of mahogany rather than ormolu-inlaid rosewood; and there were none of the light-hearted touches that rendered her own rooms so charming. Having taken in all these details, Anne dismissed them from mind and turned her attention instead to the room's occupant.

Since she had left him in the hall, Stephen had shed his top-coat, waistcoat, and neckcloth, and had loosened the collar of his shirt. He was seated before the fireplace with his legs stretched out in front of him, gazing pensively into the fire. Anne stood watching him for a minute or two, delighting in this opportunity to observe him unawares. He looked very good to her as he lounged there, the lean, muscular lines of his body evident beneath his thin shirt and form-fitting trousers, and his dark hair spilling over the back of his shirt-collar as he leaned back in his chair, resting his head on his hands.

At last he seemed to sense he was being watched. He turned his head and saw Anne standing in the doorway. His pensive expression at once vanished; he got quickly to his feet and came over to where she stood. For a moment he stood looking down at her, then reached out to smooth her hair back from her forehead. "Have I already told you that you look beautiful this evening?" he said softly.

"Several times, but I have no objection to your telling me again," responded Anne. The touch of his fingers on her skin sent a little shiver down her spine. He noticed the movement and took her by the hand, rubbing her fingers between his.

"You're cold," he said. "Come over here by the fire where it's warmer."

Anne let herself be led toward the hearth. When they reached it, Stephen turned to her again. This time he did not speak, but took her hand and raised it to his lips. It was a formal gesture, yet in this context unmistakably erotic.

Another tingle ran down Anne's spine as his lips traveled from her fingers to her wrist and along the inside of her arm. All the while he was insensibly drawing her closer, until at last only a few inches separated them.

His mouth moved now from her arm to her shoulder. Anne stood perfectly still, expecting every moment that he would take her into his arms, but this he was maddeningly slow to do. Only his mouth continued its leisurely exploration of her shoulder, now straying higher to her neck, now dropping lower, with a touch as light as the lightest whisper.

The result was the sweetest kind of torment for Anne. Her every nerve felt on fire with anticipation; it was unbearable to feel him so close, actually to feel the warmth of his body and his breath on her skin, and yet experience no more of him than those delicate, maddeningly deliberate kisses. Just when she felt she could endure it no longer, his arms closed around her, his mouth found hers, and he kissed her.

It was a long kiss, to which Anne abandoned herself without reserve. She shut her eyes and clung to him tightly while his mouth and hands took all manner of delightful liberties with her. These last, in particular, soon grew so audacious that Anne was emboldened to take a few timid liberties of her own. He did not seem to mind. On the contrary, her touch seemed to inspire him to make a yet more determined attack on her dress buttons, which had thus far stubbornly resisted all his efforts to unbutton them.

"Turn around," he whispered.

Anne turned around. Under so much direct pressure, even the most stubborn buttons could not fail to give way; he unbuttoned them one by one, while his mouth took instant advantage of every fresh inch of skin bared to view. Anne's breath was coming fast when at last her dress slipped from her shoulders and fell in a circle around her feet.

Stephen drew her into his arms again and kissed her, running his hands up and down her back and molding her body against his. With only the flimsy muslin of her chemise and the thin cambric of his shirt between them, Anne was acutely conscious of the warm, solid, masculine feel of his chest next to hers.

She was overcome by a sudden urge to feel it without all those intervening layers of fabric. Impatiently she tugged at his shirt, trying to free it from the waistband of his trousers. He obligingly lent his own assistance to the task, then turned his attention to her hair, pulling out comb and hairpins with a reckless hand and scattering them across the hearth-rug.

When her hair finally tumbled loose about her shoulders, he made a noise of satisfaction deep in his throat and swept her up in his arms. Anne supposed he meant to carry her to the bed, which destination she was by that time fully as eager as he to reach; she was therefore quite surprised when he deposited her instead on a chair in front of the fireplace.

He smiled at her look of surprise and leaned down to kiss her. "You must humor the King's pleasure tonight," he informed her.

"I think this King business is going to your head," said Anne, eyeing him a little nervously. "And surely you haven't forgotten, sir, that I am a republican, not a royalist?"

For answer, he kissed her again, then knelt down on the carpet before her and began to remove her shoes and stockings. No one but herself had ever performed this very intimate office. Anne found it almost too embarrassing to watch, but at the same time she was obliged to admit that it was not in the least distasteful.

In a leisurely fashion he unlaced her slippers, untied her garters, and drew the stockings from her legs, letting his hands linger over the task and pausing now and then to drop a kiss upon her feet and ankles. Anne, who had never supposed a kiss on the foot could arouse such sensations, shut her eyes and felt positively dizzy.

When the stockings had gone the way of Anne's shoes, dress, and hairpins, he got to his feet again and pulled her to hers. Again he kissed her, and while his mouth held hers captive, his hands were busy untying the ribbon that closed the neck of her chemise. Anne eventually noticed his occupation and roused herself to a languid protest. "This is not at all fair, Stephen. You still have *your* clothes on!"

He spared a brief glance at himself before continuing with his task. "So I do," he said, as he pulled the ribbon free.

"It's not fair," said Anne again, and made a half-hearted effort to pull away from him. Then his hand closed over her breast, catching the nipple between two of his fingers.

"Oh," she said weakly, and "oh," again, when a moment later his hand was succeeded by his mouth.

There were no more objections from Anne after that. When Stephen slipped the chemise from her shoulders, she made no objection; when he sat down in the chair and pulled her into his lap, she made no objection; and when one of his hands found its way between her legs, while the other began to unbutton the waist of his trousers, she was so far beyond objection as to beg him to hurry.

He laughed softly, put his hands on her hips, and drew her toward him. "That, dear madame, is my pleasure," he said.

Anne drew in her breath sharply, then let it out again in a shivering sigh, burying her face against his shoulder. He nipped gently at her neck, then bent his head to kiss her breast.

Once more his hand found its way between her legs, and between his hand, his mouth, and the feel of him deep inside her, her pleasure very soon reached its peak. She arched her back and cried out again and again, subsiding at last with a deep-drawn sigh.

"Oh, Stephen," she said.

"Oh, Anne," he said, and gathered her tightly against him. "Oh, Anne, I do love you," he whispered, stroking her back with his hands. "You are my wife, my own true love, and without a doubt the most beautiful, exciting woman in the whole world. How fortunate can one man be?"

Anne laughed weakly and buried her head against his shoulder again. "I love you, too, Stephen," she said in a muffled voice.

He nuzzled her neck gently and then, in one swift motion, lifted her and laid her on the rug in front of the fireplace. He was on top of her now; his breath came fast as he began to make love to her with passionate urgency.

Such was his passion, indeed, that Anne found herself becoming aroused all over again. Once more she experienced the gradual rise to a moment of aching, unbearable pleasure. She cried aloud and heard Stephen cry out, too; for a moment the world seemed to swing wildly out of orbit and then slowly settled into its normal steady course.

When Anne's senses returned to her, she found herself lying on the hearth-rug with Stephen on top of her. He was still nominally clad in his shirt and trousers, and both of them were sticky with sweat and breathing hard. Anne wrapped her arms around him and shut her eyes, luxuriating in a sense of profound contentment.

After a few minutes had gone by, however, she became aware of a strange movement on Stephen's part. He would lie still for a moment and then be seized by a fit of trembling that shook his whole body. At first Anne thought he must be shivering, unlikely though that seemed, but finally it dawned on her that he was laughing. This was such an unexpected phenomenon that she knew not whether to be alarmed or offended.

"Stephen, why are you laughing?" she demanded.

Another paroxysm of laughter shook him as he lifted his head to look at her. "I was just thinking how deceiving first impressions can be," he said in an unsteady voice. "You seemed such a *cold* woman, the first time I met you. . . ."

Twenty-one

It was Anne who awakened first the next morning. On opening her eyes, she experienced a moment's disorientation to find herself in a strange room and a strange bed, but the sight of Stephen lying beside her quickly restored her to a sense of her surroundings.

For several minutes she lay studying him as he slept. He looked quite as handsome asleep as awake and very nearly as stern, she was both amused and touched to note; his mouth was set in a thin, uncompromising line, and a slight frown furrowed his brow, as though even in sleep care weighed upon him.

Not wishing to wake him, she cautiously pushed back the covers and began to ease herself from the bed. But her feet had barely touched the floor when she found herself suddenly pinioned by a strong arm and pulled back into bed. Anne let out a stifled shriek. "I thought you were asleep," she said accusingly.

"I was asleep," said Stephen. The careworn look had vanished; he was grinning now as he looked at her. "I was asleep, but now I am awake. Very much awake . . ."

He insinuated his body a little closer to hers as he spoke, so that she might be in no danger of mistaking his meaning. Anne pulled away from him, however, and made a determined effort to remove the arm that was still firmly clamped around her waist. "I must go to my own room now, Stephen," she said.

"But why?" he said, nuzzling her neck. "You seemed to find this room perfectly satisfactory last night."

Anne sighed deeply and gave him a look of affectionate exasperation. "Must I spell everything out to you, Stephen?" she said. "It is *necessary* that I go to my room!"

Stephen laughed. "Oh, I see," he said. He let go of her waist and raised himself on his elbow to watch as she got out of bed. The appreciative grin on his face rather nettled Anne, who was already extremely self-conscious about her state of nudity; she snatched his dressing gown from the chair beside the bed and put it on with a look that dared him to make any objection. He made none, but as she hastened toward the door he called, "Hurry back."

Anne waited until she had reached the doorway before replying. "Perhaps I will, and perhaps I won't," she said. "Twelfth Night's over, and you're not King any longer, my lord." Having settled him with this crushing speech, she then proceeded to mitigate much of its effect by throwing him a saucy smile over her shoulder as she went into the next room.

When she returned a few minutes later, she found Stephen sitting up in bed. The bedclothes covered him below the waist, but his chest and shoulders were bare, and Anne paused in the doorway to survey him with pure feminine appreciation. He surveyed her in turn, letting his eyes travel slowly from her red-gold head (hastily smoothed with a hairbrush only a minute before) to the bare feet just visible beneath the dressing gown. "You look very fetching in my dressing gown," he said huskily. "Come here and let me take it off."

"No, *you* come *here*," said Anne, crossing her arms over her chest and regarding him with a challenging smile.

He promptly threw off the bedclothes, jumped out of bed, and came toward her. Anne continued to stand where she was, letting her eyes wander over him with the same air of critical appraisal he had subjected her to a few minutes earlier. He returned her look with a good deal of amusement. "Do I meet with your approval, my lady?" he said.

"Yes, indeed," said Anne. Deliberately she lifted her hand and ran it slowly down his chest, to close at last over that member which, until now, she had scarcely allowed herself even to look at. Stephen's eyes widened. He regarded her silently for a moment, then set about divesting her of the dressing gown with all possible dispatch. Anne made no demur; neither did she demur at being returned to bed, or at any of the things he subsequently chose to do to her there. The morning was considerably advanced when she took leave of him a second time and went to her room to make her toilette for the day.

This business did not take her long, but even so Stephen managed to be dressed and ready before her. When Anne came out into the hall she found him waiting for her, clad in frockcoat, boots, and breeches, and looking his respectable self once more. As they went down the stairs together, he spoke of taking her on a tour of the property later that morning.

"You haven't yet seen the full extent of it, and it looks to be a beautiful day for a drive. I noticed from my window that we had a fresh fall of snow overnight. Should you object to taking my curricle? If you were bundled up well enough, I don't think you would feel the cold."

Anne graciously gave her approval to this plan. "With the sun shining so brightly, I'm sure I should be perfectly comfortable, Stephen. Indeed, I don't think I should mind even if the sun wasn't shining. Your northern English winters aren't so bad once one grows accustomed to them. I never would have thought to hear myself say such a thing after that dreadful night we spent in the mailcoach, but I'm starting to find something almost invigorating about cold weather—assuming, of course, that I am properly dressed for it!"

Stephen, with a gleam in his eyes, said he much preferred her in a state of improper dress. Anne was still scolding him for this remark as they entered the breakfast room. Mrs. Etheridge was already there, talking excitedly to Diana; she turned to her son and daughter-in-law a face in which distress struggled with a kind of incredulous satisfaction.

"My dears, the most astonishing thing," she said. "I suppose there is no harm in speaking of it before the servants, for it is bound to come out sooner or later."

"What's happened?" said Stephen, looking sharply from her to Diana.

It was the latter who answered him. "Lydia has eloped, Stephen! She took her clothes and her maid and went off in the night without a word to anyone. Mother found a note pinned to her pillow this morning when she went to see how she was feeling after her—ah—injury yesterday."

Stephen's face wore much the same expression as his mother's as he regarded Diana. "Lydia eloped?" he said. "Eloped with whom?"

"That's the most amazing thing of all," said Mrs. Etheridge. "Do you remember that nice Lord Francis Rowland who was staying with the Moorhavens? It appears that Lydia has been seeing a great deal of him lately, at the Moorhavens' and other places. I knew she had been spending a great deal of time at Moorhaven Manor lately, but I didn't realize that he was the attraction."

A noise halfway between a gasp and a giggle escaped Anne. Mrs. Etheridge glanced at her curiously as she continued, "I don't pretend to know all the details, but it seems that Lord Francis persuaded Lydia to marry him, and she went off this way 'to save everyone trouble,' as she says in her note. I still can scarcely believe it. It seems such an odd way of going about it—and surely she could not think we would have begrudged her a proper wedding. I know I, for one, would have been very happy to see her marry again. Indeed, if one is to speak frankly, it is a great relief to have her gone, but I cannot help feeling it on Amy's account. To go off in such a way, with no warning—and not a word does she say about Amy in her letter, so that I do not know in the least what I am to do about the poor child."

"Lydia eloped with Francis Rowland," said Stephen. There was a peculiar smile on his face as he looked at Anne. "That's a development I wouldn't have expected, but I can't say I disapprove of the match. It seems like a pretty good solution all around, in fact."

"But Amy," worried Mrs. Etheridge. "What am I to tell her?

She will want to know where her mother is, and though Lydia says in her note that she and Lord Francis will probably go to London after the wedding, she says nothing about sending for Amy later on. I am in quite a perplexity what to say to her. Oh, dear, yes, and that's not the only difficulty, either—the jewels, Stephen! Lydia had them, you know, and when I finally got my wits enough about me to check, I found that she had taken all the family jewelry with her, including the diamonds. Those diamonds ought to have gone to Anne on her wedding day. And though I don't like to speak ill of Lydia, I can't help feeling that there may be a good deal of difficulty getting them back now that they're gone."

Anne and Stephen looked at each other. "Speaking for myself, I don't care about the diamonds," said Anne. "It seems to me that Amy is the more important issue. If Lydia means simply to abandon her here, without a word—"

"She does," said Diana with conviction.

"—then something must certainly be done for her. Again speaking for myself, I shouldn't have any objection to her staying on here at Etheridge Hall. If Stephen agrees—"

Stephen did agree and said so, with a warm look at his wife. Mrs. Etheridge shook her head, however.

"That's very generous of you, my dears, and for the time being it would probably be better if she did stay on here, so as not to disrupt her life any more than is necessary just at present. But if Amy is to live with anyone, it ought to be with me, and I think the best plan would be for me to take her with me when I go to Ash Grove this summer."

"To Ash Grove?" said Stephen "I hadn't realized you were planning to spend the summer there, Mother."

"Well, I hadn't been planning it, precisely, but you know I have been talking for some time about returning to Ash Grove, and this business of Lydia's has decided me. As soon as the Season is over, I'll take Amy and Molly and remove to Ash Grove. I have grown very fond of Amy these past few years, and I would be very glad to have her company now that my own children are growing up and getting married."

"Aren't you being slightly premature, Mother?" inquired Diana with a sardonic smile. "I may be going to be presented this spring, but I haven't yet heard that I was getting married."

"Well, no, but you *might,* you know, dearest. And even if you don't, I expect you'll be traipsing off for parts unknown as soon as you're twenty-one, the way you're always talking about. Either way I should be left by myself, and then I should be very glad of Amy's company."

Diana had nothing to say to this, and Mrs. Etheridge proclaimed the matter settled. "Though I suppose nothing can truly be said to be settled until we know Lydia's plans," she added with a sigh. "Really, I am quite put out with her over this whole business. It seems a very inconsiderate, underhanded way to manage things, not to say any worse. She is of age, after all, and quite her own mistress. There wasn't the least need for her to elope, unless indeed it was because of the diamonds."

Diana said coolly that it was Lydia's nature to do everything in an underhanded way. Mrs. Etheridge admitted that the late Lady Etheridge's nature was not so open as might be desired, but she continued to shake her head over Lydia's conduct as long as she and Diana remained in the breakfast parlor. When at last they had left to pursue their separate occupations, Stephen looked at Anne.

"Lydia's conduct isn't such a mystery to me as it is to Mother," he said in a low voice. "Before dinner last night, I sent up word that I wanted to speak to her as soon as she felt well enough to receive visitors. She must have guessed the game was up and decided to take this way out to avoid a confrontation. And it would have been a confrontation, too! I still can't believe she told you the story she did—a story that could have been easily disproved by so many people. She can't have expected to get away with it."

"You forget how close she did come to getting away with it," said Anne with a smile and a shiver. "And really she wasn't taking so much a chance as all that. I never got around to telling you this before, Stephen, but the fact is that Lydia knows the whole story about how we met and about that night we spent in the mailcoach. Francis told her on the afternoon of Boxing Day, that same day you were called away to Ash Grove. I meant to tell you about it at the time, but I never had a chance before you left, and afterwards, of course, Lydia had already got her work in. She must have thought that since we'd known each other only a few days, there wouldn't be any risk in telling me a few convenient lies about your past."

"I see," said Stephen slowly. "Yes, that would explain a lot that's been puzzling me about this business. Boxing Day . . . I recall now Lydia coming to me in the study that afternoon and being very—affectionate. She hung all over me and talked a lot of stuff about forgiving and forgetting the past—"

"Indeed?" was all Anne permitted herself to say.

"Yes, I rather wondered about it at the time. It seemed strange that she would behave as she did when she knew you and I were just married. But it makes more sense in light of what you've just told me. After hearing Francis's story, she must have assumed that we'd married solely out of necessity, and that there couldn't be any real bond between us. She probably figured that one good misunderstanding would be enough to drive us apart—"

"And so she set herself to provide the misunderstanding! How happy she must have been when you got called away to Ash Grove so suddenly. That gave her a wonderful chance to work on me when you weren't around to defend yourself. She probably thought I'd be so shocked and disgusted that I'd pack my bags and leave right then and there. And in fact that's almost what happened—it must have been a great disappointment to her that I was still there when you got back. No wonder she's been sticking to you so closely all this week, Stephen! All her schemes depended on the two of us remaining estranged, and it would have taken only a few minutes of frank conversation between us to clear up the whole misunderstanding."

"As it did," said Stephen, smiling at her. "And not a moment too soon, either! But it's still a wonder to me that Lydia risked doing what she did. I can't imagine what she hoped to gain by it. Even if she'd succeeded in driving you away, she can't seriously have thought I'd be willing to take her in your place, after all that business years ago."

"I don't know," said Anne hesitantly. "I think perhaps she did, Stephen. From what Diana says, it sounds as though she had become obsessed these past few years with the idea of getting you back. She might well have felt that it was worth any risk to try to separate us. If she succeeded, she had everything to gain, in her own mind, at least, and if she failed—well, she probably felt that if she lost you, she'd lost everything anyway."

Stephen was quiet a moment, considering this idea. Finally he shook his head with a wry smile. "It'd be flattering to my pride to think I had inspired such devotion, but somehow I doubt that Lydia is very broken up on my account. You see how quickly she found consolation with Francis Rowland and the family diamonds!"

"Yes, Francis! That is the part *I* find difficult to believe. Francis must have worked very quickly, to have convinced her to marry him in such a short time. They can't have seen each other more than three or four times in the time he's been here."

"Actually, I suspect it was a little more often than that, Anne. During that week when you and I weren't on speaking terms, Mother took me to task for spending all my time with Lydia, but in fact I wasn't spending more than a few hours a day with her. I'm more than half inclined to think she was merely using me as a blind, and that Francis was her real object all along."

"If he was, then she went to a great deal of unnecessary trouble about it! No, Stephen, I think you are wrong there. Lydia may have flirted with Francis, but I'm sure you would have been her first choice if her plans had worked out as she hoped. But just in case they didn't, she probably felt there wasn't any harm in having two strings to her bow! And while we're on the subject of bowstrings—" Anne's eyes held a sparkle of laughter as she looked at Stephen across the table. "I have a confession to make,

Stephen. I'm afraid Diana's 'accident' yesterday wasn't entirely accidental! I had told her a little about the problems I was having with Lydia, and though I didn't expect her to do anything as drastic as to shoot Lydia, I know she did it to help me. If you are angry about it, Stephen, you must be angry with me, not her."

"So she did deliberately mis-aim! I suspected as much at the time, but without any proof I couldn't be sure. I must congratulate her next time I see her upon her wonderful restraint. My own inclination would have been to shoot Lydia somewhere rather more vital, if not actually to wring her neck."

"Yes, mine, too. It's a good thing she's gone, isn't it? If she wasn't, we might be tempted to really do it!"

"It *is* a good thing she's gone, in every respect. It would have been very difficult to get her out of the house under the terms of Marcus's will, and to go on living with her after everything that's happened would have been intolerable. She and Francis ought to do very well together. They're neither one of them troubled by an excess of principle!"

"Yes—although I can't help feeling a little sorry for Francis. He is a rogue, to be sure, but a very likable rogue, and after he's lived with Lydia for a while I'm afraid he may think his fortune rather dearly won."

Stephen gave Anne a long look. "Should I be jealous?" he said.

She shook her head, smiling a little. "No, Stephen, you don't need to be jealous. There was a time in my life when I was very fond of Francis—a time when I even considered marrying him—but so much of that had to do with my situation at the time. I was feeling terribly alone and unhappy after Mother's death, and the idea of having someone take care of me and my affairs was—well, very tempting. But you must remember, Stephen, that I did refuse Francis, or at least put him off when he asked me to marry him."

"Yes, I remember. I recall you speaking of it that day in the mailcoach. You said you were reluctant to enter into an engagement so soon after your mother's death."

"That's right, and I think now that even if Francis had waited and renewed his offer properly at the end of six months, I wouldn't have married him in the end. I had always had a few doubts about his character, deep down—and of course he was a nobleman, too, and you know my opinion of those!"

"Yes, I'm not likely to forget it. Such a dressing down as you gave me, that day at the inn! My ears still ring when I think of it."

"I know, and I'm sorry for the way I spoke that day, Stephen, but it really wasn't you I was upset with. It wasn't even Francis so much—the person I was really upset with was myself. Francis would never have been in a position to abduct me if I hadn't compromised my principles in the first place, and of course that made me doubly reluctant to compromise them a second time."

"Yes, of course. You mustn't think I was blaming you, my dear. After an experience like that, anyone might be pardoned for a little prejudice on the subject of noblemen!"

"You pardon me more easily than I can pardon myself, Stephen. It was inexcusably foolish of me to assume you were like Francis simply because you both had titles. And what makes it even more inexcusable is that I felt you were different, right from the start—if I had only trusted my instincts about you both I would have been a great deal better off. But it's all straight now, I hope, and I can assure you that you haven't the least cause to be jealous, Stephen. Even before I found out Francis was a fortune-hunter, I never felt for him one tenth of what I feel for you."

Anne hesitated, then added rather diffidently, "I suspect I have more cause to be jealous myself. I don't mean to plague you by constantly referring to what's past, but it's pretty obvious that you cared very much for Lydia at one time."

Stephen was quiet for a moment, frowning a little as he considered the question. "I thought I did," he said at last. "The thing was, you know, that what I cared for wasn't Lydia at all. It sounds ridiculous now, but I saw her as a regular piece of perfection—pretty, and gay, and bright, and possessed of the whole catalogue of virtues."

"She is a talented actress," said Anne with feeling.

"Yes, she is, but still that doesn't excuse my folly. I would have seen her faults if I had looked for them. The truth is that I was willfully blind—blinded by infatuation, and blinded by pride, too, I have no doubt. Lydia was quite a belle in these parts, and I felt I'd done a clever thing to carry her off in the face of so much competition. It wasn't until she threw me over for Marcus that my eyes were finally opened."

"Much like mine were with Francis," said Anne with a grimace.

"Yes, very much like that. I was pretty bitter about it at first, as I mentioned before, but once I got past the initial shock, I was cured of any lingering infatuation I might have felt for her. It's a funny thing," Stephen went on, looking ruminatively at Anne. "What I feel for you is entirely different."

"You don't find me a piece of perfection?" said Anne with mock indignation.

"Well, no." A fleeting smile crossed Stephen's face. "I don't see you as perfect, but then I don't pretend to be perfect myself, you know. The thing is that you're perfect for me. I don't express myself very well, I'm afraid—"

"On the contrary, you're expressing yourself very well," said Anne. "Do go on. Which of my imperfections did you first fall in love with?"

Stephen laughed and shook his head. "No, it wasn't like that either, Anne. I can't explain very well how it was, but from the moment you stepped into that mailcoach and sat down across from me, there was something about you that caught my eye . . . something that attracted me to you. It wasn't just the way you looked, though that was certainly attractive enough, and it wasn't just that you seemed to be in trouble. That gave me an excuse to interest myself in you to begin with and for a lot of what you called chivalry later on, but though I hope I would have behaved as well by any woman in your situation; I'm afraid my chief motivation was simply a desire to get to know you better."

"Oh, dear, and I was so rude to you, Stephen! I wonder you wanted to know me better after the way I spoke to you at first."

"You certainly didn't give me much encouragement," agreed Stephen with a reminiscent smile. "But later, after the blizzard had shut us in and we began to talk . . . I don't know. Perhaps you didn't feel it, but it seemed to me that there was a kind of natural sympathy between us. And then I was so impressed by the way you behaved through the whole ordeal. Even when things looked worst, you were so brave about it all, and even managed to joke about it—I can't tell you how impressed I was."

"You're making me blush, Stephen! If we are to deal in compliments, I may as well go ahead and admit that I was very impressed by you, too, that day."

"Were you really?"

"Yes, I was. And I *did* feel something of the sympathy you spoke of. If the circumstances had been different, I think I would have felt it as strongly as you did, but at the time I was still in a state of shock over everything that had happened. It wasn't until a few days later that I finally got my feelings sorted out and realized that I had fallen in love with my husband. A most remarkable turn of events, don't you think?"

Stephen laughed and dropped a kiss on the back of her neck as he got up to go to the sideboard. They were alone in the breakfast parlor by now, the attendant footmen having taken themselves off to other duties. Stephen helped himself to cold beef while Anne took a second roll from the basket on the table and began to break it apart and butter it. When Stephen returned to the table with his plate, they settled down to eat in companionable silence. But only a few minutes had gone by when Anne observed a frown settling over his brow.

"Why are you scowling, Stephen?" she inquired. "Are you still brooding about Lydia's misdeeds, or is it that your roast beef's not done to your satisfaction? Of all your English customs, I think that is positively the most barbaric. I can't see how anyone can go filling their stomach with cold meat at this hour."

"No, it's not the roast beef that's at fault. I *was* thinking about

Lydia again, and about this business of her eloping with Francis
Rowland. Although I'm glad enough to see the pair of them go,
it does vex me a little that the family jewels seem to have gone
with them. You made light of it before, but those diamonds
ought to have been yours, Anne."

"I really don't mind," Anne assured him. "I already own quite
a bit of jewelry, as it happens, and though I can't say how it
compares to your family jewelry, Stephen, you must remember
that I've never so much as laid eyes on that. I'm not likely to
miss it much."

"I suppose not, but still it's galling to think of Lydia and Francis having it. If it weren't that it'd cause such a confounded scandal, I'd be tempted to go after them and see if I couldn't make
them hand it over again. At the very least, I could relieve my
feelings by blackening both of Francis Rowland's eyes for him!"

"I'm sure that would be a delightful relief to your feelings,
Stephen, but it would undoubtedly cause a scandal, as you say,
and there's another thing you ought to take into consideration."

"Oh, yes? What consideration is that?"

"Well, it seems to me that it might not be such a bad thing
to let Lydia keep the diamonds, as a sort of guarantee of good
behavior. She does know about our experience in the mailcoach,
after all, and though Francis promised to try to keep her from
telling anyone else, I don't know how much influence he really
has with her. But if we could make it in her interests to keep
quiet . . ."

"I see what you mean," said Stephen, his brow lightening
somewhat. "It's true that the diamonds would give us a certain
leverage if we were forced to have any future dealings with
Lydia. As long as she behaved herself and said nothing about
us, we wouldn't say anything about the diamonds, but if she
ever threatened to cause trouble, we'd only got to turn around
and threaten to sue her for the theft of entailed property."

"Yes, that's the idea. But of course it would mean sacrificing
your family diamonds."

"I suppose I must resign myself to it. Much as I hate to lose them, I can see it might be worth it to let Lydia keep the diamonds as a means of insuring her future good conduct. And if I find my feelings still need relief here in six months or so, I'll relieve them by buying you a set of diamonds twice as nice as the others."

"Well—if it makes you feel better, Stephen," said Anne, laughing.

Her face grew serious a moment later, however, and she sat watching Stephen finish his cold sirloin with a rather pensive expression. She was still wearing the same expression a little later, when, having finished breakfast and put on outdoor garments for the drive, they were standing in the portico waiting for Stephen's curricle to be brought around.

"I was just thinking, Stephen," she said. "Diana says there is no use in not facing facts, and we must face the fact that some word of that business with the mailcoach may eventually get about in spite of all we can do to prevent it. Even besides Lydia and Francis, a great many people know about it—the landlady at the inn, and the coachman and guard, and heaven knows who else."

"Yes, I suppose it's possible the story may get about," said Stephen, looking down at her. "People do like to talk, as my mother is fond of saying. I suppose our best strategy is to make sure that from now on they have as little as possible to talk about. If we both appear to be perfectly happy in our marriage, people will soon discount the rumors and start talking about something else."

"I think I can keep up my part in that bargain well enough," said Anne, smiling up at him.

"And I, too," said Stephen, reaching out and drawing her into his arms.

And if any people had happened to be looking on at that moment, they would have been very satisfied to see that Lord and Lady Etheridge were, indeed, perfectly happy in their marriage.

About the Author

Joy Reed lives with her family in the Cincinnati area. She is currently working on her next regency romance, *The Seduction of Lady Carroll,* which Zebra Books will be publishing in August 1996. She is also the author of another regency romance, *An Inconvenient Engagement.* Joy loves hearing from her readers and you may write to her c/o Zebra Books. Please include a self-addressed stamped envelope if you wish a response.